GOLD, SILVER, & BOMBS

TED TAYLER

Vinci Books

vinci-books.com

Published by Vinci Books Ltd in 2026

1

Copyright © Ted Tayler 2015

The author has asserted their moral right to be identified as the author of this work in accordance with the Copyright, Designs and Patents Act 1988. This work is a work of fiction. Names, characters, places and incidents are the product of the author's imagination or are used fictitiously. Any resemblance to actual persons, living or dead, places and incidents is entirely coincidental.
All rights reserved. No part of this publication may be copied, reproduced, distributed, stored in any retrieval system, or transmitted in any form or by any means, including photocopying, recording, or other electronic or mechanical methods, nor used as a source for any form of machine learning including AI datasets, without the prior written permission of the publisher.
The publisher and the author have made every effort to obtain permissions for any third party material used in this book and to comply with copyright law. Any queries in this respect should be brought to the attention of the publisher and any omissions will be corrected in future editions.
A CIP catalogue record for this book is available from the British Library.
Paperback ISBN: 9781036700508

The EU GPSR authorised representative is Logos Europe, 9 rue Nicolas Poussion, 17000 La Rochelle, France
contact@logoseurope.eu

By Ted Tayler

The Phoenix

The Olympus Project
Gold, Silver and Bombs
Nothing Is Ever Forever
In the Lap of the Gods
The Price of Treachery
A New Dawn
Something Wicked Draws Near
Evil Always Finds A Way
Revenge Comes in Many Colours
Three Weeks in September
A Frequent Peal of Bells
Larcombe Manor

The Freeman Files

Fatal Decision
Last Orders
Pressure Point
Deadly Formula
Final Deal
Barking Mad
Creature Discomforts

Silent Terror

Night Train

All Things Bright

Buried Secrets

A Genuine Mistake

Strange Beginnings

Dead Reckoning

A Normal November

Into the Sunlight

Tame the Storm

One True Friend

Whispered Truths

A Morning Murder

Quick to Anger

Red Herring Season

Gathering Clouds

Still Standing

Chapter One

Jeremy Faversham sat astride his favourite animal. His beloved hunter, Bonus Magnet, was part Irish Draught and part English thoroughbred. Bonus magnet stood at seventeen hands and was eight years old, and Jeremy knew the horse had been a good find. On a brisk January morning, he could think of nowhere he wanted to be than in the saddle, hacking across the glorious Cotswold countryside. He was among friends. The cares and stresses of the working world were far, far away.

No two fox hunts were ever alike. The continuous chaos of the chase appealed to him. Jeremy knew he must be on constant alert, and he rigidly stuck to the centuries-old protocols and accepted the inevitable uncertainty.

Jeremy reflected that Foxhunting was a way of life rather than a mere sport as he negotiated a tricky downhill slope. Over the years, it framed his life. While working in the City at the bank, he often saw himself viewing his financial experiences in a hunting context.

Just like himself, the fox was a predator. Jeremy Faversham might have appeared to be the country gentleman, suitably attired for the occasion, but there were skeletons in the closet. Those skeletons attracted several groups of people. People from those groups now watched the banker ride across open ground towards Downend Farm.

The Phoenix was one man with a pair of field glasses fixed on the edge of the woods. He not only followed the banker's progress; Phoenix kept an eye on the hunt saboteurs too, who lurked in the cover of the trees. From time to time, he switched his attention to the hunt followers. At least having a moving target eased the boredom.

"Is everything going as planned?" whispered Colin.

"Faversham's heading in the right direction," replied Rusty, a few hundred yards ahead. He watched events unfold on the opposite side of the field.

"I'll keep tabs on the great unwashed and the hunt supporters to make sure they don't interfere," Colin replied. "It's good to have them on the scene, though. Unfortunately, it will muddy the waters when they investigate the accident."

"Roger that," replied Rusty. "I'll move ahead and confirm the equipment is in the correct position. I'll double-check too that our clean-up crew are alert and poised to move in as soon as our target is down."

The Olympus agents resumed their duties; communication needed to be minimal on a mission. Many parties were scattered across this small corner of the West Country. Each had its agenda. The days when the hunting crowd rode in these fields and woods by themselves following their sport were long gone.

Donald Chalmers had worked at Downend Farm for over fifty years. He went straight from school to work on the land. Now retired, Donald lived in a cottage half a mile from where he stood. He had been part of the hunting scene in these parts the whole of his life. Donald's wife, Catherine, passed away seven years ago, and they had no children to help fill the cottage with warmth and laughter. Instead, they spent much of their lives outdoors. They enjoyed the companionship of and working with horses and dogs daily — an uncomplicated style of country living fast disappearing.

Donald rose early, just as he did every morning of his working life. Nothing had changed. He saw no reason to stay in bed now that he was retired. He walked across from his cottage to this spot, which was his usual vantage point. It was a place he had occupied on dozens of occasions. This was a spot that gave him a glimpse of his old life. He might not be in the midst of the action anymore, but he could tell anyone who listened to him what was what.

The trees thinned out as he made his way up the path to the step over the fence. Donald spotted a small gathering of watchers huddled against each other by the fencing. They had dressed for sitting in their cars rather than standing on a chilly stretch of Cotswold countryside in the early morning. Donald smiled to himself, not because of their discomfort but because he knew he had an audience.

Donald nodded a greeting as heads turned to acknowledge his arrival.

"Hello there," he said. "Shall we see good sport today, do you think?"

Few intelligent comments came in response to his question. Donald knew his educational commentary would fall on virgin territory. These townsfolk were trying to experience a slice of authentic country life without getting their brand-new boots dirty or snags from thorns or branches in their fashionable jackets. Thank goodness he had not stumbled upon a group of bloody saboteurs. If they found his favourite spot, he would have to walk another mile to get as good a viewing point.

Donald enlightened his unwitting students about the fox and his many attributes. "A fox can sense changes in temperature or a subtle change in the speed of the wind; he knows the lie of the land and the distances between strategic points accurately. Mr Fox knows who you are and who I am. He can tell the difference between a human being wearing a hunting kit and when they are not."

Donald pointed to the far left-hand side of the field. "Can you see the way the land drops away over yonder? If they have picked him up, the fox will head there. We will watch him dart over the brow of the hill. When he reaches the bottom level, he will have earned himself time. The hunters will be slow negotiating the steep descent, and the hounds will fall back a touch. Mr Fox will dash into a covert in the woods and emerge later to descend to the stream. He might choose to lie low for an hour or two. By the time the hounds re-discover his scent, Mr Fox will be miles away. He will stroll back to his den at his leisure. If they are lucky and keep on him, the fox will take them further into the woods. Mr Fox understands that the hunter is disadvantaged on rough terrain. Not every pack of hounds can negotiate the thick, clinging undergrowth they will find there. You mark my words. The fox decides when the chase has ended, not the hunter or the hounds."

Donald took his hip flask from his inside pocket and took a swig. The fire of the brandy warmed him as it made its way down his throat. He basked in the glow of admiration from his students, who had soon recognised they were in the company of a real countryman. They resumed their vigil in silence.

A little further on, closer to the sounds of the approaching hunt, Wayne Saunders had his binoculars. He checked his other saboteurs, ensuring they stood in the ideal spot to disrupt proceedings. Wayne had been at this game for a decade. Wayne got involved at Bristol University, although he hadn't needed much persuading. When the ban came into force, they thought they had won. Seven years later, they were more active than ever.

Wayne knew most hunts understood the exact woods which harboured fox-cubs. Patches of forest or brush, owned and protected by hunt supporters, were where the fox might have their litter. Many foxes stayed in the same coverts from generation to generation. Wayne and his cronies had learned this and kept records of which woods to police and which to ignore.

A lot of the saboteurs' work went on before the meeting started. One of the best methods was to pre-spray. Wayne delegated that job. He had done it when a rookie, but it meant getting up early. Wayne was no fool. As this was one of the first meets of the season, he had several saboteurs out in the fields, ready to blow their horns and call. This blowing and calling confused any new hounds and tried to wrest control of the huntsman's pack.

This morning he asked his rookies to lay a few false trails too. Then, if the dogs became interested in the incorrect path, the saboteurs could increase the blowing and shouting. Wayne had often seen this tactic work, and soon he would know whether their preparation paid dividends.

Jeremy Faversham still galloped in pursuit of the bulk of the mounted field. He was not a fit and healthy young man any longer. There had been too many executive lunches and fine dining for that. His horse was sound and keen as mustard, but the extra weight he carried meant that Jeremy was way off the pace these days.

Many of the field, who paid their subs money on the day for a good ride across the countryside, rarely saw a kill or the hounds at work. The majority cared little for the technicalities of hunting, and the Field Master kept them in the background until the hounds were well on the fox's scent. Only at the death were they encouraged to follow on at close quarters.

The overweight banker and Bonus Magnet were nearing the woods. Each rider had their particular route through familiar parts of the ground they were hunting. Jeremy had used the same approach many times. This path led to the five-barred gate and access to the scrubby bushes and trees lining the wooden fencing that marked the boundary to Downend Farm.

The Phoenix and his Olympus colleagues had discovered this route too. They had studied Jeremy Faversham for months. Jeremy would take the simple course and thread his way through the trees and bushes until he reached the far side of the woods. Then, as he lost the momentum his gallop provided, he dismounted, opened the gate, and led his horse into the next field. Finally, he would close the gate behind him and set off again.

This less dangerous shortcut often brought Jeremy closer to the action while many of his companions risked life and limb trying to jump fences and fallen trees. On other occasions, if the fox led the pack in a different direction, then Jeremy was one of the last to arrive at The Old Bell Inn, which was the place where riders and followers gathered.

Bonus Magnet gamely galloped onwards. The gate was now clearly visible. Jeremy and his horse were alone; they were isolated from the leading riders by physique and design in equal parts. Bonus Magnet weighed up the obstacle. He recognised its construction and its size. To clear this gate would not be a test for him. Landing on the other side with his rider thumping back into the saddle after the exhilarating leap was another matter.

There were two strides to the gate as Jeremy heard a sudden noise and sensed something on the other side. No, not something, someone. In those final seconds, Jeremy Faversham saw a figure spring from the bushes. His brain tried to process what it was as he catapulted forward out of the saddle.

Bonus Magnet had cleared the gate but crumpled on landing. The poor horse had spotted something that appeared to be materialising out of the ground, just where he intended his front hooves to land. The horse's brain could not compute what he saw. Jeremy realised it was a commando in camouflaged combat gear pointing a rifle straight at him.

Both Jeremy Faversham and Bonus Magnet died in the fall. The Olympus clean-up crew rose from their hiding places in the nearby bushes without a sound. First, they removed the cardboard commando, so familiar on the firing range back at Larcombe Manor, and the spring mechanism which had released him when Bonus Magnet prepared for take-off. Next, the crew eliminated any evidence of anyone else in this part of the woods apart from the stricken banker and his horse. Once the team completed their task, they disappeared as quickly and quietly as they had arrived.

The news of the infamous banker's death covered the front page of every newspaper. There were features on every television news bulletin. However, nobody openly celebrated

Jeremy Faversham's end, as his shady financial dealings had blackened his character. The public shed more tears over the death of Bonus Magnet than over the demise of the wealthy banker.

There were pictures of his four-hundred-acre estate in Gloucestershire. The weekend supplements contained details of his ski chalet in Chamonix and his *pied a terre* in South Kensington. The red tops concentrated on the complete chapter and verse of his salary scale, share options, and latest bonuses. Every part of Jeremy Faversham's life was exposed to the world.

The media circus moved out of town within days and on to the next big news item. In time, the picture became more apparent for those who watched more intently.

A few newspapers carried a report of the autopsy for Bonus Magnet. The eight-year-old thoroughbred died from head and neck trauma because of a sharp fall. No medical evidence emerged that might have caused the animal to collapse suddenly. The saddle and tack appeared to be in position and firmly secured. The coroner determined that the horse lost foot control during a fast gallop and Bonus Magnet's death was accidental.

In due course, the inquest into Jeremy Faversham's demise occurred at the Gloucester Coroner's Court. The Medical Examiner's report showed that the banker broke his right collarbone and suffered multiple skull fractures. The Master of the Hunt told the court Jeremy had been an experienced and enthusiastic rider for many years. The coroner looked around the sparsely populated room. He recognised the banker's family and friends; he spotted a few local reporters. The other people in the room might have been from the national press. He could not tell. Considering what a swine this Faversham had been, it was a surprise not to see more faces.

After all, Jeremy Faversham committed a fraud that almost led to the collapse of a City of London bank. That fraud costs investors millions of pounds — investors such as Mr Michael Kent, the Gloucester coroner. Much of the forty million pounds Faversham raised from two hundred-odd clients at his private investment firm vanished. Rumours spread that he had misspent and embezzled twelve million. Michael Kent wanted to dance on this man's grave. Kent wished he had a bigger audience to watch him do it. Individuals need to be held responsible for their actions, he thought. They needed to know the actual consequences of their behaviour. It was no good for the Government to bail out these banks; that would not give sufficient incentive for them to mend their ways. They needed banging up in jail, locked up for a bloody long time, and the key should be thrown away.

As Michael Kent listened to an old codger called Chalmers rambling on about what he saw that morning, he mused on the prospects for his old age. He had been looking forward to retirement, looking through the glossy brochures for the cruise ships. Michael Kent was a confirmed bachelor. He had a close circle of friends who bored him to tears. So he toyed with the idea of selling up and spending his time on a series of ships. What could be better? Travel broadens the mind, and he would have new companions at the dinner table every couple weeks. That seemed attractive until Jeremy Faversham got his sticky fingers on Michael's expanding pension pot, and it disappeared without a trace.

The Gloucestershire coroner dragged himself away from his fading vision of the Captain's table and caught the last few words of Donald Chambers's diatribe.

"Hunting takes place in all weathers unless there is a risk of injury to the horses, such as hard or slippery ground. The hunt will always pack up as dusk falls. That morning the conditions underfoot were perfect. When I saw Mr Faversham riding by me on the far side of the field, he was going at a full sprint."

At the back of the court, a well-dressed observer with a military bearing sat listening. Major Michael Purvis had not suffered at the hands of Jeremy Faversham. Instead, he was enjoying a day away from Larcombe Manor. Alastor noted every tick in every box of the due process that a coroner's inquest took. In time, he would deliver a detailed report to Erebus and his colleagues in the Olympus Project. It would show that after the coroner's deliberation, Jeremy Faversham's death was an accident, no more and no less.

Once again, the meticulous planning and first-class execution that typified the work of Phoenix and his fellow Olympus agents turned up trumps. Those two hundred clients might only retrieve a small proportion of their lost money. Even so, Jeremy Faversham would never again have his hand in the till.

After the banker met his maker in the copse overlooking Downend Farm, the people out on such a lovely morning carried on their business. The Master of the Hunt arrived at The Old Bell Inn with his Field Master. They were not the first to arrive.

Several dozen riders, both men and women, milled around in the car park and on the approach road to the seventeenth-century watering hole. Some walked their mounts towards horse-boxes, while others engaged in warm equestrian conversation.

The scene greeting the Master was one his predecessors had met over the centuries. This idyllic moment was soon spoiled as the riders mingled with hordes of so-called supporters and the noisy arrival of a rag-tag army of saboteurs.

The Master knew a hundred riders rode with him today. Many now made their way home and were scattered abroad in the lanes and tracks across the shire. The social side of hunting had been so much more agreeable when he rode as a boy. So many oiks followed the field in their flat caps and wax jackets these days. These oiks drove like idiots, squeezed into their people carriers, had no affiliation to country pursuits significantly, and had no respect for the countryside. They worked in towns and cities from Monday to Friday and played country folk on the weekends.

The saboteurs pestering his hunt were mild by comparison with those that followed the horses in the neighbouring county. Last year, a hooded thug attacked a fellow Master during a hunt trying to drag him from his horse. Later in the day, as the Master prepared for the drive home with his horse and hounds in the lorry, a group of masked men set upon him with baseball bats leaving him on the ground unconscious.

So far, the local saboteurs were only guilty of the more run-of-the-mill crime of trespassing. Those still involved in hunting across the country knew the police were reluctant to get involved. It was fair to say that seven years after the hunting ban came into force, the cruel sport of the hunt saboteurs was as popular as ever. The hunts don't get much help from the police when they are attacked by hunt saboteurs, whether they blow a hunting horn to get hounds to run onto main roads or launch vicious attacks on humans.

The Master dismounted and joined a group of familiar friends. A stiff drink would be welcome over the coming hour. The food on offer in this beautiful old country inn would take away the bad taste of the unsavoury elements they attracted these days left in the mouth.

"Hello there," he called to the small crowd of riders. "Has everyone returned safe and sound?"

"There's no sign of Faversham as yet."

A few sniggers and negative comments were whispered among the banker's fellow hunters. He was not as popular as he had imagined. Jeremy Faversham had lived locally on his vast country estate for many years, but he was not entirely accepted. He splashed his money around, or more correctly, other people's money. Several of the hunt supporters having a go at him had been happy to be in his company when his generosity extended to buying rounds for everyone in the bar.

"I expect that poor horse of his protested at the extra weight Faversham expected him to carry," someone shouted.

An hour later, the hunt's staff left the Old Bell Inn car park, and the grass verges by the side of the road. Meanwhile, back in the woods overlooking Downend Farm, the emergency services had arrived, summoned by a woman walking her dogs.

Wayne Saunders had seen Jeremy Faversham riding by. Wayne was supposed to concentrate on the leading pack of riders well in front of the banker. However, Faversham's face had been in the media so much that Wayne immediately recognised him.

"Arrogant bastard," he thought as the banker galloped towards the woods.

With his mind back on the hunt, he reflected on how things had gone so far that morning. The rest of his fellow saboteurs did everything he asked of them. There was no sign of the local press providing much of a presence, so they shelved a banner demo on this occasion. His instructions had been to mingle and chat with the supporters, acting the part of followers, to find out which way the hunt was heading. Several of them were to spray their hand with Intimate and pat the hounds if they could get close enough to rub it well into their coats.

As the hunt progressed, Wayne kept an eye out for the police. He spotted a couple of cars, but they were well away from the action. They waited for the saboteurs to regroup by their vans and vehicles to move out after the hunt finished. Wayne was happy about that. It meant they would not be blocked in by hunt supporters trying to score a cheap point after having the saboteurs sniping at them throughout their so-called sport.

Wayne had headed towards Downend Farm on foot after the few riders not now cooling off after their workout. As usual, he kept his eyes peeled. Wayne did not want to get too close to the riders; they knew him too well. He also steered clear of confrontation with the followers, the beaters, and the rest, just in case a few turned nasty. Wayne wondered where Jeremy Faversham could be as his eyes darted from side to side for danger. He looked over his shoulder towards the copse. Wayne could see no sign of any horse and rider. Surely, Faversham must be through the spinney by now, he thought, but looking ahead towards Downend Farm, he could not pick out the portly banker among the handful of riders he saw.

Wayne Saunders had met up with his colleagues, and they carried on making themselves unpopular with the hunting fraternity. They sounded their horns, shouted, and protested about the continued existence of the hunt, even in its much-altered state since the ban. The whereabouts of Jeremy Faversham soon became the last thing on his mind.

Wayne remembered one odd thing that morning when the news of the banker's death reached him via a local radio broadcast. He spotted a few walkers as he glanced over his shoulder towards the woods. On reflection, it was a strange place to view the hunt. Wayne was unsure whether they had been regular supporters or the casual brigade from town. They wore dark clothing, hooded jackets, and balaclavas. They cast their eyes down or to the side when he looked towards them, so Wayne did not see their faces. The man at the back carried something in a canvas cover, around two metres long. In that few seconds, he surveyed the scene behind him. The image of a surfboard had leapt into Wayne's mind. He discounted that straight away as being just plain daft.

When he read the inquest verdict in the local press later, Wayne remembered that group of strangers and the item one of them had been carrying. He could not fathom what it meant. There were other fox hunts to follow and saboteurs to recruit. Wayne Saunders forgot all about Jeremy Faversham, the woods near Downend Farm, and the surfboard.

Chapter Two

Colin and Rusty had met the clean-up crew in a lane leading to the Old Bell Inn. But unfortunately, they could not partake of the sumptuous spread the Master and his friends would soon be tucking into after their morning exercise.

Colin knew that before the food and drink had time to settle in their digestive systems, they would hear the news about Jeremy Faversham. He knew their mission had been one hundred per cent successful. The whispers and the rumours would creep around the walls and low ceilings of the old coaching inn, bouncing off the brasses and the pictures of hunting scenes.

Long before the horses, dogs, and 4x4s returned to their various paddocks, kennels, and garages, their owners would have learned of the death of the crooked financier — a man who robbed around two hundred unsuspecting, innocent investors of their hard-earned cash. Colin Bailey would lose no sleep over his passing; he did not imagine many others would either.

The Olympus agents climbed into plain vans with tinted windows that they had parked on the quiet stretch of countryside. They moved off without fanfare and merged with the lunchtime traffic. The trip back to Larcombe was uneventful, and just over an hour later, they drove between the stone pillars and negotiated the winding driveway that led to the Olympus headquarters.

"Home Sweet Home," muttered Rusty.

"Another day, another dollar," chipped in one of the clean-up crew from the back of the leading van.

"Another day, another dead villain," said Colin quietly.

"Amen to that," said Rusty.

The agents left the vans with the transport section and walked across to the old stable block, where the staff had their quarters. After a brief conversation and removing their communication devices, several went to the ice-house. They returned the kit to the store and handed the camouflaged commando to the lads in the indoor firing range. The subject of the conversation had been food. Thinking of the Old Bell Inn and its excellent food had made everyone hungry.

Colin and Rusty were out of luck. The rest of the crew headed for the canteen in the terraced cottages where the estate workers lived many years ago; however, Colin and Rusty made for the orangery. Colin phoned Erebus and told him they were back from the Cotswolds mission and ready for their debrief. The elderly gentleman awaited them. He saw the vans coming up the drive and had already walked over from the manor house to their usual meeting place.

The three men met in the orangery. Erebus had anticipated his two agents' needs. A large pot of coffee and three cups stood on a tray between them, and another plate was piled high with bacon rolls.

"Dig in, chaps," said Erebus enthusiastically. "I've eaten my lunch, but after a fresh morning's exercise in the country, I expect you both need something appetising."

Rusty and Colin tried to express their gratitude without losing any of the roll, butter, and bacon they were devouring.

"While you two are catching your breath, I'll just recap today's events, and you nod in the right places."

Erebus went through the agreed itinerary for that morning's direct action. Colin and Rusty nodded when he looked over the top of his glasses to confirm the successful completion of a specific objective. Eventually, Colin could reassure his leader that the morning had gone without a hitch, thanks to their fieldwork beforehand.

Erebus sat drinking his cup of coffee, deep in thought. Colin and Rusty sensed the meeting was not over yet; Erebus wanted to share something with them. They had learned to read him well over the time they worked for the Olympus Project. Erebus was deciding how much he should reveal.

After a few minutes, which the two agents filled by further demolishing the food on their plate and washing it down with a second cup of coffee, Erebus began to speak.

"It is common knowledge among our country's intelligence chiefs that it will be impossible to prevent a well-planned terrorist attack on mainland Britain. As we learned earlier this year, the Olympic Games in London is the most likely target for suicide bombers. Our section here at Larcombe Manor supports this view without reservation. A secret government report on possible threats from Al-Qaeda and other Islamic terrorist organisations indicates a conservative estimate of the deployment of two hundred terrorists. The threat is likely to be much greater. The influence of homegrown terrorists is of even greater concern. Despite the deaths last year of Bin Laden and Al Awlaki, their organisation is still strong. The terrorists are developing new measures for the new countermeasures that MI5 and MI6 have devised. They are more security-aware. They will avoid wearing certain types of clothing and overtly praying before carrying out a suicide attack because they know the police will watch for those types of signs. The London Games will be subject to the biggest security operation in our nation's history. The highly patrolled sporting venues and stadia are unlikely targets. Public transport will be an option, as will the more isolated venues. We must be watchful and not underestimate the internal threat. We know recruitment and radicalisation are rife within our prison system. The internal threat is growing more dangerous. Extremists are conducting non-lethal training without ever leaving the country. We can no longer expect to track potential terrorists by monitoring passenger manifests between this country and Pakistan. Should these people evolve into suicide bombers, our umbrella of intelligence resources would struggle to find them on any radar screen."

Erebus had sat forward in his chair as he addressed the two agents. He now sat back and looked closely at them.

"This could prove to be the toughest nut we've had to crack so far, gentlemen."

Colin sighed.

"What are you thinking, Phoenix?" Erebus asked.

"I dislike nuts, Sir."

Rusty nearly choked on the last bacon roll. Erebus placed his cup back on the tray and rose from his chair.

"Well done this morning, gentlemen. We will have to wait until the inevitable 'accidental death' verdict from the Gloucestershire coroner. Then, if no complications arise, we can draw a line under the Jeremy Faversham case. So rest up this afternoon, chaps; I'll see you both later at the meeting."

"A meeting, sir?" said Colin.

"Ah, you haven't seen the message I sent you this morning. You can catch up with things after you return to your quarters. Time is ticking ever onwards. August will be upon us before we know it, and we must devise our plans posthaste. This evening will see the start of that process."

Erebus left them in the orangery. As Colin and Rusty finished the last pot of coffee, they chatted over the likely themes of any plans that Olympus might conjure up to combat the terrorist threat. Erebus had been right. It was a difficult nut to crack. London was going to be teeming with people of all nationalities. Identifying potential dangers could be extremely difficult. The Olympus Project agents were familiar with the task. Security around the Olympics would involve many other agencies and possibly even the armed forces. It could become a case of too many cooks.

"We'll be bumping into one another at every turn," said Rusty. "This will be a nightmare, mate."

A steward from the manor house came into the orangery to remove the tray and the crockery. Colin and Rusty took that as a signal to return to their quarters. Erebus wanted them rested for the meeting this evening.

Colin checked his emails. Sure enough, Erebus's invite to the meeting was there. So were various updates on intelligence surrounding cases Colin would be involved in over the weeks before the Games. First, a mother had reported her daughter missing in Oxford, but the authorities were slow in responding. There was a note about the potential transfer of prisoners from one high-security prison to another. Colin was interested in that one in particular.

Finally, who was likely to be on the passenger list? He filed both items away and then opened a series of messages from Athena.

"Are you free?"

"Do you want company?"

"Why aren't you answering? Is there something wrong?"

Colin delayed replying to these until after he had been to the pool. A few dozen lengths of exercise were what he needed. Colin had spent too much time standing around on the damp ground in the countryside for his liking. When he got back, he was dog-tired and lay on his bunk, intending to take a nap. Colin forgot Athena and her messages. He slept until Rusty knocked and stuck his head around his door.

"Come on, mate. We need to be somewhere."

When they entered the drawing-room for the meeting, Erebus was deep in conversation with Henry Case. Finally, Erebus nodded to acknowledge the agents' arrival.

The others filed into the room soon afterwards. Minos and Thanatos walked in together as usual; Athena followed them, and Alastor came behind her. Several of the more senior ex-SAS operatives attended too.

Erebus looked around the room to check everyone was ready. Then, satisfied that they were, he asked Henry Case to go through the past few weeks' events.

"As we agreed at our last summit meeting, the radicalised students involved in the Euston Station caper were dropped off at the service station near Spaghetti Junction. We have monitored their movements since that time, and no direct action is currently necessary."

"Did we have any luck in converting them," asked Athena, "and bringing them around to a less radical way of thinking?"

"We deemed it in the best interests of Olympus to

nurture the other contact we identified in the local Muslim community. He has had to work with caution. However, his information will prove to be most valuable to us. As for Habeeb Rehman, he was of no further use after he told us everything. He is now at rest, alongside the body of his colleague, Zunairah Jaffri, in the pet cemetery. We have identified the contacts Rehman interacted with in the ring and are keeping a close eye on their movements. We have used the list of names, addresses, landlines, and mobile numbers that Rehman provided in the end. The majority are of only a minor concern. We removed those deemed to be a real threat to national security."

"Did this create any response from the cell?" asked Minos.

Henry Case allowed himself a brief smile.

"We used subtle methods to remove these people, Minos. Have no fear. It is normal for people to return home to Pakistan to deal with family affairs, such as bereavement or a wedding. Accidents happen over there, too, you know. Older people succumb to sudden heart attacks. We placed notices in the local press in the Midlands to explain why these links in the chain had not returned and were no longer active. So far, the remaining cell members and any recruits are happy in their ignorance. As you will recall, the most important information Rehman gave us was regarding the trial run at Oxford Circus. Al Qaeda's plan is for the main strike to occur during the London Games. They planned coordinated attacks on the Olympic Village, the taking of high-profile hostages from both Britain and the USA. More terrifyingly, they plan to target several medal ceremonies on the penultimate day of the Games. The fallout from these attacks would be catastrophic, as you can imagine. Any prospect of going ahead with the final day's action, the pageant of the Closing Ceremony, and joie de vivre associated with such an event are lost forever."

The room fell silent as the Olympus agents and their masters absorbed these images. Then, finally, everyone realised the importance of Henry Case's comments. The next few days and weeks spent preparing to counter such a threat would take every ounce of their intelligence, resourcefulness, and courage.

Henry 'Head' Case had completed his initial report. Erebus stood up and took his time rearranging the folders and other items on the table in front of him before he finally addressed his audience.

"Thank you, Henry. I am sure we can agree we have a significant problem. Before I put forward my suggestions, does anyone wish to comment on what we've heard so far?"

Athena was the first to speak.

"Habeeb Rehman and Zunairah Jaffri have been eliminated. We have removed the most dangerous personnel from the cell operating in the Midlands and closely monitor everyone else involved. What possible threat can this group represent? They can't mount a credible attack on the Games with the scrutiny they are receiving. We may not be alone in watching these people; our lacklustre national security services might have stumbled across them by now. So why are we not concentrating our attention on potential terrorists arriving in the country from Pakistan, Afghanistan, and similar locations?"

"If we have a mole inside the cell," said Colin, "we should analyse the information Henry has gathered before we dismiss their threat. As for arrivals, good luck with that. Terrorists come in all shapes and sizes. The world will descend on Heathrow this summer to participate in or watch the Games. So let's concentrate on plans that counter any hopes of kidnapping and bombing within the environs of the Olympic venues that our intelligence section earmarks as confirmed targets. Whether Leicester, Lagos, or Lahore, where these beggars come from, does not matter a jot. Stopping them is what matters."

Athena was miffed. As one of the five leaders of the Olympus Project, she was not used to an agent questioning her views. Moreover, her relationship with Erebus over the years was stable. Her mentor had told her that when he felt it was time for him to stand aside, Athena was his natural successor.

Erebus paced around the room for a moment or two; then, he returned to stand by the head of the table. He looked at the assembled gathering of his most trusted and valued people.

"We have to make a decision. We have divided opinions on how we should best go ahead. I suggest we take a vote. But first, considering how important the matter is, I want you to go away and think carefully. We will reconvene at nine o'clock tomorrow morning. We will vote then, and, whatever the outcome, the Olympus organisation must receive your total support."

The meeting ended. The silence as the agents and their leaders left the room was deafening. Colin and Rusty made their way to the stable block. Colin saw Athena turn and look in his direction as she strode out of the room with Erebus. What was Athena thinking? Was she angry at his blatant opposition to her proposal? Or was she hurt because he had ignored her since his trip to the Cotswolds?

Colin and Rusty chatted amicably on the walk back to their quarters. Rusty had been thinking along the same lines as

Colin as far as their next moves were concerned. He favoured being proactive wherever possible; he would probably have taken direct pre-emptive action by now.

"How many terrorist organisations do we have operating in the UK, Phoenix?"

"Fifty of all creeds and colours, maybe a few more."

"Yes, but how many are interested in or have the capacity to attack the Olympic Games?"

"Just a couple, I reckon. The intelligence gatherers in the command centre will have a better handle on it."

Rusty slowed his walk and glanced over his shoulder to ensure they were alone.

"Exactly my point. There are just a couple of outfits and a dozen, perhaps twenty, faces to identify and take out of the game. Twenty bodies, unlike something far, far worse if an IED makes it into the Olympic Stadium when it's packed with athletes, officials, and spectators. Munich was bad. Atlanta was bad. The last thing we need is London's legacy being a major tragedy. If we did things my way, there might well be a bonus. Once word got out that we had removed several of the main players from the picture, it would deter any fringe extremists who might have been contemplating a solo effort."

"We must see which way the vote goes in the morning. Erebus was right when he said this was a tough one to tackle. Neither choice guarantees success. A single bomber working alone would be hard to stop. There will be too many people and venues, and the Games security will never cover everything."

The two men stopped outside the door to Colin's room.

"It sounds daft," Rusty grumbled, "but we'd better pray that any threat comes from an organisation with a load of people on the ground, working together. At least we will have a chance of picking up their communications or spot their activity en route to a venue."

Rusty strolled off towards his quarters with things on his mind.

Colin entered his room and flopped onto the bed. He intended to spend the rest of the evening relaxing. Colin thought through both his preferred scenario and that of Athena. Although both plans had merit, he had to admit that he felt hers potentially too conservative. If the vote went against him tomorrow, he would throw his weight one hundred per cent behind Athena's suggestion and then cross his fingers that the proverbial did not hit the fan.

The knock on the door was quiet but insistent. Colin was surprised to ascribe so much meaning to a few simple taps of the knuckle on wood. Despite being dog-tired after the busy day in the country, he knew there would be no rest until he found out who was calling at this late hour. He dragged himself off his bed and opened the door; it was Athena.

"I'm sorry, but I had to see you," she said, gently pushing Colin back into the room. She closed the door and locked it. Colin flopped back on the bed, his hopes of a good night's sleep forgotten for now. It must be important if Athena needed to speak to him urgently. He patted the foot of the bed and asked her to make herself comfortable.

Athena perched on the end of the bed. Her hair was loose and falling across her face. Colin was unsure what she came to say, but she seemed to struggle to find the words. She moved closer, tucking her long legs up under herself. Her right arm rested on his knee, casually enough, but it was a closeness that Colin found disturbing. It was unexpected but far from unpleasant, and, despite his tiredness, he felt deep in his body that something stirred.

Cancel that previous notion, he thought. If she stays much longer, a good night's sleep could be forgotten, full stop, let alone for the time being.

While Colin revised his overnight schedule, Athena moved closer still. She leaned her face in, kissed his forehead and eyelids, and then eagerly found his mouth. Colin fought the temptation at first, but then, as he realised resistance was futile, he responded, kissing Athena enthusiastically in return.

Colin realised he had been way off the mark, thinking Athena was mad at him for suggesting a different approach to the Olympic security problem. But, if she was, this was a strange way to show it. I should ignore her text messages more often, he thought, as Athena grew more amorous.

His hands slid across her back as she was now virtually on top of him. He broke the kiss temporarily, despite her groan of protest. Colin pulled her blouse and dragged it over that mane of hair, which fell over her bare shoulders and hid her face from his searching eyes.

Seconds later, they kissed again, and his hands moved to her breasts. She sighed, and her fingers trailed across his chest. "Wait," cried Athena and rose from the bed. She removed her bra. Colin clawed at her jeans, and they somehow removed the rest of their clothes. They collapsed onto the bed, and time stood still. Athena kissed his chest, his neck, and his mouth. Gently, she caressed his hips, thighs, and buttocks; she neglected the obvious. His erection was massive.

"How on earth could she have missed it?" thought Colin.

He kneaded her breasts and lowered his head to suck on them. Athena fell back, and Colin kissed her stomach and thighs. In turn, he pleasured her with his mouth and fingers, and she responded by taking the length of his shaft in her hand and stroking it. Colin knew he had to stop her before he lost control, and he parted her thighs and entered her. Athena cried out. It had been so long since she had been with her late partner, and Colin was much bigger.

Colin felt more confident now and moved inside her again, slowly at first. Athena moaned and arched her back as he made love to her gently, increasing the dance rhythm until both of them climaxed, leaving their bodies vibrating with intense pleasure. Colin lowered his face to her lips once more.

"I've wanted to do this since the first day I saw you at Larcombe Manor."

Athena kissed him and moved her hips. She encouraged him to stay where they were, locked together as one.

"Perhaps you should finish what you started then?" she whispered.

Colin's first thoughts of what Athena's late-night arrival meant were correct. It was over two hours before they finally fell asleep in each other's arms. Nevertheless, Athena was content; she finally set free the ghost of her lover from seven years earlier. She would never forget Simon, cherishing his memory and their time together. Now with Phoenix, she hoped she could look forward to a future filled with promise, a promise of loving and being loved.

Before he dropped off to sleep, Colin wondered what the last few hours would count for in the morning. He had always wanted to make love to Athena. She intrigued him from that first lunchtime here at Larcombe Manor. He realised she was a strong, forceful, and independent woman. That she was gorgeous was plain to see; what concerned him most was her breeding and intellect. Colin was unquestionably a clever man whose education had been cut short by his mother. Although he was always confident he could have made it to a redbrick university and made a fair fist of studying a degree course, Athena seemed way out of his league.

"Blokes like me don't pull a bird that attractive," he thought as they sized one another up at the dining table under the watchful eye of Erebus.

The older man had marked his card, too, in the months since his arrival at Larcombe. Erebus was aware of the potential for his successor at the helm of the Olympus Project and one of his most accomplished agents to become involved.

Colin was not sure whether Erebus approved of such a liaison or not. He told him to be cautious because Athena was still vulnerable. She lost her partner in the London bombings in 2005. Nevertheless, Athena had shown him affection before and after the Oxford Circus affair. Indeed she spent an innocent night in his room on one occasion. Tonight had been inevitable, but whether their relationship would continue to develop or whether Erebus and the organisation's demands would quash it was unclear.

Colin had other problems. There was Therese for a start. What was he supposed to do about her? Why was life so bloody complicated?

For most men with this dilemma, the answer would be simple enough; to be fair, most men would not get themselves into this situation. However, Colin Bailey had always been a different kettle of fish. His parents had neither wanted nor loved him. Karen Smith had been a good-time girl who trapped him into marriage, falling pregnant after one night of passion. Colin had not known *how* to love her.

Colin discovered that he could truly love their daughter, Sharon, and he did so without reservation, but a father and daughter's love is unique and very different. Sue Owens taught him about sexual desire, and their affair had been passionate to the extreme. Over their decade as lovers and, eventually, as man and wife, that passion had never diminished. Over time, it had matured into a loving relationship that both partners contributed to and savoured in equal measure.

Colin loved Sue Owens; his grief at losing her to cancer turned his heart to stone. It was this lack of feeling that had allowed him to hunt the targets he identified. Eight of the names he had added to his list while in The Gambia. More names had been on that list, but the close attention of DCI Phil Hounsell diverted him from his mission.

He should never have kidnapped the police officer's wife; that had been a mistake. It was a mistake that almost cost him his life, let alone his freedom.

As for Therese, Slater had bumped into her as part of his preparation for the Manchester job. There could have been anyone working behind the bar that afternoon. Therese was an attractive woman with a fantastic body. Colin had an itch that needed to be scratched. He was not proud of himself. Sex with Therese had been exciting and physical. She left him wanting more.

Events in Bath had led to his plans unravelling in an instant. He had been ambivalent; the coin was in the air. He could meet up with Therese and disappear into mainland Europe for a few months, or he could go in another direction, perhaps to Ireland and rest alone until the coast cleared for him to return. Phil Hounsell took the decision out of his hands. Therese had travelled to Holland alone.

At Larcombe Manor, Colin had met Athena, and that itch resurfaced. Was that all it was? Was he capable of feeling something deep and meaningful towards her? The

Scottish trip to eliminate Donald MacDonald changed everything. Who could have predicted that Therese would be on a station platform slap bang in front of his carriage window?

She had recognised Colin, even after his minor facial surgeries in West Africa and at Larcombe. The few days in Blackpool satisfied that blessed itch for Colin, but he wondered just where Therese thought it might lead. That train trip back to Bath after he left her soon passed. As the scenery flashed by, Colin saw little of it as he weighed up whether it was time to dispose of the sexy barmaid.

Not because she had become a threat, as she had not done so yet; Colin had not tired of her. It was Athena. He had to admit that Athena was in his head every hour he spent in Blackpool. She was a constant presence in his thoughts these days. As his eyelids grew heavier and heavier, Colin wondered why relationships were so bloody complicated. He dropped off to sleep without finding the answer.

Chapter Three

Mornings at Larcombe Manor followed a regular pattern. Agents were either leaving for a mission at the crack of dawn or returning from a job well done. Erebus and his closest cohorts breakfasted early and arrived promptly for their morning meeting at nine o'clock. Permanent staff in the stable block had been out of bed, ready for work in the ice-house by eight.

When Colin awoke, Athena had left.

He looked at his watch — a quarter past eight- and needed to move fast.

As he headed for the shower, he spotted a post-it note stuck to the screen of his computer. It contained a heart, a kiss, and 'A.' Colin sighed. The conversation he knew they needed to have would not happen immediately, but it had to occur sooner rather than later.

Almost as soon as he re-emerged, showered, shaved, and was ready to face the day, his phone rang.

It was Erebus.

"Good morning, Phoenix. I trust you slept well?"

Colin wondered if the boss knew about last night. Did he spot Athena creeping back to the main house? Erebus was a crafty old bugger; he did not miss a trick.

"Like a log, sir. A clear conscience helps," said Colin, with his fingers crossed.

"Touché, Phoenix. I need to see you after the morning meeting. We have this damned vote to get out of the way first, plus other items on today's agenda. It should be over in an hour, though. So let's say we'll meet up in the orangery at half-past ten, alright old chap?"

"That's fine with me, sir," replied Colin.

Erebus ended the call.

Colin finished dressing and walked across the manicured lawns towards the manor house. You could not help but be impressed by the magnificence of the old building, especially on a bright morning such as this. The Georgian edifice towered over him as he climbed the slope towards the patio. The secrets of the outbuildings had to stay hidden away from prying eyes, but the manor house deserved to be open to the public. What a shame they could never wander unaccompanied in the grounds or go on tours to see the exquisite furniture and paintings graced the interior.

"A penny for your thoughts, mate," called Rusty, running to catch him.

"I was thinking how beautiful this place is," said Colin.

"Whoa. Something's perked you up, and no mistake."

"Yeah, well," said Colin, a little flustered.

Rusty gave him a light tap on the shoulder.

"Only kidding, Phoenix. Whatever has made you believe this world's a beautiful place, long may it last. I reckon things will get worse before they get better, but I was always a miserable bleeder."

The two agents covered the last few yards into the

meeting room in companionable silence. Colin respected Rusty; he was a tremendous ally. You would not want to be on the wrong side of him. That was a certainty.

Rusty respected Phoenix too. When Phoenix arrived at Larcombe Manor, he had been wary of what Erebus saw in him. Rusty had questioned why Erebus had brought him into the fold. Everyone else who worked for Olympus was ex-service personnel. Most field agents were ex-SAS with a proven track record. Even Giles and the intelligence people wore a uniform for part of their careers.

Phoenix had a dark and troubled past. Rusty knew little or nothing of much of it. Erebus and the others at the top table kept secret what exactly he did before he arrived. Rusty knew he was a killer.

As the months passed, he had grown to appreciate just how good Phoenix was at his job. Phoenix did not take pleasure in killing or glorifying what he did. He believed when the system failed the victims, it was only proper that an agency such as Olympus should exact the punishment.

He's a perfect fit for the organisation, thought Rusty. Erebus had found the final piece of the jigsaw. The Olympus Project may have considerable adversaries ahead to face, but they were well equipped to conquer them with Phoenix on board.

The two men entered the room. Stewards moved back and forth with cups of tea or coffee. A folder for each attendee waited for them on the table in front of their chairs. On the side table, Colin saw a black tin box.

Colin wondered who was looking after the 'swingometer' this morning. It was akin to election night on TV. He and Rusty bid good morning to their colleagues. The clock on the wall showed one minute to nine.

Erebus and the rest of his inner sanctum swept through

the furthest door, and the morning's business could get underway.

"Good morning. I hope you have given the matters we discussed yesterday much thought. When you open your folders, you will find a ballot sheet. Please indicate which of the two options you wish Olympus to pursue. Fold your sheet in two and place it in the box provided. Minos will not vote. He will be responsible for the count."

A rustle of papers and a scramble of feet followed as the people around the table followed Erebus's instructions. Everyone voted in little more than a minute, and Sir Julian Langford QC unlocked the black box and tipped its contents onto the table.

Colin quickly checked the table to see how many Olympus people there were at the meeting today. He counted twenty. Bloody typical. No sign of 'Head' Case and the rest of the intelligence section people.

Minos handed Erebus the result; he read it out.

"Votes cast in favour of Option A; supported by Athena, ten. As proposed by Phoenix, the number of votes cast for Option B is also ten."

Colin had feared that this might happen. He did not know whether Henry or the others would have gone with his idea or not. But Erebus was now in a spot. He held the casting vote; surely, he would go with his future successor Athena?

Erebus sat at the head of the table, his thin, elegant hands steepled in front of his lips. His elbows rested on the arms of his chair. Eventually, he spoke.

"After consideration, I have determined that I shall vote for Option B."

Colin was stunned. There were several gasps around the table as people realised Erebus had gone against the wishes of his second in command. He had done so to follow a course of action proposed by the newcomer.

"Let us move on to the next item on our agenda," said Erebus.

Colin looked across to Athena at the right-hand side of Erebus. She gave a brief smile and a slight shrug of her shoulders. The woman was a class act, Colin mused. It must hurt, but she will never show it.

They dealt with the remaining agenda items in their usual efficient manner. There was updated terrorist cell activity and the latest report from the mole.

Further details have emerged about the proposed movement of high-security prisoners. A report covering the preparations for London 2012 by the authorities was in the folder for future reading and analysis.

Colin tried hard to concentrate, but he was fighting a losing battle. Erebus wrapped everything up before a quarter to ten. Everyone then left the room except Athena and the Three Stooges. They stayed behind with Erebus.

Colin had hoped to talk to Athena to clear the air, but not about what happened last night. That could wait a while longer. He was more concerned with the vote result, with Erebus siding with him instead of maintaining a united front.

Colin and Rusty walked back to the stable block together.

"Never saw that coming, Phoenix," Rusty said. "I mean, your idea was superior, but when the votes were level at ten apiece, I thought the old man would go for Athena, for sure."

"So did I," replied Colin.

"What are you going to do now, mate? I'm going for a swim."

"I'm going to take a rain check, Rusty. Erebus has summoned me. He wants another get-together in the orangery in thirty minutes."

"You are fast becoming his blue-eyed boy, Phoenix. Athena will be miffed."

Colin let Rusty have that one. He didn't want a long conversation about his relationship with Erebus and Athena. That was dangerous ground. Rusty was not daft. It would only take one ill-advised comment, and he could add two and two to make a 'relationship'.

"See you later," said Rusty and strolled to his quarters.

Meanwhile, Erebus and his colleagues finished discussing Option B's itinerary in the manor house.

"I have another meeting now. I know I can rely on your support for our chosen strategy. So I suggest we meet this evening, after dinner, to finalise our detailed plans."

Alastor, Athena, and Thanatos stood up and left the room.

Minos lingered behind on the pretext of tidying up the ballot box and sheets until he and Erebus were alone.

"Why did you give your casting vote in favour of Phoenix? Your ballot sheet in the box carried a vote for Athena. The way you fold a piece of paper is so distinctive. It could not have belonged to anyone else."

Erebus smiled.

"Caught out by one of my trusted colleagues," he said. "You are right. Based on people's comments and body language yesterday, I weighed up the likely number of votes for each option. I felt sure that Phoenix would have won the day convincingly if Henry Case and the others had been here. I hoped I could allow her to save face by voting for Athena, losing by a narrow margin. In the end, I had to use my casting vote, and given that scenario, I hoped she could reconcile her loss as a 'toss of the coin'. I needed her to believe it could have gone either way. I am a sentimental old fool, Minos. She will still succeed me as leader of Olympus in time. But it will do her no harm if, now and then, she doesn't get her way. She will be a better leader if she learns from the experience."

Minos nodded sagely. He wanted Erebus to think he understood completely, but in all honesty, it baffled him. Exciting times lay ahead.

At half-past ten, Colin left the stable block to meet his boss. Colin found Erebus in the orangery awaiting his arrival. He sat in a chair holding a sheaf of papers. He gave a deep sigh as Colin approached.

"Take a pew, dear boy," he said without looking up from the material he had been studying.

"Am I needed for something, Erebus?"

"I have a job for you, Phoenix, that requires your particular talents. Despite other pressing matters that need our attention, this nest of vipers is too much of a menace for us to ignore any longer."

"May I?" asked Colin, leaning forward and offering to take the papers from his boss.

"Certainly, Phoenix," sighed the old man. "Just holding these sheets of paper makes me feel unclean. I despair of the depths to which a few depraved members of our so-called society can descend."

"I'll study this and plan our response as soon as I finish," said Colin.

Erebus stood; he rested a bony, liver-spotted hand on Colin's shoulder.

"Plan, by all means, dear boy; it's what you do best. But make sure the bastards suffer, please."

Colin nodded, "Understood, sir."

When he returned to his quarters, he started reading. Over two years ago, Tanya Norris ran away from her family home in Oxford. Tanya was fifteen. She stayed with a school friend and then drifted from town to town, seeking temporary work. Instead, she ended up homeless on the streets in Swindon.

Tanya was vulnerable. A sadistic gang who manipulated and controlled a crop of underage girls in the sprawling Wiltshire town had groomed her and sold her for sex in a few weeks.

The Olympus Project investigation team uncovered a staggering amount of background detail. It impressed Colin. It did not make for pleasant reading, but he couldn't deny its thoroughness. Tanya's mother had reported her missing, but the police had few resources available to find a delinquent teenager. They were too busy filling in forms and persecuting motorists to hit their traffic offence quotas.

There were four men involved in the grooming and abuse. They were two sets of brothers who had preyed on pre-teen and underage teenage girls for the past five years at least. Six weeks ago, Tanya Norris became pregnant. The gang attempted to make her miscarry. Her condition went into a rapid decline. One gang member drove her to a local hospital, not out of concern for her safety but to dump her on someone else's doorstep. They had no further use for her, so she got shoved through the passenger door onto the pavement outside without slowing down. Tanya was very sick; without quick action, she may have died.

Fortunately, the staff spotted Tanya and hurried her into the emergency room, where they treated her immediate injuries. The doctor looking after her noticed other scars and bruising, plus the usual demeanour and pallor associated with a habitual drug user. She interpreted this as indicative of her young patient suffering abuse over a long period, whether self-administered or by a third party. She became concerned for Tanya's welfare, but Tanya shut down. Months of abuse, the frequent misuse of alcohol and drugs and the Svengali-like control the gang members exerted over her left her afraid of her own shadow. She trusted no one.

As Tanya recovered in the hospital, the doctor spent as long as she could, often in her own time, building up the young girl's trust. There was no mention of police or social services. The doctor did not interrogate her about her family or friends. She gently probed, trying to get the youngster to open up to her more on each visit. In time, the dam broke. Tanya cried, and the entire sad story tumbled out between the sobs and the tears.

Once the full horror of Tanya's treatment at the hands of the gang became apparent, the young doctor made a phone call. That first call was to a national newspaper. Giles and his team at Larcombe intercepted that call and opened a case file. A male and female field agent drove to Swindon and took steps to relieve the young doctor of any further responsibility in Tanya's case.

Tanya Norris had gone when the doctor reported for her next shift. She discovered that Tanya's parents so-called had arrived from Newbury. The friendly reporter meeting the young doctor for a scoop on what happened to these vulnerable girls was working on another political scandal. He had been notified by a concerned senior colleague at the hospital that his informant was a stressed-out young NHS doctor. She was a doctor who worked incredibly long hours and was prone to flights of fancy.

Tanya was in a safe house in Devizes where a nurse looked after her, ensuring her physical wounds healed.

Someone else would need to be with Tanya over the coming months to help her back to something approaching normality because her mental state would take far longer to heal. Over the next couple of days, the male and female agents who posed as her parents interviewed her and the sheets of paper that Phoenix now read contained Tanya's tale.

Colin read what was becoming a familiar pattern across the country. The four men came from Muslim backgrounds, in their early to mid-thirties. Their victims were almost exclusively white. Over the past five years, people with suspicions about what was happening contacted the police and social services. Unfortunately, no one had followed up on those suspicions. Colin shook his head.

"I can hear the conversation. 'We will be racists if we accuse them of something'. Either that or because of their backgrounds, they wouldn't have believed the girls might be telling the truth. The authorities discounted any rumours or complaints as unreliable."

He continued reading.

These girls were between twelve and fifteen years of age. Most of them came from broken homes; some had run away from home, like Tanya Norris. Others were already in the care system and were frequent absconders. In a matter of weeks after meeting the men, they received presents, and then alcohol was followed by coke and heroin.

They were ferried to the town in expensive cars and lulled into believing the men cared for them. It was easy to see why they fell for these tactics. They never had much love at home. For a few, it was the first time in their life that anyone had shown them affection.

In time, the drugs made Tanya and the others dependent on the gang, and it soon became impossible for them to leave. That was when Tanya's nightmare began. She described her ordeal to the Olympus agents. Page after page detailed where, when and how the rapes and torture occurred. If she showed any sign of resistance, her punishment was severe.

Colin had only read a few pages, and he understood why Erebus reacted as he did. He felt the same disgust — the same wish to punish these men without mercy.

After the four men had used and abused her for days, they set her to work for them. Tanya travelled in the same expensive cars she enjoyed in those first innocent days. Now she went to various addresses around the town where dozens of men paid hundreds of pounds to her captors to have sex with her.

Inevitably, Tanya became pregnant. Her treatment at the hands of the brothers was horrendous. The gang blamed her for being stupid and not taking precautions. The beatings and verbal abuse continued until the bodged attempt at a miscarriage and that final car ride to the hospital. After that, they continued to exploit the remaining girls under their control without a single thought for Tanya.

Colin closed the file. He took it back to his quarters and locked it in a drawer. He took a shower because he felt unclean. Colin then dressed in casual clothes and visited the gym. He knew he needed to keep active. Colin always found that punishing his body allowed him to forget his pathetic minor problems. He used the time he lifted weights and rained blows on the punchbag to plan his response to what he had read. It was time for the four brothers to answer for their crimes.

Colin's workout had exhausted him. He showered yet again and threw on a sweatshirt and jeans. He rested on his bed, going over the file and awaited the knock on the door.

It never came. He spent the evening putting the final touches on his plans. Once satisfied that he had covered everything, his last task was to email the armoury, listing the requirements for his mission. Colin decided to turn in early. He was tired and asleep before his feet touched the pillow.

He was out of bed early the following day. When he looked out of the window, he saw that overnight the clouds had rolled in, and it was murky with the threat of rain. Luckily, he was not spending the day on the high ground because the temperature had dropped fast. Any rain that fell could fall as sleet or snow in parts of the West Country today.

His first visit was to the armoury in the ice-house. Barry Longdon, the ex-SAS Sergeant, was on duty. Bazza had been on hand to pick the most appropriate weapons for Colin over the past few months for his missions. He had also been there to help pull him out of the waters below Pulteney Weir.

"As you can see from my email yesterday evening, I need the right tools to take out four guys in Swindon, Bazza. What do you recommend?"

"Where did you have in mind? There's the County Ground, the railway museum, or perhaps you prefer somewhere quiet? There isn't much choice compared to the lovely city of Bath, Phoenix."

"These guys drive around at night in flash cars. They ferry young girls to pubs and clubs, show them a good time, and then have them turning tricks later. That means moving them around the town in the daytime too. Sometimes they even pop into the country if a bloke living in a big house fancies underage company."

"Tricky. I'm guessing that rules out the pipe bomb under the car or an RPG; too much collateral damage," said Bazza, referring to the specification that Colin had sent.

Colin knew Bazza would give him the answer in the end. He had to let him have his bit of fun. There was not a lot of that available in the ice-house armoury. Apart from a rare foray into the evil world above ground, they entertained agents who needed to sharpen their shooting practice. They checked guns, knives, and other materials in and out of the stores. Now and then, they helped with burial duties for visitors to Hotel California that exceeded their usefulness.

"I can tell that you are a busy man, Phoenix," the armourer said, turning to his racks and boxes of available items.

He produced an array of items from the shelf nearby. It was plain he had been awaiting Colin's arrival.

"Here's something I prepared earlier, Phoenix. As you can see, everything will fit into your hands-free carrier of choice, the ubiquitous backpack."

"Sweet," said Colin picking up the SIG Sauer pistol from the counter. "This baby has serious stopping power; I take it?"

"More than enough for what you want. Just shy of a kilo of weight, and you know you have it in your hand. It's the P226 model with a twenty-round magazine of nine millimetres Parabellum cartridges."

"Twenty rounds?"

"You said four blokes?" replied Bazza with a twinkle in his eye.

"That's right. Only the four, but Erebus is anxious that these guys and any others of their type get the message, you know?"

"I won't ask what they've been up to, mate, but if the boss wants them hurt, it must be nasty."

"Very nasty," said Colin.

"When are you off, mate?"

"When I get the green light from Erebus. If I grab him after the morning meeting and take him through my itinerary, I can be in the targets' backyard in an hour."

"Day trip, do you reckon?"

"Maybe, I'll need to book myself in somewhere just in case and do an on-the-spot 'recce' tonight. Then, if I can quickly confirm the target's whereabouts, I can improvise. I shall do my best to be back tomorrow."

"Have a successful trip, mate," the armourer shouted as Colin scooped up the equipment and headed back to his quarters.

Colin looked at his watch when he off-loaded the kit in his room. He had plenty of time to load up his backpack before Erebus and the others would be out of the meeting. So he telephoned the main house to arrange a ten-minute session with the elderly gentleman as soon as he was free.

While he waited for the call, he leafed through the file that Erebus gave him yesterday.

Anjum Ahmed 35

Kamal Ahmed 31

Farhan Hussein 37

Bassam Hussein 34

These were to be his targets. There were no details of education or occupation. These men had worked the system ever since they arrived in the country. If they had filled in a form in the past five years, they might have put 'entrepreneur', provided they could spell it. Colin read the analysis of the gang supplied by the Olympus intelligence section through again.

According to an imam from a local Islamic congregation, race and religion linked these grooming rings inextricably. The more radical preachers encouraged men such as the Ahmed and Hussein brothers to believe young white girls were naturally promiscuous just because they were non-believers, non-Muslims. They see the way British girls dress in skimpy, revealing clothes. Their provocative nature was encouraged by the images portrayed in the media by their screen and music idols. The four brothers believed they were justified in exploiting and degrading them. It was what they deserved.

The authorities appeared eager to ignore the exploitation, desperate not to undermine the official creed of cultural diversity. They had failed to act, even in the face of evidence of blatant abuse.

Colin shook his head as he read the swift public whitewash the authorities had received. 'There was no apparent evidence of willful professional misconduct; senior managers were unaware of the problem.' Colin circled the piece that said, 'no one was to be disciplined or sacked' Typical, he thought; no one will 'carry the can' despite the errors made.

Colin made a note of a few names. He was determined to mention them to Erebus. Several of these people deserved to suffer for their lack of action. Maybe they did not deserve to die, but at least they should lose their jobs or experience pain.

His mobile chimed in with its ring tone of 'Breaking The Law' by Judas Priest. It was a steward up at the manor house. Erebus wanted to see him at eleven o'clock in the orangery. Colin packed his backpack and an overnight bag. With an eye on the weather, he changed into the clothes he intended to wear for the first part of his mission.

From the disgust Erebus showed yesterday towards this gang, Colin knew that getting the green light to take them out was a formality. He wasn't presumptuous, packing everything ready for the off. He expected to be on the station platform at Bath Spa in good order.

Dodging the puddles after a sharp shower earlier than he had expected, he darted to the orangery before the heavens opened again. Inside he found Erebus waiting for him. His leader had sensibly worn a winter coat, and his umbrella lay on the floor by his chair — a trilby perched on the coffee table in front of him.

"Did you get caught in that shower, Phoenix?" Erebus asked.

"Just missed it, sir."

"Right, what have you got for me?"

Colin took him through his plan of action. Erebus queried a few minor items, which Colin answered to his satisfaction.

"Everything looks perfect, dear boy," said Erebus, "but one query. When you have achieved the complete success of our primary aim, what will you do about the poor, unfortunate girls that these swine have been exploiting?"

"They are being collected either tonight or tomorrow by the same agents that picked up Tanya Norris. First, they will take them to our hospital for check-ups, then to the safe house in Devizes over the next couple of days. How long they stay in the hospital and at the safe house will depend on the conditions we find. It's open-ended, I'm afraid."

"It can't be helped, Phoenix. We must support them as much as possible without drawing attention to our activities. We must try to avoid getting on the radar of the authorities."

Colin saw his opportunity to raise the matter of his little list of bonus names.

"The authorities haven't shown their radar to be that sensitive, sir. I think we can assume they will be in the ostrich position. What do you think we should do to these senior police officers and care system managers? They appear to have a blatant disregard for what was happening on their watch."

He handed the list to Erebus.

"Let me have a day or two to consider that one, Phoenix. It will need delicate handling."

"Oh, so I can forget it then, sir?" said Colin.

Erebus threw his head back and laughed aloud.

"There will be no extreme measures; you are correct in your assumption. Olympus needs to tread with care. Each extra covert mission we carry out has the potential to provide another grain of information. It may provide something that the security services, police, or our great British public might stumble across. In time, they could recognise that a common hand controls events."

"I understand. Do I have your permission to carry on, Erebus?"

"Godspeed,"

Erebus picked up his hat and retrieved his umbrella, giving it a final shake. Without a backwards glance, he disappeared towards the door and away across the grounds to Larcombe Manor. He was undoubtedly thinking of his lunch or whatever international or domestic crisis Olympus was attempting to tackle today.

Colin watched him stride away into the distance, then returned to his room, collected his bags, and phoned the transport section. An Olympus mini-cab pulled up outside the stable block within two minutes. Fifteen minutes later, despite the best efforts of Bath's traffic nightmare trying to delay them, Colin was on the concourse, walking into the station. He purchased a ticket for Swindon and awaited the next train; he did not have long to wait. The service was regular, and the journey time was only twenty-five minutes, provided no blessed engineering works existed.

He could make out the female station announcer rabbiting on as his train arrived at his destination. It was disappointing. Phoenix had half expected to see Andy Partridge from XTC there to greet him. Instead, he tried to hear the distinctive male tones from the days he travelled here on the train as a boy.

"Swindon. This is Swindon."

Nothing is ever forever.

Colin was hungry, so first things first. He left the platform and made his way into the town. Colin took his map from his bag. He soon found a place to grab a snack. While Colin ate, he looked at the map and tried to work out where to look for the brothers. Tanya had provided lots of information, and he had marked a few likely spots the gang frequented during daylight hours.

Swindon is a sprawling, shapeless conurbation. Thousands of people commute to it every weekday. Then they get the hell out in the evening. Colin had heard the rumours surrounding the four Ps—the vast council estates and tower blocks that dotted Pinehurst, Penhill, Park North, and Park South.

The gang had the girls housed in flats dotted around the town. Keeping them together in the same place would have attracted attention from the resident patrols that had sprung up in recent years. The Broadgreen area and Manchester Road used to be home to the town's red-light district. Over the years, there has been a dramatic reduction in the number of on-street sex workers. However, the locals would spot a 'knocking shop' a mile away.

The band of brothers had helped cut the numbers of on-street girls, although civic pride had little to do with it. Their girls were scattered everywhere. They kept them supplied with drugs and drink. In return, they were driven to clients, even out of town, to earn their keep. In the evenings, the brothers often took the girls to nightclubs. It was supposed to show them they still cared, but they were not above making them work if punters willing to pay. When the clubs emptied, the gang piled their charges into the cars and returned them to the flats.

Colin had wondered at first why none of them tried to make a break for it. Tanya's testimony had soon put him right on that score.

'The brothers own the flats. They rent them either to family members or friends. The girls have a place to sleep if they're lucky. If it's an occupied flat, the tenant or tenants rape them. The lucky ones are those in a flat with a second bedroom locked overnight. One girl tried to escape while I was there. They burned her with cigarettes, beat her, and nearly choked her to death. Nobody tried to run away after that.'

Colin checked in at the Holiday Inn at two o'clock. It was soulless, but he craved anonymity, and it was close. The middle-aged care-worn employee in Reception looked up as Colin arrived with his overnight bag and backpack. He attempted a smile but failed; it only made him look like he had a touch of wind.

"Good afternoon, sir," he gushed.

Colin let him carry on with his corporate banter and tried to nod in what he thought were in the right places. He saw a card slide across the desk and a pen; this was the first hurdle. Colin considered what name to use. He filled in the card and passed it back.

"Welcome, Mr Partridge. I hope you enjoy your stay."

Colin gave the bloke a look that told him to get on with it. After that, things speeded up, and Colin soon found himself in his comfortable little room. He placed the backpack and its goodies under the bed. The overnight bag went on the floor beside it. There seemed no point in getting his change of clothes out and putting things on hangers.

Colin took the opportunity to sleep with the prospect of a late night and a busy day tomorrow. When he woke up, it was dark, and the weather had not improved. He freshened up, slipped on his hooded jacket, and set off to track down the gang.

As soon as he left the Holiday Inn and mingled with the early evening pedestrians, he became invisible. That was the way he liked it.

Chapter Four

Old Town has plenty of pubs and clubs; Colin found a fast-food takeaway that served up something edible. He kept away from brightly lit shop windows as he ate and then stashed the remains in a bin. Colin was too polite to add to the detritus that littered the streets and pavements. As another short, sharp shower hit, he pulled his hood forward, tucked his head down, and began his search.

Colin liked pubs. His favourites were those with bands playing his brand of music. The places he visited were dead. They had a handful of punters, and apart from a few tunes from a jukebox or a lacklustre karaoke night, no sign of a group playing anywhere. So far, there was no sign of either of the brothers out on the town. Colin persevered.

He relied on his mental list of places to visit and the best routes to take to reach them. He would have been labelled a stranger, ripe for a mugging, if he stood around looking at a street map on every corner, asking for directions. The bus service was one big plus in a town as large as Swindon. Colin could move around to the most distant places on his list, using relatively quick and cheap transport. Buses were more anonymous than taxis.

There were loads of taxis on the roads too. However, Colin did not want to risk a driver in a day or two telling his fellow cabbies,

"You'll never guess who was in the back of my cab the other night."

Over the next couple of hours, Colin used the bus shelters in Old Town to get out of the rain. He saw the time of the upcoming arrival conveniently displayed above him. Nobody paid him any attention. It was usual with buses heading for the four corners of the town for the next to pull in, or the one after, not to be the service you wanted to board.

The shelters he used gave him a good view of the pubs and clubs circled on his map. He revisited some of them because everywhere he visited came up empty. There was no sign of the gang yet. It was cold and damp. He even started thinking that the room at the Holiday Inn would be more welcoming. Then he spotted a BMW X5 turning into the street fifty yards away.

"Flash gits," thought Colin, stamping his feet to keep warm. His only companions in this glass and metal haven were an elderly couple. He thought he had seen them earlier; they rode the buses to keep warm. Their bus passes gave them a free journey anywhere they fancied going, and it saved on their heating bills. Oh well, something for him to look forward to when the time came.

Colin kept his eyes on the SUV. It pulled into the bus lay-by on the opposite side. Whoever sat inside seemed in no hurry to get out. Colin soon realised why. A top-of-the-range Lexus roared towards him and executed a noisy u-turn, drawing up behind the BMW. It made sense. They collected the girls from different points on the compass.

The bus the elderly couple awaited arrived. Colin moved from the shelter for a more unobstructed view of the cars over the road. Doors opened, and girls of all shapes and sizes fell out of the vehicles. Their drunkenness was the one thing they had in common. Two large men walked them towards the nearest nightclub, and door staff nodded them through without checks. These girls were frequent flyers.

The two cars drove towards the multi-storey car park in the distance. He decided to hang on until the drivers returned to check if they would join the rest of their party.

"I might yet have the chance to kill two birds with one stone," he muttered as he resumed watch from the shadows of the bus shelter.

Sure enough, he spotted two men fitting the descriptions of the brothers. They stood on the opposite pavement. It looked to be one from each family, echoing what he had seen ten minutes ago as the noisy crowd of girls made their way into the nightclub.

Colin gave it two or three minutes; then, he crossed over. Suddenly, the door staff had something to do. The gang and the girls breezed inside the dark interior without a second glance. As Colin approached the entrance, one man stepped in front of him. He was as wide as he was tall.

"Arms out and legs apart," he grunted and frisked Colin. "Turn out your pockets too, please, sir, just to make sure you have no drugs on your person."

Colin thought that was a bit rich, considering the state of the girls who went in with their pimps, but he decided to play dumb. He was just glad he left the SIG Sauer in the hotel room.

As every Olympus direct action field trip was on expenses, he handed over the ten quid admission fee to the girl at the desk with a smile. In return, she switched her gum from one side of her mouth to the other.

Colin walked inside the club. The place was Swindon, not Ibiza, and it was half-empty on a cold, wet weekday night. The crowd he was interested in occupied a semi-circular booth on the far side. There were loads of drinks on the tables, primarily alcopops for the females, and the Muslim Brotherhood looked to be on soft drinks.

As he strolled to the bar, he took in the rest of his surroundings. The décor was faded eighties chic, not an attempted retro look, just untouched since the eighties. The music was louder than loud, and Colin had heard enough. That frantic dance, trance, pants music encouraged people to look stupid on the small dance floor.

Almost on cue, a few women began gyrating, bouncing, and shaking that booty. They waved their arms manically above their heads, making them look like extras from Day of the Triffids. Colin bought himself a pint of lager and was pleasantly surprised to receive much change from a tenner. He sat at the end of the bar to watch his targets on the opposite side of the room.

He checked out the four men. They were well-built but more flab than muscle. They were suited and booted, with chunky gold rings, chains, and bracelets. Colin had watched the way they walked when they approached the club. They had that exaggerated gangster swagger that looked cool in Thirties America. It looked pathetic in Swindon Old Town in 2012.

The music seemed to get louder and faster. The brothers mingled. A click of the fingers towards a skinny girl with long blonde hair summoned her to join one of the gang members at another table. Colin identified Anjum Ahmed as he leaned his big head close for a brief conversation with a middle-aged white bloke. Anjum patted the man's shoulder and left the girl with him.

Colin never saw money change hands.

"Perhaps he has an account," thought Colin.

"You can buy me a drink if you want."

Colin turned his head towards the voice. She looked like mutton dressed as lamb.

"I'm not looking for company," replied Colin.

"I'm not fucking selling it, you stuck-up bastard."

Nobody else heard this verbal exchange above the sound of the music.

Colin thought she meant to whack him with her oversized handbag, but in the end, she stomped off, cursing him with every step. This mission was turning out to be a nightmare, Colin thought. The music was driving him mad. The thirty or forty locals belonged to the fake tans, tattoos, cheap jewellery, and dodgy clothes brigade. He half expected to spot a shell suit if he stayed around long enough. Only the four blokes he needed to watch kept him there.

His would-be partner retreated to a table behind him and looked daggers at him. He felt the heat without turning his head. Farhan and Bassam Hussein still mingled. They appeared to have a handful of regular contacts in the place. The brothers struck a deal and made brief introductions. The client either carried out preliminary fumbles with the young girl in the booth or disappeared straight away for a good time. Well, a quick time for the most part.

Colin referred to his watch. Shit, only half-past twelve. If he was a proper punter, he had another couple of hours of this. It would be four hours if it were the weekend; he didn't see the attraction. He finished his pint and went to the Gents. On returning to the bar, he stopped in the corridor and flipped open his mobile. He rang a Devizes number.

"Can you have a van and a good car here in an hour to pick up our packages?"

"If the traffic is light, we could do that. Where are you?"

"We'll meet at the entrance to the multi-storey near the Wyvern Theatre."

"What do we need to bring?"

"Two pairs of strong arms should be enough."

"Will do. See you in a while."

Satisfied the targets would be in the club for an hour, Colin returned to the Holiday Inn. His middle-aged sparring partner from this afternoon had gone. The older man who had replaced him looked half-asleep, so there was no problem then. Colin went up in the lift to his room and retrieved his backpack. Then he descended to the foyer again by the stairs. The man in Reception turned his back and did a few stretching exercises. Maybe he had dropped off to sleep with the boredom and was taking desperate measures to wake himself up.

Colin slipped quickly and silently into the chilly night air. He checked his watch; he had plenty of time with less than five minutes' walk to the car park.

Wandering around a multi-storey car park late at night is not a safe occupation. Colin could tell this ageing building only had a fraction of the vehicles that a more modern construction could hold. So he moved to the three levels searching for the gang's large, flashy motors. In the early morning, it wasn't too difficult to find them. They parked on Level 2 and were only three or four spaces apart.

Colin returned to the ground floor in the shadows and looked for signs of the brothers and their female companions. They were still in the club. The streets were almost empty, with occasional cars or taxis on the nearby main road. A few unsteady pedestrians went home after visiting a local kebab house. He waited.

It was a quarter past one. Two vehicles turned off the main road and entered the small car park in the shadow of the multi-storey. As the people carrier pulled up opposite him, the driver flicked his headlights twice. A Porsche 911 slipped alongside it, and a few moments later, the two drivers got out and walked over to where Colin stood.

"What's the latest Phoenix?" asked the male driver of the people carrier.

"Our targets are in a nightclub five minutes' walk away. I doubt the packages you are here to collect can walk that far on the heels they're wearing. So somebody must collect the cars and then pick the girls up outside the club. We must be ready to follow them wherever they go in Swindon."

"What is our exact role in this job?" the female driver of the Porsche asked.

"Did you come equipped?"

"You suggested a pair of strong arms on the phone," said the man tapping the shoulder holster at the side of his chest. "We can play our part."

Colin briefed the two agents. He had imagined two or three different scenarios and, as usual, worked through them in detail. Two things could prevent things from going as planned. First, the route the gang members would take when dropping the girls off was uncertain. Second, they could not be sure how the girls themselves would react if they attacked the vehicles and took out the two sets of brothers.

For now, they must sit and wait for the party to return

from the club. Colin joined his new colleagues in the relative warmth of the people carrier.

Hayden Vincent was now twenty-eight years old. He served in Iraq and Afghanistan as a medic. Under fire in Helmand, he met Kelly Dexter, a Lance Corporal in the Logistics Corps. Kelly, now twenty-six, took shrapnel in the legs after a mortar attack. In 2010, Olympus approached them and invited them to join the team when they returned to the UK. They were a couple. Where one went, the other followed, so they headed to Larcombe at once for training.

Over the past eighteen months, they had been living and working in Devizes. Colin knew Olympus had 'sleeper' agents scattered across the country. Direct action missions involved experienced professionals or gifted amateurs such as himself, but Hayden and Kelly received the same level of training as himself. He was happy that they would cope with anything this job threw at them.

Colin sensed the two men's approach before they materialised by the entrance to the car park. He motioned his companions to cut any chatter and keep down until the men had gone for their cars.

Once the coast was clear, Colin nudged Kelly, and they got out of the people carrier and into the Porsche.

A minute later, the BMW and the Lexus descended the ramp and exited the multi-storey. As the cars eased onto the main road heading back to the club, Colin signalled to Hayden to follow them. Kelly followed behind him, keeping a sensible distance.

"Who drove which car? Do we know?" asked Kelly.

"Kamal Ahmed in the BMW; Farhan Hussein in the Lexus. The same as on the way into town."

Outside the club, twenty-odd people stood on the pavement. Taxicabs picked up fares. Colin noticed the woman who wanted him to buy her a drink earlier. She gripped the arm of a large black man; he had to be twenty-five stone at least. She looked drunk, but she seemed happy enough. All's well that ends well, Colin thought.

A few yards farther, Colin spotted a group of girls being shoved unceremoniously into the back of the flash cars. Doors slammed. The shouting died, and the vehicles pulled away.

"Okay, the Hussein and Ahmed brothers use the same motor."

Hayden watched to see which direction the Lexus headed. His task was to follow at a discreet distance and photograph the address details where each girl got out. Then, they could be collected later. Phoenix anticipated trouble at some addresses on his list, but if they needed reinforcements for the morning, they were only a phone call away.

Farhan and Bassam Hussein were unaware a car was tailing them; they set off along Queen's Drive towards the A419. They dropped off girls in Walcot, Covingham, Stratton, and Pinehurst and headed back towards Old Town.

Hayden moved his vehicle closer. They were on a deserted tree-lined road at half-past two in the morning. There were no cars or people anywhere in sight. Hayden accelerated. Farhan Hussein didn't appreciate a people carrier overtaking him and 'cutting him up.'

"Bastard," he yelled.

"Let's teach that white boy a lesson," shouted Bassam.

Hayden saw the headlights of the Lexus getting closer and closer. He turned off the main road into a quiet side street as if returning home after a night out. He slowed and parked. The Lexus swerved around him and screeched to a halt sideways in front of him.

"What the fuck do you think you were doing?" screamed Farhan as he came around the front of the Lexus. Bassam had trouble opening the passenger door. Farhan had come to a halt so near Hayden's vehicle that he couldn't move.

Hayden slipped his gun out of the holster and removed the safety. Farhan was kicking the headlight on the passenger side of the carrier. It was time to carry out his orders. Phoenix had told him what Erebus specifically requested.

Hayden stepped from the car and walked calmly towards the Lexus. He shot Farhan and turned toward Bassam, who frantically tried to clamber over the driver's seat to climb out of the car. The younger brother's bulky frame made that impossible. Hayden shot him in the same area as he had Farhan. It was not an agent's standard choice for a kill shot. The blood they lost from where their wedding tackle had been was significant, and the two Hussein brothers lay bleeding and whimpering.

Hayden sat in the car for a few minutes and checked his watch. He made a quick phone call to a clean-up crew in Shrivenham. He received confirmation they knew the precise location they had to come to and were close at hand. Hayden shrugged and got back out of the car.

"You haven't suffered enough, but I'm needed elsewhere."

He finished the job with two headshots and drove towards Old Town.

Kelly Dexter was an expert driver.

Colin Bailey was a novice by comparison. Driving to the

shops in a beach buggy back in The Gambia didn't give him the credentials to carry out this job.

Anjum Ahmed was a boy racer, even at thirty-five. He ignored the rules of the road and was a nightmare to tail, but Kelly Dexter coped admirably.

The Ahmed brothers only had two girls in the back of the BMW. When they left the club, the route suggested that the flat or house they delivered them to was in Toothill or near The Link centre.

Anjum's driving style alternated between aggressive acceleration and braking. He changed lanes whenever he pleased. He tried to see how close he could get to running a red light and used his mobile phone throughout. Anjum only ever had one big mitt on the wheel at any time. Sometimes not even that if he wanted to light a cigarette.

"If the police pulled him over, he'd be riding a bike next week," Kelly muttered.

"Points on his licence are the least of his worries," snorted Colin. "As for riding a bike, no chance."

Kelly followed the same procedure as her partner. Don't let yourself be spotted. Photograph the addresses. Colin sat beside her, watching and waiting in silence. In time, both girls were out of the car and indoors. They may not be one hundred per cent safe yet, but their ordeal at the hands of their abusers was at an end.

Kelly and Colin had to follow the men back to their homes. However, as the BMW began the trip back towards Old Town, it suddenly turned off at the Mannington roundabout. Then at the Mead Way turn-off, the BMW sped away towards Blunsdon and the countryside.

Colin thumped the dashboard.

"Shit. The brothers have spotted us. Put your foot on it, Kelly; you have to overtake them. Get as far as you can in front of them as soon as possible. We can't let them get past the park further up on the left."

"You're the boss," Kelly cried and floored it. The Porsche 911 growled and leapt forward like a caged animal. Kelly fought the wheel with the skills her advanced driving courses had drilled into her. She had been born to chase criminals in hot pursuit. It was the ultimate turn-on. The distance between the cars narrowed dramatically.

Anjum Ahmed weaved across both lanes as he sensed the little car was trying to overtake. Kelly darted left, then right, and feinted left again. Anjum moved to counter, and Kelly went for the gap. The offside wheels spat gravel and damp grass as the cars travelled neck and neck at eighty-five miles per hour. Kelly had two things in her favour. She had plenty more under the bonnet yet, and once she got one hundred per cent on the tarmac, she would pull away.

The other thing in her favour was that Anjum was bricking it big time. Kamal screamed at him to ram the Porsche, but he wanted to slow down. Every second on the limit of his driving ability was closer to him losing it and piling into those trees on the side of the road.

Moments later, Kelly got in the clear. The headlights of the BMW receded. As they approached the far edge of the country park, Colin shouted for Kelly to stop. He told her to drive into the hedge on the right-hand side and leave the engine running. He ordered her to stay in the car.

Colin grabbed his backpack and leapt out. Right, Colin thought, let's hope this kit works. He opened the bag and unloaded the magnum spike. The wrap and roll system was fast and easy to deploy. The fluted design made deep sizable punctures in tyres, which gave the user a controlled deflation and, therefore, no accidents.

"As if we care whether the buggers crash," thought Colin as the BMW sped around the corner.

Thinking the Porsche driver had lost it on the bend, the Ahmed brothers ploughed on with a cheeky blast of the horn. They were still laughing at their pursuer's misfortune when the magnum spike did its job. The BMW slowed and rolled to a stop. Kamal got out of the passenger door.

"The bastards have done our tyres."

"A lovely night for it," said Colin as he emerged from the trees. He raised the SIG Sauer, fired, and dropped Kamal where he stood. Anjum was out of the car and running; it was more of a waddle and a stumble. He sprawled full length on the tarmac, and Colin wandered across as calm as you like.

"Tanya asked me to give you this, Anjum."

Anjum tried to remember anyone called Tanya, but Colin pulled the trigger, and it didn't matter anymore.

Colin waved for Kelly to join him, so she eased the Porsche back out of the hedge and stopped behind the BMW.

"I could have helped," she said, revealing her Smith & Wesson MP Shield in her handbag.

"Impressive," said Colin. "That's a nice bag too. Do you think you could cram any more in there?"

Kelly grinned.

"A girl never knows what she might need when she goes off with somebody she's just met."

"What we need now is a helping hand. Where are our nearest clean-up crew?"

"Shrivenham. Shall I call them?"

"Please. Can you order a two plus two? Then you can help me move these two over to the trees in case anyone is still up at this ungodly hour.

Kelly made the call.

"I got an earful about getting them out of bed, but that's the nature of the job. The crew will reach us in fifteen minutes or thereabouts.

"Fair enough. I want to turn this BMW around and park it on the other side of the road facing the town. How can we do that?"

Kelly walked to her car.

"I told you I came prepared for everything, Phoenix."

She produced a tow rope from the boot. Five minutes later, the BMW was in position. Colin delved into his backpack. He placed items on the bonnet. Kelly drove the Porsche a hundred yards further, reversed into a gateway, and waited for the clean-up crew. When Colin had finished what he was doing, he joined her.

"After the crew has cleared the scene, I'll tidy up a few loose ends. For now, all we can do is sit and wait."

In time, a dark van with tinted windows drew alongside the Porsche. The passenger door opened, and a man got out and walked over to the driver's door.

"Good morning, Kelly. I understand you've got packages to collect?"

Colin got out of the car.

"They are up there, opposite the BMW. After you've looked around to check we haven't left too much of a mess, I'll torch the car. Then, with luck, the police will chalk it up to joyriders."

"Okay, no worries. We have the kit we need to wash away any blood, and we can collect any other bits you left lying around. Just give us five minutes. Kelly put a shout in for a two plus two, was that right?"

"Yes," replied Colin as they walked up the road

together. "You should get a call from Hayden before too long, provided he met no unforeseen problems."

The driver of the van followed behind at the sort of pace you associate with a hearse. Well, it seemed right in the circumstances.

The two clean-up men went about their work, tossing Anjum and Kamal Ahmed into the back of the van. They erased every sign of anything unusual happening on that stretch of the road.

Colin torched the BMW.

"We had better get out of here," said Colin. "You two follow us back towards town and maybe park up in a lay-by to await your next call."

Kelly and Colin sped away in the Porsche, heading for Old Town. The van followed behind. As they arrived at the Mannington roundabout, the call came. Hayden heard he would receive his clean-up crew quicker than expected.

It was after three o'clock; each of the four targets was dead. However, both scenes would soon be clean, with no sign of anything untoward. The only blot on the landscape was a burnt-out high-performance car by the side of a country road; kids today, eh?

Kelly and Colin waited outside the entrance to the big Victorian house the four brothers had occupied. Hayden arrived in the people carrier several minutes later.

"Everything went to plan then, Phoenix?"

"Of course," said Colin.

"What next?"

"Drop me off at the Holiday Inn. I'm off to bed. You can drive home to Devizes and get to sleep. First thing in the morning, visit the addresses and pick up the girls. Do you think you can manage that?"

"It will be a breeze," said Hayden.

"Who will be my taxi driver?"

"I'll do it," said Hayden. "Kelly, you can get off home, stick the blanket on and warm the bed up for when I get home."

Colin looked at Kelly. Hayden, you lucky swine, he thought. I'm at the Holiday Inn; you're in clover.

The three agents were tired but happy when they awoke. Colin went for a hearty breakfast and afterwards walked across to the station. He rang the transport section for a minicab to collect him from Bath Spa. He should be back at Larcombe Manor by the end of the morning meeting.

Kelly and Hayden returned to Swindon in the people carrier with another young female agent on board and collected the victims. One or two property owners needed a gentle tap to keep them in line. Hayden saw to that. The girls were confused, and most of them strung out. The nurse and Kelly reassured them they were in safe hands.

They were on their way to the medical centre at Larcombe in an hour. The physical side of their ordeal was over. They would receive medical attention before they were transferred to the safe house. They would have their reliance on drugs tackled. With care and attention and the passage of time, the mental side of their ordeal might be behind them too. Nevertheless, they faced a long journey.

In other parts of Swindon, life went on as usual. Normal for Swindon, that is.

In a side street in Rodbourne, a Lexus blocked the driveway to No43. It was empty, locked up tight, with no sign of its registered driver, a Mr Anjum Ahmed. Miss Ethel Perkins, eighty-six, wanted to drive into town to buy cat food. She was not happy. She told the man at the council so when she rang him.

Gold, Silver and Bombs

The burnt-out BMW attracted several early-morning commuters as they drove or cycled into Swindon to work. At the police station, they received one call after another reporting the matter. The desk sergeant tried to fob people off as long as possible; he knew he would not be popular sending someone out until it warmed up. The paperwork in the office was always more appealing on a winter's morning.

In a flat near the town centre, Sondra Lovett wished she hadn't downed so many Bacardi's. It was that bloke at the bar's fault. He looked alright. She would have been more careful with her drinks if he hadn't thought she was a tart looking for business. As it happened, she got pissed. She could hear Cyrus in the bathroom. Why couldn't he aim for the side? Bringing him back had been a disaster. She hoped he would shove off home soon. Sondra hurt all over; he was so big, everywhere. Why was life so bloody unfair?

Colin stood on the station platform. There was still no sign of Andy Partridge. The Paddington train was due to arrive in two minutes. Life did go on as usual.

Except, that is, for the Ahmed and Hussein brothers.

Oh, and the Old Town nightclub would be without a few of their big spenders.

Colin chuckled to himself as he left Swindon station. Life is about balance: good and evil, right and wrong, lucky and unlucky. The brothers' luck ran out. The clients with those accounts with the gang were the lucky ones. Nobody was left to collect the money they owed.

Colin could still taste the full English he had enjoyed at the Holiday Inn. Very enjoyable it had been too. On the downside, it did not entirely stop him from remembering the smell of the BMW blazing away last night. He looked out the window and watched the pleasant Wiltshire countryside flash past him.

His senses were working overtime, you might say.

Chapter Five

Colin arrived back in his quarters at Larcombe just over an hour later. He returned the kit he had taken on his trip to Bazza in the armoury and congratulated him on his choice. After a phone call to the main building, he got the call to visit Erebus in the meeting room at the manor house.

Erebus stood by one of the floor-to-ceiling windows that looked out across the lawns. He looked preoccupied. When Colin entered the room, he beckoned him to join him.

"Good morning, dear boy."

"Mission completed, sir."

"Well done, Phoenix. What would I do without you?"

"Anything from the meeting this morning I need to be brought up to speed on, sir?"

"Yes, we have received more intelligence from the mole inside the cell, Abdul Rivzi. To fill you in on his background. Abdul runs lucrative traffic in fake brand-name clothing. We overlook this if he provides his handler with useful information on the day-to-day working of the cell. A small cluster like the one in Milton Keynes is still dangerous;

modern communications empower it. It has access to weapons and explosives. Although they are strategically unfocused at present, it makes them elusive and unpredictable. His latest intelligence suggests that the militant leaders of his group are less concerned with doctrinal depth than their obsession with their beards. They are more concerned with developing a distinctive pattern of patois speech, an open disdain for women, and an aversion to jewellery. Many cell members are born-again Muslims or converts from non-Muslim societies drafted via the prison system. That worries me, Phoenix. Life was so much easier when terrorists were fanatical but predictable. Abdul says they drive into the country and camp out on the weekends. They pretend to be akin to the Mujahideen in Chechnya and live on pita bread and tuna. They play paintball games mimicking battlefield scenarios where they kill non-believers. These activities are even videoed and sent off to their superiors. Every exercise they undertake has an overt military context. He has had handgun training every weekend. Oxford Circus was already a target when he joined the cell. As that mission failed, his cell was still in training. But they are out of the loop for 'bang up-to-date' information as a punishment. As the London 2012 Games grow closer, it is obvious preparations are needed. They expect to receive the news they are to be involved in the proposed strikes at any time. At the moment, the location and timing of such strikes are unknown, at least to the cell at Milton Keynes."

"The increased frequency of intelligence coming from Rivzi must inevitably increase the risk of his exposure as a mole, though, sir? Do we have any contingency plan for bringing him out if things go pear-shaped?"

"We discussed that matter this morning. It would be unfortunate for Rivzi if his colleagues believed he was less sympathetic to the cause than supposed. It could be far more damaging for Olympus if we lost contact with him. We believe he is one of our best assets in identifying where and when they will hit the Games."

"Although Rivzi reports that the cell doesn't have the doctrinal depth of a number of their colleagues, 'unfortunate' could still be a euphemistic description of what would happen if they uncover his double role."

"That is a risk Mr Rivzi has to take, Phoenix. We cannot afford to lose him."

"Anything else, sir?"

"A prisoner transfer will take place between HMP Belmarsh and HMP Wakefield in ten days."

"What's behind this, sir?"

"The prison population in England and Wales has hit a record high, Phoenix. The Ministry of Justice says the figure rose another five hundred in the past week alone. Officials are making contingency plans to speed up opening new buildings and bringing moth-balled accommodation into use. There are now around sixteen hundred useable places left in the system, but prison chiefs say they stay confident they have enough to cope with those imprisoned by the courts. The Prison Service says they are developing contingencies to increase usable capacity. The pressure is most acute in London, so inmates must transfer from the capital to other institutions to free up space. This removal of difficult and dangerous prisoners to Wakefield will be the first in a series of moves."

"It seems daft that logically, we need more prisons to lock up the scum I've just been handling, along with the other lowlifes we meet. Who thought it a good idea to stop building prisons? Or, more to the point, who reckoned it a good idea to give the government's hangman his P45?"

"We must handle things as they are, Phoenix, not as we wish them to be," said Erebus. He moved away from the window and sat by the fireplace in one of the comfortable chairs. Colin took a seat opposite him as Erebus continued.

"The rapid increase in prison numbers means that parts of the system are little more than human warehouses. They do nothing more than lock people up in overcrowded conditions, with hard-pressed regimes to offer any employment or education. A few first-time offenders will undoubtedly take a fast track to a criminal career. Rehabilitation work to tackle re-offending will go by the board as jails try to cope with the rapid rise in prisoner numbers. Prison and probation officers need to get the resources and support they need."

Colin was well aware of prison's adverse effects on a large percentage of offenders. But he still believed it better for them to be sent to jail than to receive a pathetic non-custodial sentence that seemed in favour these days.

"The system is what it is, sir, as you pointed out just now. How much do we know about this proposed switch? Have we any intelligence on who might be on board the van? How long does the journey take? Which route do they follow? Perhaps more importantly, do we have a plan for ensuring these prisoners do not reach their intended destination?"

Erebus smiled.

"Always eager to get on with things, aren't you, dear boy? As we understand it, the trip takes around four hours. They negotiate the M25 and then take the M1 north via Newport Pagnell. They leave the motorway at Junction 40 and take the A638 towards Wakefield. About the makeup of the transferees, they will be Muslims with known terrorist affiliations. There will be a maximum of twelve prisoners.

There may be the odd empty place in the vehicle due to illness on the day."

"Twelve? Are they sure they can round up that many?" asked Colin. He knew in his heart of hearts that the number would be a drop in the ocean. He liked winding up Erebus. He walked over to the main table, picked up a file, launched into statistics mode, and read from a sheet he pulled from the file.

"HMP Belmarsh is one of our most secure prisons and is home to many of its most dangerous offenders—including a large swathe of terrorism convicts. Many high-profile terror suspects have passed through the high-security jail of late. Muslim prisoners made up just one in seven Belmarsh inmates two years ago. That proportion has climbed to one in five, with no signs it has stopped climbing. In general, the number of foreign nationals in HMP Belmarsh has increased by a third. The situation at Belmarsh mirrors a nationwide shift, with data suggesting a doubling in Muslim inmates across the country over the past decade. There were around ten thousand in our jails at the end of last year."

"Right then," said Colin getting up from his chair and joining his boss at the table, "how are we going to reduce that number?"

"We talked through a few ideas this morning Phoenix. First, the van's route virtually negates any realistic opportunity of an attack until they leave the motorway. So, one way suggested we concentrate our efforts in the tiny window between Junction 40 and HMP Wakefield."

"Sorry, sir, but don't talk daft. That's no more than a five-minute drive from the junction."

"Hold your horses, Phoenix. I didn't say it was an option to which we gave credence. We thought of stopping the transfer vehicle on the motorway, perhaps by arranging an accident, followed by an attack designed to release the prisoners. The assailants would be wearing clothes suggesting terrorist sympathisers carried out the raid. That idea has several pitfalls too, and I'm sure you will tell me what they are."

Colin shrugged his shoulders.

"Well, the first problem is causing an accident without hurting innocent people. The volume of traffic on the M1 during daylight hours is substantial."

"It is used by ninety thousand vehicles per day."

"Enough said. Even if you stopped the truck without incident, you would have an audience. Let us assume everyone sits quietly in vehicles as the traffic builds up behind the accident or breakdown, whichever you arrange. The security of prisoner transport vehicles is paramount. Two communication systems run without the need for opening windows or doors. The driver's comms operation is usually fully hands-free. The truck's rear can also be hands-free, or the vehicle can contain headset sockets or telephone handsets. Most of the ones they use these days have high-security locking and unlocking systems with stainless steel electronic bolts. Stopping the vehicle will be the easy part. Getting inside and releasing the prisoners is one thing. The task of emptying the driver's cab and removing the truck to a more convenient place would be a different kettle of fish. The officers inside the vehicle could call for backup by mobile phone before we could gain entry. We need more ingenuity."

"Do you have something in mind, Phoenix?" asked Erebus.

"Give me a day or two, sir. I believe we can do this without any accidents and without there being any spectators. Olympus will stay off the radar too as far as any responsibility for a dozen terrorists disappearing into thin air."

"You have forty-eight hours then, Phoenix. Bring your detailed plans and present them to the executive at the morning meeting. I shall be away tomorrow but hope to return before then. Elizabeth has not been well; her condition has deteriorated. The doctors at the nursing home are concerned that she may have given up, old chap. It does not seem possible that a person could will themselves to die - but Helen's death was so catastrophic for her, it appears to be the case."

Colin understood now why Erebus stood by the window when he arrived and why he had looked so distracted. Colin knew the pain of loss. He and Erebus had found a mechanism through which they could cope. They fought back against the injustices. Now and then, the loss overtook them. Erebus had been gazing across the immaculate lawns of his family home. He may have imagined himself and his wife sitting together on the patio as they watched Helen riding her horse across the estate.

Colin often heard a song that reminded him of Sharron singing a track by her favourite group. He caught a scent that reminded him of his second wife, Sue. Colin knew that he could never lower his guard whatever challenges these next few months brought. While the threat of terrorist attacks existed and criminals remained unpunished, he must stay focused. There was no time for emotion.

Erebus returned to the window. He held the honeymoon picture of him and Elizabeth in Ibiza from the table drawer under the window. It was the image he had shown Colin on his first full day at Larcombe Manor.

Colin left Erebus with his memories.

The first person Colin saw when he left the room was Athena. She made it clear she was pleased to see him. Athena pushed him back against a massive painting of Trafalgar and kissed him passionately.

"I've missed you so much," she purred.

"I've missed you too," said Colin, pushing her gently away. A steward emerged from a doorway further along the corridor. Fortunately, they were far enough apart to appear deep in conversation rather than in a romantic clinch. "But we need to cool it. Erebus will have kittens if he hears we are involved."

"Ooh," sighed Athena, with a pout, "we *are* involved then?"

Colin realised that this was the moment. He had known that this conversation would come since the night they slept together. After meeting with Erebus, he was in no doubt that any emotional distraction would harm the chances of Olympus surviving the summer without losing a significant number of innocent lives.

Colin suggested he and Athena walk over to the orangery. He always enjoyed meeting there with Erebus. It was comforting and as private a place as one could find on the estate. They strolled over, side by side, in silence.

When they arrived indoors once more, Colin took Athena's hands in his.

"Athena," he began, "the other night was something both of us wanted and enjoyed."

"I need to be with you again soon."

"We have to focus on the enemies that this country faces. These next few months will present Olympus with a series of challenges. Any of them could be a disaster if we are more concerned with our emotions than with the cold, hard facts surrounding potential terrorist strikes."

"What about us?"

"There'd be plenty of time for us after this is over."

They kissed.

"Can we still spend quality time together if there's a chance?"

Athena raked her fingers down Colin's back, and her tongue fought its way into his mouth. Her hips pressed against him, and from the reaction from Colin's body, she knew there was only one answer he could give.

"Are you doing anything tonight?"

"Not sleeping, that's for sure," she grinned, cupping his erection in her hand.

"Hold that thought," he said, breaking away from her grasp. "I have work to do. Erebus has to visit Elizabeth. Second, I need to plan the direct action on the prison transfer in time for the morning meeting the day after tomorrow."

"All work and no play," whispered Athena as they walked hand in hand to the door of the orangery.

Colin gave her a quick kiss goodbye before they left the building. They arranged to meet up later, and Colin headed for his quarters. Now, he needed to keep a clear head and find background data. So Colin rang Giles in the intelligence section and put in a request. Giles said he would email the information to him within the hour.

Colin wondered about a cold shower but opted to run to the old worker's cottages. Unfortunately, a visit to the pool was required to clear his head and stop him from thinking how good it felt to hold Athena again.

Twenty lengths of the pool sorted him out, but all that time splashing from end to end started him thinking of Therese Slater. Now that he and Athena were a reality, might it be time for Therese to go?

Colin sighed as he towelled himself dry after his swim and got dressed. Not for the first time, he wondered why this 'relationship' lark was so complicated.

When he returned to his room, he found that Giles had furnished the needed details. So Colin began analysing the procedures that HMP Belmarsh required to follow.

- Select the named prisoner for transfer
- Check prisoner meets the criteria for receiving establishment
- Obtain the name of a person with authority to accept the prisoner at a receiving establishment
- Complete the booking form
- Fax booking form to the office by noon Thursday for moves the following week
- If the trip can get completed in a day, a contractor faxes **both** establishments on the day before the move
- The contractor collects as specified in the movement fax and delivers the same day

Colin made a note to double-check HMP Wakefield's criteria. Then he listed the actions he needed Giles and his team to carry out over the next few days. Colin had learned the KISS principle—Keep It Simple and Stupid. His plan was simple, provided the information he requested was to hand. With one problem sorted, he lay on his bed and wondered what to do about Therese Slater.

He remembered that morning in Blackpool when she asked those questions, and he had tap-danced his way around the truth.

He could hear her now, saying, "I don't know who you

are. I don't understand how you could be dead, but now you're not. Do the people you work for know who you are? How have you become entitled to the holiday so soon? What kind of job is it, anyway?"

He had spun the story well. "They were looking for people who liked hard work, didn't mind getting their hands dirty, and prepared to travel around the country chasing up clients. I got in touch, and they employed me. They offered me the job. No questions asked; as long as I hit my quotas, they'll keep employing me."

It did the trick. The couple swapped mobile phone numbers, and he promised to ring her when he had a break due. She hadn't rung him in the past two months. Colin felt Therese was a strong woman, capable of standing on her own two feet. He did not classify her as the clingy, needy type.

Colin decided to let sleeping dogs lie.

With another problem sorted, even if only for a short time, he thought of those sleeping dogs. He wouldn't get to enjoy a whole night's sleep tonight, so he had better get his shut-eye now. As the afternoon dozed away for Colin at Larcombe Manor, many miles away in Milton Keynes, the situation was to take a dramatic turn for Abdul Rivzi. Although Olympus ignored his activities on market stalls scattered around the Midlands, other agencies did not.

Today was the day for Abdul to appear in court. After he left hours later, two men in a dark saloon car followed him home.

A report appeared in the local paper at the end of the week.

"A trader who sold fake designer clothing at a market in Midsummer Boulevard has been given a community sentence and ordered to pay £800. Abdul Rivzi, 51, of

Pentagon Way, was handed a community sentence of two hundred and forty hours of unpaid work. Also, Rivzi had to pay £800 after admitting sixteen charges relating to over four hundred items of counterfeit clothing. It follows an anti-counterfeiting operation at the market by Buckinghamshire Trading Standards over an extended period. A council spokesman said having made a test purchase and confirmed it as a fake, Rivzi was arrested, and clothing and cash were seized. Magistrates considered aggravating factors, including an earlier conviction for possessing counterfeit goods and that there had been several offences over a lengthy period. They were satisfied that the cash seized formed part of the trading operation, and Rivzi forfeited over a thousand clothing items. Trading Standards believed clamping down on illegal traders such as Rivzi helped the fight against serious organised crime. The sale of counterfeit goods damaged honest businesses and lost sales to criminals who peddled these illegal goods. In addition, the profits might fund more serious organised crime."

Abdul Rivzi didn't see the report. He didn't serve one hour of his community service. Callers at his home over the next couple of weeks found the property appeared to be empty. His car sat in his driveway. There was no sign of the mole whose Olympus handler had code-named 'Top Gear'.

In the evening, while Colin sat in the canteen eating and anticipating the arrival of Athena to his room later, Abdul Rivzi was in an abandoned warehouse in Leicester. The men who had followed him from the court were there. Around a dozen other men had joined them.

A chair bolted to the floor stood in the centre of the room. Abdul was lashed securely to it. He was blindfolded and frightened.

An older man stepped forward. He spoke quietly to Abdul.

"Who do you report to?" he asked.

"No one. What do you mean?" replied Abdul.

"I thought you might remember that you reported to Waheed Shaikh, the leader of your cell."

"Him, of course, but why did you ask who I reported to?"

"You have been receiving money. However, the money you get from selling your goods on the market stalls is insufficient to explain the amounts in your bank account. Who has been paying you this money?

Abdul did not reply. He feverishly thought about how to explain away the money he had received from his handler. How had this happened? Who had betrayed him?

"If you refuse to answer a question, the beating starts."

Four men came forward from the gathered crowd of onlookers. They started with punches and slaps. They tired of that, so four other men took their place.

The older man returned to stand next to Abdul.

"It is better you talk. Tell us about the British security services. Who is your handler?"

Abdul's face bled; his nose was broken, and several teeth loosened. He tried to speak. The sound that came out was weak and barely a whisper.

"I've never spoken to the security services."

The older man shook his head even though Abdul had spoken the truth.

The group of men surrounded Abdul. He heard them curse him for becoming an MI5 spy and betraying his people.

"You will be taken out and shot for being a spy."

"Where you're going, you'll not be telling anybody a thing."

"We will skin you alive, Abdul, and nobody will hear you scream."

Finally, the Imam spoke.

"We have tried Abdul. We will leave you to consider. In the morning, you will be ready to tell us what we want to know."

They cut him from the chair and strung him up, his hands raised above his head. He was to remain in this stressful position for eight hours.

The torture continued when he was alone in the room overnight. They left the air conditioning unit on full blast. Abdul was unsure his body could take that cold on top of the beating. He felt sure he would answer their questions in the morning. The beating was preferable to the standing.

At first light, several of the men returned; the elderly Imam accompanied them.

He whispered to their prisoner. "Are you ready to talk now, Abdul?"

Abdul heard another voice.

"He is too weak to handle torture, especially electrocution."

"Perhaps we should try it anyway," said the Imam.

Abdul drifted away; the pain didn't register after a while. He was floating on his back in a swimming pool, gazing up at a clear blue sky.

They asked him questions, but his mind had gone.

When he refused to answer, they beat him on the soles of his feet.

Abdul gazed at the sky and relived the events of the last year. He was 'Top Gear', a senior figure in the cell at Milton Keynes who acted as an agent for a secret service branch. It was an agency so clandestine; MI5 and MI6 were unaware of their existence.

He was of such value to them he got paid tens of thousands of pounds with the flow of information from him handled by a special intelligence section. He was the most valuable source within any terrorist cell in the UK.

He had risen through the ranks inside the cell to become a key figure. The irony was that one purpose of this cell was to search for informers and agents of the security forces.

Many Al Qaeda members and others were picked up by the cell and interrogated for lengthy periods. Sometimes they held them in Milton Keynes, but on other occasions, they took them to isolated houses in remote areas where they held them for weeks.

Abdul had interrogated people and beaten them to death. He had told his secret security service handler many things, but not the depths of his involvement.

The beatings continued. Abdul Rivzi never gave up the name of his handler. He could not speak. Around seven o'clock in the evening, Abdul grew cold. The sky overhead filled with clouds. It was getting darker.

He was so tired.

Sinking to the bottom of the swimming pool and sleeping was much easier.

Chapter Six

Erebus returned from visiting Elizabeth. The doctor told him there was little more they could do. It was a matter of time. Erebus expected as much. In a way, he welcomed it. She was no longer the Elizabeth he had known. She was an empty shell. Her body was functioning, but her mind had decided it would no longer have anything to do with it and shut down.

Erebus had sat in the main meeting room since five o'clock this morning. Sleep was not possible. To lie in bed alone, as he had done for several years, was just as unattractive. He showered and dressed, ready for the nine o'clock meeting. Then he sat in the chair and stared ahead, seeing nothing, alone with his memories.

Colin, too, lay awake. Yet, he was alone this morning. Yesterday offered the opportunity to relax, exercise, and fine-tune his plans to disrupt the prison transfer. Thoughts of his passionate encounter with Athena the night before kept him warm throughout the day. Each twenty-four-hour period took the men and women at Larcombe Manor a day closer to their next big challenge.

Athena had used the day before to do her thinking. She thought about Erebus and how Elizabeth's situation might affect her mentor's attitude towards the Olympus Project. Could he retire and pass the reins over to her? Would he be able to commit to the cause the stern challenges that faced them demanded?

Her mind never drifted far from thoughts of Phoenix either; their lovemaking had been both tender and passionate. She had given herself to him completely, yet he was calm and distant in the morning. It was imperceptible, but she felt it keenly. He reminded her of the need for them to suppress their emotions. The tasks ahead were too important. The security of the nation depended on Olympus getting it right. There would be no second chances.

In Leicester, the body of Abdul Rivzi travelled on its way to its final resting place. The two men who snatched him from his doorstep in Milton Keynes had stowed his body in the boot of their dark saloon car. The driver set the satnav for a lake on a golf course ten miles outside Leicester.

The spy, identified as 'Top Gear', took his secrets to the afterlife. The Imam and his colleagues had broken Abdul physically and mentally, but somehow he clung to the knowledge they craved. The terrorists lost that battle. Olympus lost a vital, irreplaceable asset. Who suffered a more significant loss? Only time will tell.

The clock on the mantelpiece struck the hour; Erebus shook himself awake. Doors were opening, and people were arriving for the morning meeting. Athena, Thanatos, and Minos walked purposefully forward together to join him.

Alastor trailed behind with Henry Case. They appeared troubled.

"Welcome back, Erebus," said Thanatos.

Athena touched the old man's sleeve and asked, "How's Elizabeth?"

Erebus shook his head.

"She only has a matter of weeks, maybe even days."

"I am so sorry, Erebus," said Athena.

"Is everyone present?" asked Erebus, breaking away from the circle of his closest friends and colleagues. Regular service had resumed.

"Right then, the first item on the agenda is the prisoner switch. Phoenix, will you present your proposal, please?"

Alastor spoke.

"Might we stray from the agenda, Erebus, for a moment? We have urgent and potentially grave news from our intelligence section."

'Head' Case stood up and broke the news to the agents and their superiors around the table. Abdul Rivzi, their invaluable contact within the Milton Keynes cell, had failed to contact his handler. He had missed two scheduled contacts so far. Activity monitored via CCTV feeds hacked into by the ice-house computer geeks spotted unusual traffic movements by known cell members in the early hours of this morning.

"Trading Standards..." Henry Case continued.

"What do bloody Trading Standards get to do with it?" exploded Erebus.

Henry explained.

"Alastor and I agree. It is almost certain that the case exposed the details of his bank accounts to someone in the cell, which would have ended in interrogation, torture, and execution. Therefore, we must assume that they know everything."

"This was not very much, thank goodness. Rivzi didn't know who he worked for," said Alastor.

"It still gives us a problem," said Athena. "We rely entirely on the ice-house to intercept any email or mobile traffic to and from the cell. We are blind, but at least we can hear."

Erebus added, "It also means that the Milton Keynes cell and the other cells in their hub believe that the 'secret services' are aware of their existence. Also, they will suspect the authorities know everything they have planned so far regarding London 2012. That would encourage them to amend their strategy. They will hold meetings, request advice and guidance from their superiors, and so forth. To lose Abdul Rivzi is a severe blow, but we must keep positive. Most of all, we must stay alert. Henry, please get that message to your people on the intelligence team."

"I shall do that right after this meeting, Erebus."

Colin sat quietly, listening to this conversation. He waited for his chance to reveal his plans for the coming operation.

Erebus noticed that Phoenix looked impatient.

"Any comments, Phoenix?"

"It strikes me that if an official government authority wasn't supposed to have planted a mole in the Milton Keynes cell, then Olympus is in greater danger of being exposed. We consistently try to carry out our direct actions under the radar. If someone finds Rivzi's body or his family asks questions about his disappearance, sooner or later, MI5 or MI6 will be alerted. If *they* didn't put him inside any cell, who did?"

"Fair comment, Phoenix," said Erebus. "How do we counter that possibility?"

"By making it appear that supporters of Al Qaeda pulled off a spectacular publicity *coup* in mainland Britain. It must be a coup that switches the attention of the security services from the Midlands and Abdul Rivzi while switching the public's attention towards the authorities' failings. It might look like this."

Colin then showed them the details of his daring plan.

After he finished his presentation, the room was silent for a few moments. That silence ended in spontaneous and unprecedented applause.

"Brilliant. Dear boy, you have surpassed yourself," said Erebus, more animated than he had been for a few weeks.

The direct action received the green light.

Athena stood up and addressed the meeting.

"This mission must not be seen as a cure for the ills the system is experiencing. It is the first step. We are painfully aware that we have a prison population that is growing. We have fewer officers in prisons than ever before and not enough police to cope with the criminals on the street. So, what we have seen is the unchallenged growth of extremists. These are men capable of whipping up anti-British feelings and inspiring their followers to commit acts of terrorism. The authorities have fewer people to search them out these days, so police and prison services find it difficult to handle. The government rejects any claim staff shortages are hindering efforts to stop Islamic radicalisation within the prisons. Well, they would, wouldn't they? They also proposed that the high-security jails should have units that work with the security services to root out extremism. Removing prisoners from HMP Belmarsh and the others that will follow reduces the chance of serious levels of radicalisation. Concentrating the vast majority of potential terrorist troublemakers at HMP Wakefield is an interesting strategy, but not without risk. Over the last few years, there has been a noticeable change in our gaols, with people becoming radicalised and getting involved in violent situations. The people responsible for that coercion were the more prominent Muslims inside our prisons. We now know that HMP Whitemoor is a prison with a large Muslim population, and inmates housed there, convicted of terrorism offences, have tried to influence and pressure others. Non-Muslim prisoners often join the extremists for protection. Before long, they are also plotting terror acts and endorsing groups such as Islamic State and al-Qaeda."

"The answer is to go inside the prisons and ensure we keep the most susceptible people away from those who might turn them into extremists. Unfortunately, we cannot keep drugs out of prison. We cannot keep mobile phones out of prison, so it's clear there are not enough people to prevent radicalisation," said Thanatos.

Athena looked at Thanatos; this was not the negative response she wanted to hear.

"We cannot be defeatist, Thanatos. The direct-action plan devised by Phoenix is the first step. The government appears to believe putting all its bad eggs in one basket will solve the problem of creeping radicalisation at sites across the country. It will turn HMP Wakefield into a one-stop shop for the would-be terrorist. Wakefield houses Category A prisoners and is the largest high-security prison in the country. The thought of having every extremist together in that cauldron of caged criminality frightens me to death. The government has reduced prison officers by a fifth over the past two years, with further reductions forecast. The prisoner-to-staff ratio is between four and five to one, leading to a significant safety deterioration. Perhaps the proposed action in the next day or two will reverse the decision to cut staff numbers. It is possible. We might even see new prisons built."

"We live in hope," muttered Colin.

Erebus was tired and closed the meeting until after lunch.

He wished the executive to reconvene then. Henry Case returned to the ice-house to pass on Erebus's instructions to the covert surveillance team.

Colin walked across to the stable block and identified and arranged the recruitment of the agents he needed for the Belmarsh/Wakefield mission. He gave it the code name 'Big Break'.

He had a long list of items he needed from stores, and he needed to pay a quick visit to the transport section. But, above anything else, he wanted to reassure himself about the weather forecast. It was all-action stuff around here.

Rusty banged on his door and invited himself in straightaway. He had been at the morning meeting, so he knew the score.

"Top job, mate," he said. "What do you need us to do?"

Colin knew Rusty and several other ex-SAS men scattered around Larcombe Manor were itching to get a gig like this one.

"Sort out lads with a Yorkshire accent for a kick-off."

Rusty looked over Colin's shoulder at the list of items they needed. He spotted the code name.

"I remember that. 'Big Break'. Pot as many balls as you can."

Colin looked at him with blank face.

"You've lost me, Rusty. Am I missing something?"

Rusty shook his head. Phoenix could be dim at times.

"No, mate, it's brilliant. It was the simplicity of it that made me chuckle, mate. Have you got an update yet on the weather?"

Colin scooted his chair over to his computer and called up the latest forecast for the coming week.

'Forecasters say there will be dense fog patches in many areas on Monday, with isolated snow flurries towards the south-east. The rest of the week will be cold and dry. The battle between cold and mild air over the UK and whether rain or snow will result has been flagged up by BBC Weather and the Met Office. It was uncertain whether the mild air would win and give snow, turning to rain, or the cold air would win, resulting in heavy snow. The latest news suggests the odds against the cold air prevailing have shortened. Wrap up warm.'

"Happy days," exclaimed Rusty. "Looks as if it will be Pa Larkin."

"Sorry?" asked Colin.

"Perfick," guffawed Rusty as he left.

Colin's computer beeped. Giles had sent a file with the latest update on what was happening at the two prisons.

HMP Belmarsh had selected twelve prisoners for transfer. Colin recognised several of the names. First, that fanatical cleric who was never out of the media before being incarcerated a year or two back. Also, the young student had bomb-making material and equipment hidden in the chemistry laboratory of his local technical college. Another name on the list had only recently arrived via Guantanamo Bay.

None of the twelve transferees was ill. Nobody needed Hannibal Lecter type handling during transfer, so HMP Wakefield was happy to agree to receive them.

The person authorised to receive them with open arms was a custody officer called Joe Nethercott.

Giles attached a copy of the booking form that Belmarsh had sent and checked Wakefield had received this morning. The ice-house people would now track the final confirming movement fax on Sunday.

Colin was satisfied things were moving along well. He emailed Giles the details he wanted to be transmitted and when they should go out on Monday. Colin's stomach rumbled.

He had forgotten lunch with his plan and the preparations for the exercise. He rang Rusty, but he didn't answer. Judas Priest echoed through the corridor as he set off to walk to the canteen alone.

Colin answered his phone.

"Rusty, fancy a bite or have you already eaten?"

It was Athena.

"Food would be lovely; I'm starving. We've just finished our meeting. Wait for me."

Colin slowed down and looked back towards the house. He spotted her emerging from the side of the manor house. At first, she walked quickly, her hair blowing in the cool stiff breeze. When she saw Colin, she broke into a run.

He turned and walked towards the old worker's cottages, waiting for her to join him. If Athena thought he would start running towards her in slow motion, she had another think coming.

The weekend weather followed the projected pattern. The snow lay four inches thick across the entire estate at Larcombe Manor. In the city and the surrounding countryside, people struggled to go about their business. Everyone dreaded the return to work on Monday.

Colin's face wore a smile a mile wide.

Smiles worried many of the agents he met because Phoenix was not a man associated with light-heartedness. On the contrary, he was a ruthless killing machine. He smiled occasionally and enjoyed the odd bit of banter, but he soon got back to business.

Colin had spent the weekend checking that he had everything ready for the mission. His trip to the transport section had been fruitful. Rusty had helped find the staff they required.

Athena had dropped by for a few hours on Sunday morning to help relieve any stress that might have been building up over the task ahead. That was a good enough reason for the smile on its own. But Colin had received other good news too.

Giles had confirmed the transmission of the final fax confirming Monday's switch. The contractor would collect the twelve different packages at ten o'clock, ready for the drive north.

Colin and Rusty collected a 4x4 with snow tyres from the transport section. They loaded the vehicle with the kit they needed and set off for Wolverhampton. It was six o'clock in the evening. It was cold, and the night sky threatened further trouble.

As morning broke, a familiar scene heralded a February day. Temperatures had dropped below freezing; cars stood on driveways across the south of the country, struggling to tick over. Further up the country, there had been a covering of snow on higher ground. Lower down, fog, and ice disrupted travel. The threat of snow remained. But as Colin and Rusty listened to the radio in their vehicle, they heard, "all roads are passable with care."

"No worries then, Phoenix," said Rusty, blowing on his hands to keep them warm.

"None so far," replied Colin. He kept an eye on his watch.

A car pulled up in front of them in the lay-by.

"This looks to be Jeff and the lads," said Rusty.

The driver got out of the car and walked back to the vehicle's cab. Rusty jumped out, and they shook hands.

"Alright, Rusty," the driver said, in a heavy Yorkshire accent, "happen you've picked a good day for it."

"With luck, it will get worse before it gets better," said Rusty. "Time to move. Follow us to the meeting point."

The driver returned to his car, and Rusty climbed back into the cab and set off from the lay-by. They headed towards Milton Keynes. The wind blew flurries of snow across the road. Clouds were filling up and looking ominous.

In Belmarsh, prison officers made final preparations for the transfer of their twelve inmates. The clock ticked around to ten o'clock. Outside the prison, the contractor's truck went through check-in.

Security staff checked inside the vehicle, the engine compartment and the doors. Next, they checked the roof using fixed mirrors. Finally, they checked underneath and around the wheel arches using handheld mirrors. The truck got the all-clear at nine-fifty.

Once inside the prison, escorts brought the twelve men into the yard. They were led by the truck in pairs and secured in individual cells. After the handover, and at ten o'clock on the dot, the vehicle with twelve prisoners and four security firm employees on board began the journey to Wakefield.

As they approached the Dartford Tunnel, the snow clouds gathering throughout the morning decided to flex their muscles. Unfortunately, before the truck emerged at the other end, conditions had taken a turn for the worse.

The driver and his companion in the front cab were glad of the heater and the company the radio supplied. Their colleagues in the rear compartment had the worst of it locked in the back with their twelve charges and little chance for conversation.

"The motorway should stay open," muttered the driver. "There's enough traffic belting past us at a rate of knots to keep one lane open, regardless of how much snow we get."

"I don't fancy being on the rural roads today, though," replied his mate.

"I'm looking forward to a hot coffee when we get to Newport Pagnell; okay if we stop at our usual place?"

"Suits me. The old Welcome Break will be heaven today."

"Not just for us, but Mick and Slim in the back too."

"Hold it. Turn that radio up a minute; let's catch the news and the weather forecast."

They caught the end of a weather update… 'set for a cold and dry week after snow fell across much of Britain. The Met Office says ice is likely to be a hazard on roads and pavements across Wales and much of England. The warnings cover the period until midday.'

"There you go. We might be slower than usual travelling today, but we can still make a short stop for a coffee."

"And hot sausage rolls?"

"You are a cruel sod. Do you want to torture those Muslims in the back or what?"

"Now you come to mention it."

The banter continued to the background music of Radio 2. Mile after mile clicked by, and at twenty-five past twelve, the truck turned off the motorway between Junction 14 and 15. Finally, it pulled up at the Welcome Break.

"Mick, we're popping into Starbucks for a coffee; warm ourselves up, mate. What do you and Slim fancy?"

"Anything, as long as it's hot, mate. It's bloody freezing back here."

"Okay, give us ten minutes. The place looks busy. I expect plenty of other buggers have had the same idea: get off the motorway for a while and get warm."

"Call us when you're back. Slim says any chance of a hot pie or a sausage roll."

The driver shared the joke with his mate. As they argued over who was getting the refreshments, an urgent bulletin broke into the music. It interrupted the Kinks singing 'Sunny Afternoon'.

The newsreader painted a grim picture.

"Police warn motorists to drive with care after freezing conditions in England led to a series of accidents. There were no reports of injuries, but a twenty-five-mile section of the A1 northbound in North Yorkshire closed this morning. Drivers sat in traffic jams for four hours after collisions involving jack-knifed trucks and other vehicles. Severe weather warnings are in place across England, with ice posing a major hazard. These low temperatures will continue for several days. So please take care when travelling and allow extra time for your journeys."

"This will be fun," said the driver. "Right, who's going then?"

They played rock, paper, scissors (best of three) to

decide who was going for the drinks. The driver lost and set off, moaning, head bowed against the driving snow.

Rusty and Colin sat in the car that had joined them earlier in the lay-by. They were no longer in the truck. The four men who had followed them from outside Wolverhampton had changed clothes and now waited in position.

The two Olympus agents watched as the second-hand vehicle they had bought in Wolverhampton negotiated the slippery surface of the car park. It drew up safely alongside the prison van. The driver's mate looked across at the front cab of the new arrival. He recognised the truck's livery and the uniforms of the two men inside. He waved out. The men in the cab waved back.

As soon as the driver returned from Starbucks with the coffee and returned to the front cab, the back door of the newly acquired Olympus prison van opened. Rusty's mate, Jeff, wandered across.

The driver called his colleagues in the back. He told them he would knock on the door, and they would get their coffees when they opened it. Instead, he walked towards the vehicle's rear and nearly collided with Jeff.

"Alright, mate," said Jeff, "good to meet you. I'm Joe Nethercott."

The driver recognised the name from the forms handed to him by the staff at Belmarsh. Nethercott was the person designated as the receiving officer at HMP Wakefield.

"What are you doing here? Do me a favour. Bang on the door. These coffees are bloody hot."

Jeff rapped on the door and stood back. Satisfied it was just the driver with their coffees, the door unlocked and opened.

Jeff's mate was now standing at the front of the truck, talking to the driver's mate.

"The weather is bloody awful up north, and it'll take four hours to reach Wakefield from here, not two. Getting back home from there could mean you'll be stranded overnight somewhere. We have the paperwork with us for the switch. Come back with me, and Joe Nethercott will take you through what's happening."

Nothing suggested anything out of order. After all, the truck was one of theirs. It was apparent the van came from the same firm; the uniforms showed that. So, moments later, the four men chatted over the change of plan while the two men in the back sipped their hot coffee and listened to the conversation.

The twelve prisoners felt a draught around their ankles with the door ajar, but they couldn't complain.

The driver scrutinised the paperwork. Sure enough, the relevant details were there. He was to transfer his prisoners to the Wakefield van and return to base. With luck, they'd be home and by the fire before Eastenders.

"Everything looks in order. To be on the safe side, you don't mind if I call my gaffer from the cab to double-check?"

"No, of course not, carry on," said Jeff.

Rusty and Colin sat and watched as the driver walked to the front cab of his truck.

"Don't fail me now, Giles," said Colin.

He need not have worried. Giles had hacked into the systems at Belmarsh and Wakefield and sent the necessary fax to the contractor, authorising the new transfer arrangements. It had arrived at noon. When his driver called in, the transport controller confirmed that a second vehicle was completing the journey to Wakefield. They could make their way back as best they could in the worsening weather.

"Okay, Joe," the driver said, "that's fine. Let's switch the prisoners."

Twelve bemused men switched, two by two, from one truck to another.

Twenty minutes later, the southbound truck left the car park and headed home towards London. They stayed in touch with conditions as they drove by, listening to the radio.

'Delays are inevitable.'

'Motorists heading out this afternoon and evening should make sure they know their route and check it's open.'

'Drivers should ensure they have enough fuel, blankets, and warm clothes. If it's a long journey, they should have food, drink, and a fully charged mobile phone.'

"I'm bloody glad we're not going on to Wakefield in this, mate."

"Me too. I can tell you; I don't envy those other blokes that trip."

It was a long journey. Heavy snow had caused widespread travel disruption across southern England. Roads became treacherous in many areas, leading to calls for drivers to take more care. As the snowstorm engulfed the truck, they slithered to a halt. They were stuck in traffic on the M25 in Hertfordshire for four hours. Snow ploughs were brought onto the motorway to sweep away the snow; they finally arrived back at base at midnight.

As they turned into the truck park, they were surprised to find people waiting. They soon discovered why.

When the second-hand vehicle had moved off to join the M1 North, the car driven by Rusty had followed close behind. Colin rode shotgun. They were leaving the motorway at Junction 15 and heading into Northampton.

The weather was lousy. There was no chance they could drive anywhere today.

Jeff and his crew took the truck to a lock-up on the outskirts of the town. The truck was soon in a safe place, despite shouts of protest from the cells. The prisoners had grasped that this was yet another unscheduled stop.

The four Olympus men changed back into civilian clothes before leaving the lock-up. They joined up with Rusty and Colin in a local pub. It was warm and inviting. The conversation over a good meal and a few drinks kept everyone entertained.

"We've got time to spare before things kick off," said Rusty.

"What gave you the idea, Phoenix?" asked one of the crew members.

"I read an article online last month. The Ministry of Justice was concerned that selling former prison service vans—used by firms such as G4S, Reliance, and Serco to transport prisoners—could allow criminals to pose as corrections officers and smuggle suspects and convicts away from hospitals or courts. Fleets of the vehicles were due for decommissioning in January after new contracts were awarded to private firms to provide security services across the UK for the next seven years. Before the outsourcing of transportation of inmates, out-of-service vans got destroyed. The Ministry of Justice was concerned that while they destroy prison service vehicles that have reached the end of their service, this was not the case with vehicles operated by private contractors. Any of those vehicles, which started service eight years ago, when private security companies first won Government contracts, can now legally be offered for sale on the open market. We needed to buy uniforms and insert the relevant paperwork into the system. A little bullshit to the other crew and a big thank you to him upstairs for the weather; we were home and hosed. We picked up the truck from a decommissioned batch for just over six grand. Rusty told them we planned to strip it out to use it as a horsebox."

"What do we do with the packages we picked up?" asked Jeff.

"Almost forgot them. Our passengers will be freezing," said Colin.

He got his mobile phone out of his coat pocket. He sent a text message to a series of numbers.

'Your dinner is in the oven. I'm off to bingo.'

"We had better finish these drinks and head back to the lock-up. We'll have company over the next few hours. Weather permitting."

Chapter Seven

The agents left the pub's warmth, and Jeff and his lads returned to the lock-up. Snow still fell steadily. The streets were virtually empty. There was an eerie silence as the men split into pairs and approached the lock-up. They moved into position two minutes apart, just in case someone was foolish enough to wander around the back streets on such a stormy night. Nothing could be left to chance.

Rusty and Colin took the car from the pub car park and followed. Rusty pulled up and parked fifty yards past the garage. Colin knew Jeff was inside, keeping himself and his mates warm by burning the security firm clothing they wore. All he and Rusty could do now was wait.

"Heads up," said Rusty. "This vehicle's one of ours."

A van stopped by the double doors to the lock-up. The doors swung open, and the van reversed up to the entrance. The driver stayed in the cab with the engine running. The garage doors hid what was happening at the van's rear, not that anyone was around to see. Jeff selected three prisoners' names from the manifest. He turned to the three guards who jumped from the back of the van. They had dressed from head to toe in black clothing and wore ski masks.

"Remove these three men from the cells. Apply duct tape to the mouth, put hoods over their heads, then handcuff them to the bars inside your van."

The men did as ordered. Quickly and quietly, they completed the switch. The three guards soon sat opposite three very frightened terrorists. The van doors closed, and they began their journey to a safe house twenty-odd miles away in Bletchley.

"That's one delivery on its way," said Jeff. "It will take them several hours in this weather, but we mustn't complain. It would have been difficult to keep things under wraps on a dry, moonlit night."

"Jeff, you're getting poetic in your old age," joked one of the crew.

"That's enough of that; keep your eyes peeled for the next collection. The sooner we get rid of these prisoners, the sooner we can try getting home to our beds."

The quiet back street saw another three similar vans arrive over the next hour and a half. They had agents in the back, ready to guard their respective charges. The Bletchley-bound van accompanied transport heading towards Corby, Cropredy, and the outskirts of Reading.

Each vehicle collected its complement of prisoners and took them away for interrogation. Jeff had been with Olympus for five years. He arrived at Larcombe Manor after being injured near Sangin in Helmand Province in June 2007. Time healed his physical wounds. He had no sympathy for the men he checked off his list. As they bundled the last men into the Reading transport, he knew, whether they talked or not to their interrogators, these men wouldn't live to finish the pathetic sentences the British courts handed them.

Colin sat in the car alongside Rusty and kept an eye on the proceedings. He was impressed, but not with the smooth efficiency with which Jeff and the lads dealt with the transfers, but with the sheer scale of the Olympus Project. Wherever his missions were in the UK, there were safe houses, clean-up crews, and fully-trained agents to call upon for help.

The criminals didn't have a prayer.

"That looks to be the lot Phoenix," said Rusty. "All are accounted for."

"Odd place to send those two younger prisoners, I thought."

"Which place was that?"

"Cropredy: I guess they reckon if they play folk music for a few hours, they'll spill their guts. I would."

"Yeah, I suppose that's as close to a joke as we're likely to get from you, Phoenix. Let's see what needs dealing with inside, and then we can get off home."

The two agents joined Jeff and his lads in the lock-up. The truck would be collected within ten days after the fuss died. Destruction would take place once it was many miles from Northampton.

Rusty and Jeff surveyed the scene. They were satisfied the contents of the lock-up stood a good chance of remaining undetected for a week or more. Fresh snow covered the ground outside. The comings and goings of the vans would not be visible by morning.

"I'm sending two of my lads over to the pub; they had rooms to let. If they can't get in there, I'm sure the landlord will know somewhere they can find a bed. Nobody will bat an eyelid over two lads deciding not to drive home in this snow. We can arrange to pick them up in the morning or later if conditions are treacherous."

"Great. So you're giving Phoenix and me a lift to Wolverhampton and the 4x4 we drove here?" asked Rusty.

"We can try," replied Jeff.

Colin wondered why the six weren't finding digs, but it made sense. First, it was too big an advert. The police and the security services might be thick, but not that thick.

The journey to Wolverhampton was tricky, but they made it. Jeff dropped them off in the car park opposite the premises of the truck company that supplied the prison vehicle.

"Thanks for your help, lads," shouted Rusty.

Jeff and his mate slithered out of the car park and into what remained of the night.

The 4x4 made slow progress on the last leg of their journey. It was approaching Tuesday lunchtime when they arrived back at Larcombe. Everything around the estate resembled a picture postcard.

Colin knew someone would know they were back. Sure enough, his phone rang as soon as he closed the door to his room. Fat chance of sleep before a debrief. It was Erebus. Who else?

"I saw you return, old chap; you were right; it worked like a dream. Congratulations. If you can spare me a few minutes, we can run through the fall-out we have been monitoring here. Then you can get that shut-eye I've no doubt you need."

Colin smiled to himself. Erebus always had his finger on the pulse. Even when he must have been thinking of his wife going through her last hours, it took a particular person to set up an organisation like this. Erebus was that person. Athena had big shoes to fill.

"Where do you want me to meet you, sir?" he asked.

"I'd vote for the orangery, of course."

"Of course," said Colin.

"Ten minutes. You're a cheeky beggar."

Colin laid the phone on the bed. Had it only been seven months since his arrival at Larcombe? He recalled that first day when Erebus showed him around the estate and uncovered its secrets. They shared a joke that day about the orangery and the ice-house. Erebus hadn't forgotten it; Colin didn't believe he ever could, either. Larcombe Manor was Erebus's home. Colin had grown to feel that way too.

He was desperate for sleep. A shower would have been welcome too, but duty called. He met Erebus in their favourite spot, and the older man told him the tale.

"The vehicle that returned to Belmarsh had a nightmarish trip back. Matters didn't improve for the four security staff when they arrived. The authorities at HMP Wakefield prepared themselves for a delay in their arrival because of the adverse conditions, but they grew concerned when night fell. At first, they checked for blocked roads and traffic accidents, but nothing matched either the vehicle or the route. When the truck had not completed a journey that normally took four hours within ten hours, they no longer became concerned. They panicked. They contacted Belmarsh and asked what had happened. Where were their prisoners? Belmarsh could not help them. I'm sorry, Phoenix. You've heard this one before, but forgive me. I'm enjoying it too much to skip the minutiae."

"That's fine, sir. I'm enjoying it too. It's the way you tell them."

"As far as Belmarsh was concerned, everything was fine

when the truck left them. They rang the security firm to ask if they had heard from the personnel with the truck. I imagine the governor crossed his fingers and everything else as he waited to learn the truck driver stopped somewhere overnight. That would be irregular but a possibility, considering the state of the weather. Imagine how his career flashed before his eyes when the controller at the security firm told him the relevant parties had authorised a switch to another truck. Besides, Joe Nethercott signed for the prisoners exactly as per the papers they first received. I cannot tell you everything that passed between the two men. The swearing escalated when the controller asked the prison governor, 'What's the problem?' When the truck arrived back at the depot, security firm managers, the local police, and people from Belmarsh. There were a few men in suits from government departments, too, who nobody had the nerve to ask for identification — everything the driver and his crew said tallied with the controller's statement. A switch was necessary because of the atrocious weather. The local police visited the Wakefield governor and then arrested Joe Nethercott. Joe and his wife had just gone to bed after a night of watching TV in front of the fire. Asinine, I grant you, but the police wish the public to think they are doing something at times such as this, even if their actions are inappropriate. We can assume Joe will be back home by now. This matter has gone far higher than the local police. The authorities have a real problem. In the past twelve hours, they have secured a total news blackout. You can imagine the uproar, even panic, that would follow. Imagine if news bulletins or the morning papers headlined the sparse details known so far concerning the escape of twelve of the most feared terrorists this country has ever held in her prisons."

"Egg on the face," said Colin. "Heads would roll."

"It's conceivable something this explosive could bring down a government, Phoenix."

"How do you reckon the security services will want to play it, sir?"

"Let us recap what they know. Someone removed prisoners from the official carrier. They disappeared into a blizzard, with four men posing as security staff. There has been no sighting of the truck or the prisoners. No one has claimed responsibility for the operation, so the authorities are in the dark. They should be asking whether the men were non-Muslim ex-prisoners radicalised while in jail, men tasked by Al Qaeda to release what they view as political prisoners. Were they members of a white supremacist faction? Finally, the sixty-four-thousand-dollar question?"

Erebus paused.

Colin jumped in, feet first.

"What question, sir?"

"Who'll give us a job after this mess?"

Colin grinned. The mission provided a special moment for Erebus and Olympus. The plan worked to perfection. Every trace of yesterday's events had disappeared, either by the agents' hands or by the weather. Erebus was right; the authorities were in the dark.

"We aren't out of the woods yet, sir," cautioned Colin. "We still have to move the truck and destroy it. With luck, we can do that in ten days to a fortnight. The sight of an eight-year-old prison vehicle on the roads around the Midlands and mid-Wales isn't rare. If we are careful, we can manage the situation."

"I agree with you, Phoenix; we must not relax. The intelligence section has done a wonderful job covering its handiwork on the interception and transmission of messages, but that cannot stop there. Giles and his people need to ensure nobody can uncover the true source of the interventions. I have every confidence in the ability of the agents at the safe houses to carry out their duties in secret, and to a successful conclusion, we pick these locations with great care. However, when the time comes for disposal, we must conduct a risk assessment. I cannot believe I said that."

Erebus stood up and stretched.

"We could leave it to our people in situ to decide where and when to do the deed, or we send one of our ambulances to collect the packages and add them to the growing population in the pet cemetery."

"That sounds to be the best idea, sir. No point running any undue risks, particularly for the safe houses the furthest away from Larcombe."

Erebus stayed standing.

"Come back to the house with me, Phoenix. I have a fine Courvoisier L'Esprit that this mission merits. I've wanted to open it for a while."

Colin and Erebus set off towards the house. How had a simple bloke such as himself, who drank nothing more than lager until his thirties, changed into someone offered a glass of brandy from a bottle costing four or five grand?

Erebus led Colin up the elegant staircase to his private quarters. Colin had never seen these rooms. On arrival, he slept in a bedroom on the other side of the manor house. He marvelled at the luxury and style of the Georgian fixtures and fittings. The apartments in this wing of the manor were equally well-appointed.

They entered the lounge, and there was evidence throughout of the feminine touches that Elizabeth provided. Yet, with her absence for several years, it seemed as if

Erebus kept everything as she left it. The room had a sad tinge with vases of dried flowers that had seen better days and a magazine on a side table from a publication that had gone out of business.

Colin was glad of the roaring fire. It warded off the chill in the air that accompanied them when they walked through the snow to the house. Erebus went to the drinks cabinet and brought glasses and a decanter to the chairs by the fireplace.

For two hours, the two men talked and drank. Erebus told him of his vision for the future of the Olympus Project. As the brandy warmed them and Erebus mellowed, the conversation drifted back to his days in the Royal Navy. He talked of his pride in following in the footsteps of his ancestors. Colin recognised this to be a special moment. He had been a loner throughout his life. However, Colin was gradually learning what it meant to be valued and a loved member of a family. Maybe it's the brandy, he thought.

The shrill ring of the telephone broke the spell.

Erebus answered it and listened to the voice at the other end.

"Thank you, I understand. I shall come straight away."

He replaced the receiver and turned to Colin.

"Elizabeth passed away fifteen minutes ago. It was very peaceful. The nurse left her sitting in a chair to see another patient. When she returned, Elizabeth had slipped away; she is at peace now."

"Erebus, I am so sorry. Do you want me to come with you?"

"Thank you, Phoenix, but I shall go alone. I shall leave instructions for Athena to assume control of operations until I return."

Erebus rang for his driver to bring the car to the front

door. Colin went down the staircase with him and watched as the car disappeared up the long winding driveway.

As he returned to the stable block, he thought of the vision for the future that Erebus had mapped out. Did he still have the heart for it now that his beloved Elizabeth had died? Was the time fast approaching when Athena would assume the mantle of head of Olympus?

Difficult and dangerous times lay ahead for the country, despite the success of yesterday's mission. There might be trying and uncertain times ahead for the Olympus Project too.

The snowy weather persisted, and things at Larcombe, akin to the whole of the UK, struggled to move at a snail's pace.

Athena chaired the morning meetings while Erebus arranged his wife's funeral. The government lifted the news blackout on the fallout from operation 'Big Break', and, as predicted, they had a rough ride in Parliament and the media.

A nationwide search began for the twelve terrorists and the men who engineered their escape. All seaports and airports became subject to a massive increase in security. Police examined thousands of hours of CCTV footage and broadcast various public appeals for information.

There were reported sightings from Ascot to Aberdeen, but the police found nothing. Behind closed doors, they admitted they didn't know where to look. A few weeks later, the frantic search lost impetus and stuttered to a turgid trickle. No one noticed when it stopped altogether. It became plain that by the spring, the approach of London 2012 was uppermost in everyone's mind.

Erebus returned to Larcombe Manor in time. He took a

brief holiday to Ibiza after the burial of his wife. Elizabeth lay beside their daughter Helen in the family crypt of the nearby church. He wanted to revisit the places he and Elizabeth stayed at during their honeymoon. Colin noticed his boss appeared to have aged in the past weeks.

The whole nation had rallied in the search for the terrorists. Every odd occurrence up and down the country received an enthusiastic level of inspection. It didn't last. The Olympus agents bided their time. The truck was disposed of near Builth Wells after delivery on a low loader overnight.

Agents who interrogated the terrorists in the remote safe houses around the country extracted every piece of information possible from the 'escaped' prisoners. The agents were veterans of the conflicts in Iraq and Afghanistan. They gave the men as much time to prepare for their demise as their late colleagues received in Basra or Helmand. Their end was swift.

Athena decided the bringing of the bodies to Larcombe was an unnecessary risk. However, it's possible if you go walking with your dog in remote corners of dense forests in Hertfordshire or Northamptonshire, your puppy will earth up the odd bone. So be warned.

The morning meetings at Larcombe throughout the rest of February and March followed a similar routine. Athena questioned 'Head' Case at length about the Milton Keynes cell. Did the intelligence boys have a handle on what they plotted? Do we have any other cells or groups coming up on their radar? Is it possible that despite the extra security that 'Big Break' generated, we remained vulnerable to a terrorist attack?

Henry Case fielded every question in his inimitable style. Day after day, he reported they were on top of the situation. Henry suggested that the Milton Keynes cell could launch an attack. They still had the ability. But, he repeatedly stressed that no matter what level of security the authorities invested in, a lone terrorist could infiltrate an Olympic venue and cause havoc.

Thanatos and Alastor provided reports on how the authorities demonstrated their preparedness for the Games. Colin sat in a meeting in mid-March and leafed through a sixty-page dossier they compiled. He decided to read it later.

Colin was bored, to be frank. 'Big Break' was the last action he had seen. The massive challenges of the summer still lay ahead. He and Athena continued to snatch a few hours here and there for their clandestine affair. They became the only times when he felt alive.

He realised that those warm feelings of belonging, in front of that fire with Erebus, were inextricably mixed with his relationship with Athena, cementing everything together. He could work for Erebus and Olympus without her but just as comfortably live anywhere in the country. He could be a 'sleeper' called on to carry out a direct action as required and return to his day job for the rest of the time.

Larcombe Manor had become his home; Athena, his partner. Was Erebus bringing him closer to the fold that night? Was the vision he outlined one that Erebus planned for Phoenix and Athena to bring to fruition?

It was a heady, intoxicating thought. Colin needed to decide whether that was what he wanted to do. He took time out to clear his head. Colin worked out in the gym and swam forty lengths of the pool. He was ready to suffer the sixty pages of 'What Every Boy Should Know' about the Olympic Games.

Colin lay on his bed in his quarters and began to read the file.

In early 2012, it seemed ironic that while large areas of the country were subject to feelings of deep insecurity, the government sponsored a massive security operation for the London Games. Since 'Big Break', that operation multiplied in scope.

The operation was often more complex than the UK had ever undertaken. Who was it designed to protect? Not Joe Public, at least not primarily. It was mostly for wealthy and powerful visitors and corporations.

As well as a large concentration of sporting talent, London would host thousands of media people worldwide. Colin counted details of more troops deployed than now served in Afghanistan. The overall number of security personnel could range between twenty-five and fifty thousand.

The veil of secrecy that shrouded everything meant that nobody knew the actual number. Intelligence reports from the ice-house suggested an aircraft carrier was due on the Thames near the City of London; surface-to-air missiles could scan the skies. Drones hovered overhead to spot potential problems.

Reports suggested deploying overseas agents, dozens of dog teams, and mile upon mile of electric fencing. The London Olympic Games Act (2006) passed without much fanfare and would legitimise armed forces, police, and even private security firms. Colin had seen no sign of it in West Africa and was meticulous in keeping up-to-date with what happened back home.

A new range of scanners was available, biometric ID cards were ordered, and CCTV systems were installed with number-plate and facial recognition. Police control centres and checkpoints were scattered like confetti. If those that lived in the capital did not have a 'lockdown' feeling with the high level of intensive surveillance now in place, then in July and August, they certainly would.

Colin set aside the file for a while and considered what he had read so far. Unfortunately, there was not much more he could think of the authorities could do to protect the city and the foreign visitors, whether competitors, officials, or spectators. A couple of things, though, struck him concerning the increased security.

Despite the economic meltdown, the now so-called 'homeland security' sector was booming. It was a way for a country to aid economic recovery, creating work for their own security companies in response to heightened terrorist threats, whether real or imaginary.

Colin could see it was in London's interest to show the world the capital was a safe place to hold a global event. If it could cope with that, it boosted confidence, which meant that London was safe to invest in and visit as a tourist. It was a 'win-win' tactic, provided a young zealot wearing plastic explosive under his 'London 2012' sweat-shirt blew no one to bits.

Colin was concerned at the appointment of the old Group 4 outfit as the main contractor. They never covered themselves in glory in their first guise. These days, they were a large organisation with people in prisons, asylum detention centres, offshore installations, and airports. Colin thought he read somewhere earlier in the week they were moving into police stations too. Only in February, another private security firm lost twelve terrorists.

He stood up to stretch his legs. What did they keep banging on about when they referred to the Games? Legacy, that was it.

Another report suggested using the now-familiar security scenery at an international airport—checkpoints, scanners, ID cards, cordons, and security zones. All of this materialising right slap bang in the middle of major cities. "What are they trying to do? Put us out of a job?" asked Colin with a slight smile.

Colin finished reading the report. He had to admit that Thanatos and Alastor had been meticulous. As Colin climbed into bed that night and lay there staring at the ceiling, he kept running through the different scenarios. With fifty thousand official security staff on the ground and in the air, how would *he* find a way through the defence and score if he were a terrorist?

Sleep did not come, nor did a feasible solution. Once you added the spectators into the mix, each one with an awareness of the potential dangers stoked by the media, it was likely that Henry Case hit the nail on the head. The threat would come from a lone bomber, maybe unconnected to any known cell. That was, without a doubt, the worst scenario.

After a restless night, Colin woke to find his phone ringing. He stubbed his toe on the table as he scrambled to pick it up before the call ended. He cursed. Once for the toe. Once for the missed call. He checked the number. It had been Therese.

"Shit," he said. "What does she want, I wonder?"

Colin limped to the shower room and washed and dressed. He had a few chores to be done today. There was more reading to get done, the morning meeting to attend, and then a spot of relaxation. He found it difficult in this 'silly season' to get motivated. He needed to spend a few hours in the ice-house gym, pool, and the target range.

The last thing he needed was Therese coming out of the woodwork.

When he felt ready to face the day, he returned and picked up his phone. Therese sent a text message.

'Hi. Miss you. I guess your job is keeping you busy. If I get tickets, will you come to the Games with me?'

Colin groaned.

"I'd stick hot skewers in my eyes rather than sit and watch any sport."

He wondered how he should reply. Not responding wasn't an option. He decided to play along. If Therese thought he was meeting her in London in a few months, then that bought him time to decide what to do about her.

'Sounds fun. I can't promise. I don't know my schedule until closer to the time.'

Therese sent back a smiley face and two kisses. Colin shook his head.

His day had started badly. The bureaucracy of selling eleven million tickets was a constant source of controversy in the media. Organisers claimed they balanced income with accessibility and atmosphere, while critics claimed the process favoured the rich. Colin read somewhere that although the name didn't mean a thing, front-row seats for Usain Bolt in the 100m final would set you back hundreds of pounds, possibly thousands.

"What if he doesn't come?" Colin asked himself.

He fervently hoped that either Therese failed to buy any tickets or they would be for something vaguely exciting. The prospect of sitting in the velodrome, watching blokes in Lycra going around the track lap after lap, had him yawning.

Colin knew the odds against her were high. Their own Olympus report showed that sponsors, officials, and the media were allocated seats as a 'given' by the IOC. The same old story as with the sudden massive increase in security. Everything was with the rich and famous in mind. Poor old 'Joe Public' stood a long way down the list of priorities.

Before Colin could treat himself to exercise and then sharpen his shooting skills, he had the morning meeting to negotiate.

Erebus was back in the chair with Athena at his side. The Three Stooges looked incredibly proud of themselves. Colin wondered what they had to report to the agents gathered around the table. Something riveting, he hoped.

Thanatos eventually got his moment in the sun. Colin thought the first few items on the agenda tedious. Thanatos reminded Erebus that the application process had been open since July 2010 to find up to seventy thousand Games Makers and Ambassadors for London 2012.

Thanatos waxed lyrical about how contagious the enthusiastic approach of this band of volunteers would be. Colin listened and thought it a painful exercise. Five weeks off work without pay, to say you have been near an Olympic Games; not even taking part, but more than likely holding a door open in the bowels of a stadium, showing people the way to their seats.

The selection process had been underway for over a year. Colin suddenly brightened. That's how I would try to get inside the venues. They will wear an official uniform with badges and accreditations. The security will be less stringent. They'll have access to areas where the public, if not barred, will be restricted.

He heard Thanatos in the background. Men and women of all ages: a nurse, a physio, any of them could be a terrorist. One minute they tended to a cut knee on a young girl who slipped and fell, and the next, they placed a bomb in a strategic position designed to cause the highest loss of life.

This fellow Usain could be having a massage on his calves and then find himself drugged, kidnapped, and whatever country he comes from could be held for ransom. Colin reckoned this was the most workable choice for the terrorists. Knowing was one thing; stopping them from carrying out attacks was another thing altogether.

Chapter Eight

Abdul Bashir and Aaleyah Fayad studied at the Queen Mary University of London. They were both twenty-one years old and met when they attended their first biochemistry lecture in October 2010. In the past eighteen months, they studied hard and lived next to one another in the Student Village in Mile End.

In the first few weeks, they saw one another now and then in the laundrette or the shops and cafes on the busy campus. Abdul was a quiet boy, easily led. Aaleyah was a firebrand who lived at home with moderate, westernised parents. She was a teenager with an attitude. She wanted to change the world.

There had been no physical attraction to spark their relationship. The pair were students, on the same course, from the same background, and they got on with one another. Aaleyah told Abdul what they would do, and he did it. She decided whether to walk to lectures together, carry her shopping bags, or discuss politics, religion, and the holidays for hours.

Gold, Silver and Bombs

Aaleyah wanted to be involved in London 2012. She goaded Abdul to join her, but Abdul wasn't interested in sports. He was a serious young man who preferred to read and study. So Aaleyah decided their summer vacation together would be spent as volunteers at London 2012. Stratford was only ten minutes up the road.

In fairness, neither of them was that keen on the vast array of sports at the Olympics. However, the driving force behind this joint venture was Aaleyah. She'd found a cause worth fighting for, and Stratford would be her battleground.

When Aaleyah moved to Mile End and started university, like most students, she was eager to make new friends and to fit in, so she joined the Islamic society. She befriended a group of Muslim girls she met at the various functions they held. They seemed to know a lot about Islam.

They encouraged her to read books that helped her learn more about her religion. What she learned from these girls and the books made her think violence was acceptable. It made her want to become a suicide bomber. She believed it would make the Western world sit up and take notice. She wanted the West to understand her anger.

Aaleyah joined the increasing number of Muslim women targeted at British universities and drawn into violent extremism. As the summer break after the end of their first year ended, Abdul and Aaleyah sought to embark on a journey that could allow them to achieve immortality.

In September 2011, they received approval for their applications to volunteer as Games Makers for the Aquatics Centre. They attended training days at Wembley Arena, Hackney College, and Earls Court.

While Erebus and his team searched for terrorist cells and internet traffic between Pakistan or Afghanistan and the UK, one of their greatest threats was already in London.

The agents in the ice-house searched for intelligence that would help them prepare for the anticipated strikes on the Games. However, the students carried on with their daily business. On the surface, you saw two young people attending lectures, studying, and enjoying a social life without alcohol. There was nothing to alert suspicion.

Behind closed doors, they learned how to prepare and operate an explosive device that left its mark on the western world for generations to come.

Munaf Mansoor and Farooq Habibi were final-year students at London Metropolitan University. They met on the Islington campus and shared an interest in football. They were avid Arsenal fans and attended nearly every home match during the season.

Munaf studied Politics and International Relations; Farooq dabbled in ICT. It wouldn't be fair to say he studied. Over the last year, his attendance at lectures dropped. He was bright and intelligent. His attention had drifted. He believed his destiny lay in more important things than working for Google or another faceless corporation.

Like Abdul and Aaleyah, the two young men joined the Islamic Society when they began university courses. With his full black beard, Munaf spotted Farooq's new face in the student canteen. He called him over to the trestle table, where he was handing out pamphlets to students and shook him by the hand.

As Farooq looked through the pamphlets and books on offer, Munaf pointed to one article in particular.

"Women are man's great temptation. They should be covered up and kept apart."

Farooq picked up the item and walked towards the seating in the hall. He had three older sisters at home who teased and bullied him, but he never thought of them as a temptation. His parents had been strict, but many of the traditional ways were in the past. Farooq was eager to discover whether his parents had lost their way.

The Society arranged for an external lecturer to talk to them. While Farooq leafed through the article, a side door opened, and men from the Islamic Society filed into the hall. Half of the seats at the front remained vacant, and he sat among the men. Munaf came and sat beside him.

Farooq watched as the women entered through another door. Then they sat as far back as possible, well away from the men. Although there were no signs enforcing segregation, it appeared tacitly accepted. Farooq soon appreciated that the more traditional elements dominated London Met in common with several other University Societies around London. So, such segregated seating became the norm.

The speaker who arrived a few minutes later was an old man and a 'hardliner'. He emphasised the need for gender division and that the current relationship between men and women had led to a crisis in Muslim society.

Islam laid down prohibitions because, without them, other sins could follow. It was essential to lower the gaze, learn the etiquette of modesty, and avoid touching and unnecessary socialising.

Farooq listened, and like a sponge, he soaked up everything that the older man said. Munaf was pleased. He could tell Farooq was a suitable candidate. Munaf had been educated privately and could challenge an argument or at least know where to look for information to make a challenge. Farooq was a different matter.

None of the schools that Farooq attended encouraged critical thinking. He could regurgitate information and become adept in the technical world of computers but was vulnerable to extreme views. However, Munaf was more than willing to educate him. He thought of it as his duty. Without Islam, Farooq might fall under the spell of the gang culture rife in the capital or succumbs to the thrill of drugs.

Completely independent of the two Queen Mary students, Munaf considered London 2012 an excellent opportunity to spread the message their Society speakers gave them. Men and women competed together in many of the stadiums. The women were not covered. It was immodest.

He preferred that Muslim women not compete, but the IOC allowed them to participate but could not wear the hijab. Such a ruling was monstrous. They had no appreciation of their religion. The final insult was the timing of the Games.

Ramadan lasted from mid-July to mid-August. The Games started on the 27th of July and ran for five weeks. What more could they do to show their hatred and ignorance of Islam and its teachings?

Munaf pointed out to his colleague at The Emirates on a Monday evening that many volunteers were required. They sent off their applications and, in time, received good news. They, too, found themselves on training courses in the city in the months leading up to the Games.

On one of these courses, they met Abdul and Aaleyah. For Munaf, it was a meeting of minds; he mistrusted Aaleyah at first because she was merely a girl. He thought

Abdul was weak and Aaleyah's lapdog. They met several times to share their radical views. The trio discovered they shared a common goal.

For Farooq, that first encounter had been a meeting of hearts, not minds. As soon as he saw Aaleyah, he was smitten. All the literature and lectures in the world couldn't block his body's reaction to the lovely young woman he saw before him. She looked into his eyes without fear and smiled as if she knew the effect she had on him.

As the last home games of the season at the Emirates Stadium drew near, Munaf and Farooq went through the same learning process as Abdul and Aaleyah. Studying was cut to a minimum, and socialising was too. It was only necessary to learn how to make the bomb and how to detonate it. Nothing else mattered.

One hundred miles away in Aston, Birmingham, Khadim Salah and Shamila Javed sat in a busy coffee shop. They were at separate tables. Khadim graduated from Aston last summer with a first in Politics and Sociology. He was halfway through what he told friends and family was his 'gap' year and had recently returned from Pakistan.

Khadim was twenty-seven. After he left school at eighteen, he found it hard to find a job he truly wanted to do. His father urged him to stay on, but Khadim saw his less able friends earning money and wanted to join them. Everything he tried turned sour after a few months, sometimes weeks, as the work became repetitive and boring. There was nothing to stimulate his brain.

Khadim went to work at a call centre for a mobile phone firm. Three years later, he had climbed the ladder to a senior post within the parent company. He proved to be an efficient, ruthless 'go-getter'. His abilities shone far brighter than the colleagues he trampled on as he made his way towards the top of the pile.

At last, he had found something he wanted to do, yet he still felt unfulfilled. The top jobs seemed to be out of his reach. The only explanation could be his ethnicity. What other reason could there be for them to deny him a promotion?

Suddenly, his firm was taken over by a rival firm. Many thousands of jobs were lost. Khadim studied his redundancy cheque and decided that his father had been right. He should have studied more. Instead, he used the money to get him into university, and his results after his final exams placed him in the country's top one per cent of students.

The students he mixed with, the Politics and Sociology course, and the changing nature of the Islamic world he saw around him shaped the mind of Khadim Salah. Things had to change. His trip to Pakistan reinforced that view.

Many young British-born Muslims return to their parents' and grandparents' land to visit relatives or discover their roots, but others come to learn how to destroy the West. Pakistan housed the Taliban and Al Qaeda. It was a breeding ground for terrorists.

Khadim met with family members at first, but later, he was introduced to Jundullah, the Army of God, a violent extremist Islamic group. He spent time at a madrassa, a religious school that preached a fundamentalist form of Islam. During his stay in Pakistan, he spent most of his time in a village north of Faisalabad. An explosives specialist visited him. The man was a veteran of terrorist training camps along the remote Afghan-Pakistan frontier. He had trained the terrorists responsible for the London bombings of July 7, 2005.

When Khadim returned home to Birmingham, the British authorities logged him as a 'person of interest'. However, staff cuts and inefficiencies meant that no one had followed up on their concerns since he had been home.

Khadim looked across the café to the table where Shamila sat. She dressed in the traditional attire of shalwar kameez: loose trousers and a long embroidered shirt. Khadim noticed the high collar, not low-cut, as many of the university's women favoured. He was impressed. He looked away when he realised that the young woman had seen him staring at her and how she dressed.

Shamila Javed had risen at six o'clock that morning and knelt to pray in the bedroom of her flat in Aston. She always prayed before dawn and then four more times during the day. It was very early, so Shamila climbed back into bed for more sleep. At half-past seven, she had risen, showered, and dressed. She grabbed breakfast and dashed out the door to catch the bus to college for her class.

Sitting on the bus, she felt uncomfortable; it was not just her. There was a growing resentment and hostility towards Muslims, whether they had been born here or not. Shamila was in her first year at the Wolverhampton University School of Media, where she took Media Studies. Her class finished just before noon. When she returned home, she prepared kofta for her lunch. She sat and ate her spicy lamb kebabs alone.

Shamila then wandered to the shops, looking for a pair of shoes and, possibly, a sparkly top. It turned out it was not a good day to buy beautiful things. She couldn't see anything she liked. Before returning to her flat to pray, she had popped into the coffee shop. As she left, she saw a man looking at her most intently. She blushed. As she stood up to leave, he came over and spoke.

"I hope you live nearby. I very much wish to see you again."

Shamila studied this man. He was tall, dark and very handsome. He seemed a little old for her, perhaps, or maybe not. She felt sure that her parents would approve of him, although they had not chosen him. She wanted to have a say in who she married. Her father had made enquiries, looking for a suitable candidate. She opted for a preemptive strike.

"I live near here. Hi, I'm Shamila."

Khadim and Shamila left the coffee shop together. They chatted for a while, and then Shamila agreed to meet her tall, dark stranger again. She thought they might have a future together. In her innocence, she was perfect for Khadim. He felt sure the security services would be less likely to be looking for an amorous-looking couple when the time came for his act of martyrdom.

Spring at Larcombe Manor was always a special time. Erebus and Elizabeth had enjoyed walking around the grounds and watching the transformation in the borders and the wooded areas they were so fortunate to have on the estate.

Alone, Erebus strolled past the forsythia with a carpet of hellebores and crocuses at its feet. Elizabeth would have loved this display. The weather seemed at odds with the seasons he remembered as a young boy. Yet nature surprised us with her resilience and capacity to adapt.

Larcombe had seen the warmest and driest March for over fifty years. A chill set in as soon as April arrived that threatened to last for weeks. Then came the rain; lots of rain, and any fears of drought were banished.

Erebus now neared the edge of the lawns and borders. Ahead lay the wooded areas and, beyond that, the pet cemetery. The profusion of snowdrops and bluebells scattered among the crab apple trees astounded him. The welcome sight of bees darting from plant to plant here and there comforted him. Spring was a difficult time. Mornings like this would help him get through the dark days after Elizabeth's death.

It was time to return to the main house. He turned and began the walk back across the lawns. Over to his left stood the refurbished worker's cottages that housed the canteen, swimming pool, and other facilities to keep the Olympus agents entertained. This spring had been frustrating. Day after day, the intelligence section in the ice-house reported that they were no further forward despite their close monitoring of internet and mobile phone traffic. The Opening Ceremony was only eight weeks away. The agents in the field and at Olympus HQ shared a similar experience to his father in World War II. He often talked to his son about the 'phoney war' and the agony of anticipation.

"To know it will happen, William, and having to wait for it is agonising. You know something more terrible than you have ever seen is just around the corner, and you may not live through it. We just wanted it to happen. We willed it even. Not because we welcomed the prospect of death, but to sit around and wait, it's bloody awful," his father had said to him. It had been just here by the ice-house, where he paused to think of his father and the legacy he left him.

That statement led Erebus to use the ice-house as the secret underground heartbeat of Olympus. Inside the building, they housed the best equipment and people possible to provide Olympus with the knowledge to arm them in the struggles they faced. The interrogation suites, which the agents termed Hotel California, were a distasteful but necessary facility to add to that knowledge.

Despite the range of tools at their disposal, his people found it particularly challenging to make progress. Identifying potential target sites was not the problem; dozens of them existed. Instead, it was how to link known terrorist organisations, of whatever denomination, to those sites that caused a headache.

Erebus continued to walk towards the house. As he drew level with the old stable block, he spotted Phoenix emerging from his quarters. The younger man slipped casually into step with him, and they strolled together.

"A beautiful morning, Phoenix," said the old man.

"Too quiet for my liking," replied Colin.

Erebus could tell that his trusted aide was straining at the leash. Like Erebus's father many years ago, Phoenix was desperate to be doing something positive. Instead, it was the hanging around and waiting that drove everyone mad.

The two men ascended the steps that led up from the lawn to the patio. Colin noticed Erebus glanced over to where Elizabeth sat with him in the old days before the death of their only daughter. Colin wondered if he imagined her sitting there. Did he see her sipping a cup of coffee, reading the paper or one of those magazines he had seen in their rooms a while back?

"Not long now, dear boy," the old man said.

Colin was not sure what he meant. Maybe he referred to the morning meeting. On the other hand, he might have related to the decision when he stepped aside and handed control over to Athena was imminent. The answer was not going to come just yet; the older man wallowed in his thoughts and memories.

Colin held the door open for his leader, and they entered the manor house. Once inside, the spell broke, and Erebus resumed his usual demeanour. He had a meeting to run. There were matters of national importance to discuss. Personal feelings had to be put aside at times, such as these.

The agenda for the meeting was brief. The team completed several items with little more than an acknowledgement that there had been reports of nothing new since yesterday. Minos had one new topic to discuss.

"The Charity Commission has contacted us. On this occasion, the financials aren't what they need to look at; instead, it will be a day's advisory visit."

"Bloody hell," said Erebus, exasperated. "Why can't these people leave us alone? What do they think we need advice on now, for goodness' sake?"

"They are checking how we look after the personal information we hold. Historically, we have informed the Charity Commissioners that we have ex-service personnel suffering from PTSD following their experiences abroad in a theatre of war. This visit is to make sure we comply with the Data Protection Act. After their review, they report their findings and offer practical advice where required."

Erebus was unimpressed.

"When are they coming, and how will this visit be conducted?"

"The Commissioners have sent an information sheet and a questionnaire to complete. They will review that when they visit. No date as yet, I'm afraid. They need a list of names of members of staff who will be available for them to interview then, too. These days we should be telling people what we are doing with their data, supplying adequate training to new staff, and other things."

Erebus took a long breath, and at last, he said, "Let me study the completed questionnaire. Give me the list of names you suggest we parade for these people when they decide to descend upon us."

Little more remained to cover that morning. As soon as the meeting broke up, Colin went to leave the room. In front of him dragged another delightful day whiling away the hours, praying for a direct action mission to materialise.

Athena hurried after him.

"I don't suppose you're busy for a while? Shall we go for a swim?"

Colin welcomed the opportunity for the exercise; a little company didn't go amiss either. They met up at the pool ten minutes later, and Colin watched as Athena strode out from the female changing rooms. She wore that grey costume again he remembered from last autumn. She was all woman with her long, sturdy legs and toned body. He was a lucky devil.

They spent the rest of the day together and the night.

"Just like an old married couple," said Colin in the morning as they got ready for the day ahead.

"I wish we could be like this always," said Athena as she brushed her long mane of hair.

Colin knew she expected him to say something here, but he could not bring himself to commit to anything permanent. They still had the summer to get through yet.

"If we don't get a move on, Erebus will be down on us like a tonne of bricks," he replied.

They made their way separately over to the main house. Just another day at the office. Except that today was different. The Information Commissioner's Office people had arrived without fanfare. Their advisory visit was today.

Larcombe Manor held many secrets. How they protected those secrets was to keep the public and various government officials well away from the property. The transport section collected letters and parcels from the city post office and newspapers. They also brought in any magazines requested and so forth.

The organisation had gone to considerable expense to ensure that the utility people could read their meters by the front gate. These meters kept the number of strangers who came up the long winding driveway to the house to a minimum.

The presence of a handful of officials with access to paperwork, computerised records, and staff members was a nightmare. Minos tried to keep calm. Erebus was apoplectic, while Athena poured oil on troubled waters.

"What do you want to take a look at first?" she asked, thrusting her ample bosom towards one of the would-be inspectors. He seemed at a loss to choose.

"We… we need to see the completed questionnaire," the inspector managed to blurt out, running his finger around the inside of his collar.

Minos searched through the paperwork he carried, files scattering across the table.

"Ah, here we are," he said. "All present and correct."

"I'll be the judge of that," one of the elder inspectors snapped.

Erebus excused himself and left the room. Athena was glad. If he stayed, she feared he might either say something rude or, worse still, punch the pompous oaf.

Erebus left because he wanted to warn the ice-house of the snap inspection. They went into a 'lockdown' situation on visits such as this. There would be no surveillance, no interrogation, no target practice, and definitely no burial in the pet cemetery.

Henry Case remained in the manor house. His name appeared on the list of people to be interviewed. Erebus deemed it safest to include the chief interrogator's name, along with a few of the stewards and gardeners.

Inside the meeting room, Athena attempted to get the ICO people on their side. The last thing they needed was for these people to leave in a few hours with the idea that the Olympus Project had something to hide at Larcombe Manor.

"Can we get you something to drink, gentlemen, tea or coffee?"

Slowly, the tide turned and systematically, Minos and Athena stepped carefully through the data. They demonstrated that the registered charity had a firm grip on the paperwork, the digital records, and the training of their staff. A false grip, of course, but it sounded convincing.

"That appears in order," said the pompous oaf on his second cup of coffee and third chocolate digestive biscuit. "We're ready to talk to a few of your staff now."

Henry Case and the others were ushered into the room and trotted out their well-rehearsed back-stories.

"I was wounded in Helmand…."

"Ever since Goose Green…"

"I wake up in the night and am back below decks. The Exocet punctures the hull, and everything changes…."

The inspectors lost track of the questioning as they heard what these men suffered. Each related the experiences that left them with PTSD and brought them to Larcombe Manor for rehabilitation.

As the last of the men closed the meeting room door

behind him, the senior inspector said to Athena, "We should be eternally grateful to these men. You are doing a wonderful job bringing them back to good health in mind and body. The work this charity does is outstanding."

"Thank you," said Athena.

The door opened, and in walked Phoenix. Athena swallowed hard. What was he doing here? Erebus had sent him to a meeting in Swindon. It was a follow-up initiative to the disposal job Phoenix had been involved in earlier in the year. Those people in authority, who should have protected Tanya Norris and the others, were to be identified and set aside for further action. Of course, there would be no killings, but they would gather evidence so that, at the very least, those authority figures lost their jobs and, in rare cases, faced prosecution.

Colin looked around the room in a wild search for any familiar faces.

"And who might you be?" asked the officious inspector.

Colin stared at him. He couldn't reveal his code name. He couldn't tell him he was Colin Bailey; the world outside believed him to be dead.

"Where did you serve? What regiment did you serve with?"

Colin did the only thing possible. He collapsed in a heap on the floor.

Athena rushed to his aid. Minos called for the stewards. The inspectors were at a loss. Could this be an extreme case of PTSD? From what hell hole had this poor chap returned? On the other hand, should they be sharpening their pencils?

The stewards helped Colin to his feet and removed him from the room. In the corridor, he met Erebus. After chasing around, he was out of breath, trying to make sure the agents at risk, such as Phoenix, made themselves scarce.

"Dear boy, are you alright?"

"Had a shock, sir. My mind went a complete blank there for a minute."

Colin explained what had happened.

"Couldn't be helped, old chap. We had no idea the inspectors were coming today. Fingers crossed, Athena can explain your behaviour away. She has worked miracles already this morning. Another hour or two, and we will be in the clear. We have ten times more pen pushers in fluffy, unnecessary jobs than fighting men. Priorities are all wrong."

Stewards hurried Colin out of a side door, and he was soon back in his quarters. His debrief with Erebus about the Swindon meeting would have to wait. One thing he would bring up with Erebus when he saw him was his cover story for visits such as today.

He had not needed one so far because Olympus generally knew when the Charity Commissioners visited. It was less frequent now the charity had become well-established. They could audit financials remotely, and every visit had left Larcombe with a perfect record of success. Unfortunately, each successive Government thought it vital to add further layers of red tape and more checks and balances. They needed to document evidence that organisations were 'going green', promoting diversity, and any other rubbish they could muster.

Judas Priest interrupted Colin's reverie.

He'd received another text message from Therese on his mobile phone.

'I bought tickets for Greenwich Park. Friday, Aug 3rd. Hope to see you.'

Colin thought it must be for a football match.

"Oh well, that won't be so bad for a few hours if it keeps her sweet."

He sent Therese the reply she wanted to hear. Colin marked the date on his calendar and forgot it for now; he had two months of hard work in front of him first. At least, that's what he hoped.

The ICO inspectors left Larcombe Manor later that afternoon. As they travelled in the hire car back towards the city of Bath, they chatted over the day's events. The manor house and grounds had impressed them; the gardens looked so beautiful at this time of year—a pity they didn't have time to explore them more.

Annabelle Fox and Sir Julian Langford had assisted them admirably too. The analysis of their questionnaire presented no apparent problems. After they dropped off their car and boarded the train to start their journey north to Wilmslow, the conversation turned to the staff interviews.

"How long has Larcombe Manor been open?"

"Around five years."

"There appear to be several ex-servicemen still with PTSD, many years after the action in which they fought. I was surprised to find veterans of the Falklands still being treated. I wonder where they were before the Olympus Project started."

"I have no idea. What did you make of that poor chap who collapsed?"

"Odd that. He looked exceptionally fit for a man, what, in his early forties, would you say?"

"Around that, I suppose. I wonder where that soldier served. Probably Kosovo or somewhere in that region, I expect."

"We never got a name for him, did we?"

"No, we didn't. Now you come to mention it. Do you think we should follow up on that?"

"It's something to bear in mind, certainly. If that *was* odd, then it makes you wonder whether everything we saw and heard today is as genuine as Olympus led us to believe."

"Perhaps we're reading too much into it. What can we possibly know of the effects the heat of battle has on the minds of the young men we send off to fight on our behalf?"

The inspectors grew tired due to their long day's work and the warmth of the train compartment. One by one, they dropped off to sleep. The senior inspector was the last one to fall asleep. His final thought was to make a mental note to include a note of concern in his report to the Charities Commission.

Chapter Nine

Erebus sat at the head of the table and frowned.

A frown was becoming his most frequent expression. Colin wanted to tell him what his late mother used to say to him, in between slapping him around the ear and reminding him that his being born had ruined her life. She would tell him his face would stay like that if he didn't take care.

The actual Games were enough of an issue for Olympus to counter any potential acts of terrorism without drawing attention to it. They also had to contend with lengthy exercises like the Torch Relay. So Erebus had good reason to frown.

An attack could occur in hundreds of places while that carnival was underway. The relay lasted ten weeks, with celebrations almost every night. Thousands of people were taking a turn carrying the torch. There were famous faces, and others were 'the great and the good' from whichever area the flame visited.

Erebus had enough white hairs without considering the

dangers that visiting national heritage sites, sporting events, green spaces, festivals, and points in between might cause.

"How are we going to cope with this minefield?" he asked one morning towards the end of May.

"To be frank, we should leave it to the authorities," said Alastor.

"I agree," said Athena. "The relay has an escort of trained officers from the Met who run with the torchbearer. A wider team of cyclists, motorcyclists, senior officers, and operational planners supports them. If we intercepted intelligence that specifically identifies an attack on a leg of the relay, then we can react to that; otherwise, we should switch our resources elsewhere."

"Is that the view of each of you?" asked Erebus.

Although not unanimous, it was a well-supported view, and Erebus reluctantly agreed.

"I know concerns remain over the vulnerability of the relay runners, but on this occasion, we must leave it to the police and hope for the best."

Colin looked up from the file in front of him on the table.

"The Diamond Jubilee celebrations are giving the authorities an extra-long Bank Holiday weekend to manage. Would any of our known terrorist organisations attack the Royals or the spectators watching the planned events, do you imagine?"

Minos shrugged his shoulders.

"The public outrage at an attack on the Queen or Royal Family would be so great that most groups refrain from attacks on such occasions. There's no evidence to suggest a risk. Further to the concerns over the torch relay, true this weekend will bring several opportunities. There are ten thousand ticket holders for a Diamond Jubilee Concert in front of Buckingham Palace. The Queen travels to St Paul's Cathedral to attend a national Thanksgiving service; after that, she moves to Westminster Hall for a formal lunch. The finale will be in an open-top carriage, and she rides back to the Palace. Later in the day, there's a 'feu de Joie and a fly-past."

"I hope that meant fireworks," said Colin. "Not a firing squad?"

Athena tried to suppress a giggle. Erebus peered over his glasses at Colin.

"I think the authorities have their work cut out ensuring no one gets hurt, whatever their blood colour. There will be thousands of people and dozens of places to carry out an attack, whether by a sniper or a bomber," he said.

"I reckon we are in the same position as we are with the torch relay," said Colin ."We do not possess the personnel to cover every eventuality. We must rely on official channels to do their job."

Erebus reluctantly agreed. He did not fancy the odds. Every day, there seemed to be more and more attractive scenarios for a terrorist strike emerging. It was bound to happen in the end. He feared that because there were so many targets, the odds against them knowing which one to offer the most protection grew greater and greater.

Abdul Bashir and Aaleyah Fayad had completed the term's studies and examinations at Queen Mary University. They still met with the two male students from the London Met regularly. Several weeks ago, the four collected their uniforms, ready for their roles as Games Makers.

Munaf Mansoor took his younger colleagues and Farooq Habibi back to his flat in Islington. They had several things to discuss. But, first, they had to rummage through their brand-new kit bags and check out the paraphernalia they received.

They had a jacket, polo shirt, trousers, trainers, socks, cap, bag, water bottle, and that vital accessory for every British summer—an umbrella. The design of the deep purple and poppy red uniforms made the volunteers stand out from the crowd.

"How are we supposed to blend into the background and do what we want in this?" cried Farooq as he paraded around the flat. Aaleyah laughed at her friend. He had his cap on back to front, and his trousers were tucked into his socks.

"If there are seventy thousand of us across the different venues, don't you see? We will hide in plain sight. It's perfect," said Munaf.

"Anyway, we won't be just seventy thousand, will we? Because the general volunteers wear the same colours, too," said Abdul.

"Exactly. This uniform suits us well," said Munaf. "We can move around with far more freedom in this than if we wore normal streetwear. It is functional and comfortable. The bag is part of the outfit. When the time comes, it will be normal for people to see us carrying one. No one will suspect what's inside."

"What about us, though?" asked Aaleyah.

"What do you mean?" said Farooq. He had grown closer to Aaleyah over the past few weeks.

"Not us, silly," chided Aaleyah, "I meant us as Muslims. When we first attended our training session, we didn't see many others at Wembley Arena."

"I thought the McDonald's guy running that session said they were pleased with the diversity," said Abdul.

Munaf sneered. "This is Britain. There *must be an equal split of males and females,* old and young. They would face criticism if they didn't have numerous ethnic groups involved. So, there won't be only us four Muslims."

"It's no big surprise that Maccy D's got involved, is it?" laughed Aaleyah.

"Why?" asked Farooq.

"Because most Brits are fat, lazy spongers who eat fast food, do you mean?" said Munaf.

"No," said Aaleyah, thinking what a knob Munaf could be. "Because it's great publicity for the business and it adds to people's perception they have a great training scheme. Look at the materials they handed out too."

"The travel cards we got will be vital," said Farooq.

"And the meals vouchers," said Abdul.

Munaf became serious.

"As long as the vouchers aren't exclusive to a McDonald's, I suppose we'll get good use from them. Now listen up. The time is over for laughing and joking. We must set up guidelines for communicating in the next few weeks. From today, we must stop phoning one another on our mobile phones. It is too risky to discuss our plans on an open line. We need to buy a cheap pay-as-you-go phone. When we meet next, we will add each other's numbers to the phones and use code names for our identities. We will no longer call one another by our name in a message. Is that understood? Farooq and Aaleyah, you are Popeye and Olive Oyl."

Aaleyah looked towards Farooq, and they both burst out laughing.

"It is not funny. You two will work together at the Aquatics Centre. Abdul and I will be at Greenwich Park. Your new disposable phones will let us text one another and keep our true mission secret."

"What are your code names then?" asked Aaleyah.

"I shall be Spider-Man, and Abdul is to be Roadrunner."

That set Farooq and Aaleyah off, laughing again. Abdul was happy with Roadrunner. He had visions of Munaf lumbering the two of them with Batman and Robin. No, Roadrunner was bearable.

"But if we text one another too often, won't people will get suspicious? Our purpose is to show spectators to their seats and give directions to toilets and so on," said Farooq.

Munaf had worked on a solution to this. He handed over a sheet of paper.

"This list of phrases covers everything we might need. Each begins with a three-number code. If we stick to these, then if anyone from the security services monitors mobile traffic, they will miss the significance. Only the four of us will know."

The other three students flicked through the list that Munaf had written,

- 321 means 'Meet at noon'. I will add the location 'my flat', for example.

- 412 means 'Go underground'. Keep mobile silence until I contact you.

- 543 means 'Collect kit'.

- 632 means 'It is time'.

"I studied the event timetables and noted three days when we might attack. My choice is on Friday the 3rd of August. We shall pray together now. Aaleyah, you should stand behind us three."

Aaleyah did not argue. While they stood, the four students raised their hands and said: "God is most great."

With their hands folded over their chest, they recited the first chapter of the Qur'an in Arabic. Munaf ensured they completed two cycles of prayer. Then they recited the second part of the Tashahhud, turned to the right and said. 'Peace be upon you and God's blessings'. Then they turned to the left and repeated the greeting.

As the prayers ended, the meeting finished. Abdul stayed with Munaf, and they discussed the days that lay ahead. Finally, Aaleyah and Farooq left the flat together and walked to a local park, where they sat in the warm summer sunshine in companionable silence.

In the flat, Munaf told Abdul, "I have one major task left. I must buy the items needed to manufacture the bombs we will carry." There were just over three weeks until the day of reckoning.

It was now early July, and the meetings at Larcombe became more and more fraught. Intelligence was lacking in the areas they craved. There was nothing to suggest an organised attack was imminent, yet they believed it was out there, somewhere.

Alastor gave his latest update on the authorities' security status. There was plenty of intelligence via the official channels. It should reassure them, but Colin grimaced throughout Alastor's statement.

"Dummy runs in June by security staff achieved a ninety per cent success rate in foiling attempts to smuggle devices into the Stratford site."

"So that means only the main stadium, the velodrome, or the pool got bombed," grumbled Colin. "Or they could plant a device in a waste bin on a thoroughfare. They might dump it because the security was too tight to get it inside."

Alastor gave him a stare and carried on talking.

"They are pulling back the Army's explosive search dogs from Afghanistan; that should confirm the level of threat and the growing unease over their preparedness. These dogs are like teenagers; they get distracted or bored after half an hour, so the thirty-odd teams they now have available to deploy are not enough by a long way. Troops will now search members of the public entering the site, whether for the Olympics or Paralympics. Armed forces personnel will need to cover twelve-hour shifts because the GS4 people cannot get enough people recruited, let alone trained."

Colin interrupted him again. Erebus peered over the top of his glasses but did not comment.

"The logistics of protecting athletes, spectators, and VIPs over six weeks are horrendous. If you have doubts about how difficult this situation is, experts reckon the greater risk of attack is away from the venues. Targets might be railway and bus stations, the Tube, and large shopping centres. These targets are what we always predicted. What would the knock-on effect of a bomb in a mainline station be apart from hundreds of potential deaths? We would see increased security at the Olympic Park, with every visitor needing to be body searched. With no vehicles in or out, you can expect queues halfway to Slough and the 100m Final run in October."

Colin's frustration boiled over, and he slammed his fist on the table.

"Wait. The Home Office just issued a statement. They have a robust safety and security strategy that is intelligence-led and risk-based. Great, we're in the shit good and proper then."

"Thank you, Phoenix," said Erebus. "We get your drift."

"Well, sir, if you could keep people safe by using a well-turned phrase, the Home Office are the people to consult. We might as well pack up and go home if we think the terrorists carry out a risk assessment on their suicide missions. So that statement is just bollocks."

"Sadly, I must agree with you, old chap," chuckled Erebus.

Colin looked towards Athena.

"Don't look at me," she said. "We did what we could to uncover the likely source of an attack. Unless our luck changes, we will deploy as many of our people as we can spare around the Olympic venues and add our eyes to the official authorities. Instead of being proactive, we will be reactive; that's not the Olympus way."

Khadim Salah had moved out of his home in the Birmingham area. His chance meeting with Shamila Javed in the café that afternoon had been a lucky break. They saw one another every day. She was smitten.

Khadim had two objectives. First, to convince Shamila he loved her. That was not a difficult task, as Khadim was an experienced lover. Second, it was no hardship either, as Shamila was an attractive young woman if a trifle innocent.

His main aim was to put distance between him and the possible scrutiny of the security services. After returning from Pakistan and visiting the terrorist training camps, he suspected he was under surveillance.

He had persuaded Shamila to come with him south to the outskirts of Salisbury. She was on holiday now from university. He suggested that she might enjoy a few weeks away from the city. He told her he had to go for job interviews in the region.

Shamila jumped at the chance of spending time alone with him. Khadim rented a two-bedroomed holiday cottage in Downton on the Hampshire-Wiltshire border. They arrived and got settled. Shamila was pleased to see that

Khadim respected her so much that he ensured she had a room to herself.

In the mornings, Khadim set off in the hire car with the pretext of attending interviews. Shamila took the fifteen-minute bus journey into the 'city in the countryside' daily. She found plenty to occupy her mind: a thriving market, a buzzing arts scene, museums, and several of England's most elegant historic houses. The old streets contained plenty of shops where she browsed clothes stores and shops where she could buy the things she needed to cook a meal for Khadim when he returned.

Khadim took the A31 that first morning and headed for Weymouth. The torch relay headed into the town at the end of the week. He wanted to see if everything he had read about this resort was right. Might it be the perfect place for him? For a perfect seaside holiday, location counts. Khadim found Weymouth ticked every box.

With its elegant Georgian seafront, a fantastic sandy beach, and a deep harbour, it has been a favourite destination for thousands of visitors each year since the eighteenth century. So Khadim headed first for Portland Harbour and the National Sailing Academy. That was where they would stage the main Olympic events in a couple of weeks.

Behind the Olympic village rose the Isle of Portland. Khadim soon realised it was an island in name only; the four-mile slab of solid limestone joined to the mainland by Chesil Beach. He spent a few hours looking around the area; it was bleak and windswept. He decided that this was not the place for him.

Spectators had snapped up five thousand tickets for the main viewpoint at the Nothe Gardens long ago. So Khadim spent Wednesday morning cruising around by the Fort, then drove to the central part of town and parked on The

Esplanade. It was not practical to gatecrash the pay-per-view site. It would attract too much attention.

As soon as Khadim had seen the beachfront, he made up his mind. Far better for them to head for the two giant screens on the beach. The hoardings advertised 'an accompanying commentary, so you will know what is happening'.

Khadim wondered what the presenters would say about his proposed change to the programme. He walked along the sands and imagined thousands of people sitting around him, enjoying the summer's warmth and the excitement on the big screens. It would be an afternoon they would never forget. That was certain. The slight problem was getting through the security turnstiles into the fenced-off enclosure. Khadim had a few ideas on that score. His plan meant they would have no difficulty persuading the staff to let them onto the beach.

On Wednesday evening, Khadim drove back to Downton. He was in a good mood. Everything was coming together. When he walked into the holiday cottage, the smells emanating from the kitchen were delicious. Shamila was ready to dish up dinner.

There was just one week to go until Ramadan. A Sindhi biryani with mutton, basmati rice, naan bread, and all the trimmings was the perfect end to a perfect day. After they ate, Khadim told Shamila that he had now attended his interviews; he had to wait to hear if either had been successful.

On Thursday morning, Khadim asked Shamila if they could spend the day in the city.

"Show me around," he said, "and let me see the places you discovered."

Shamila was excited to learn that she had Khadim to herself. She naively hoped that marriage was on the horizon. Khadim grew bored with the shops and museums, and they drove out into the country after lunch. The couple visited Old Sarum and the prehistoric monument of Stonehenge. As the early evening sun warmed them in the lee of the ancient stones, Khadim and Shamila took photos of one another, just like any typical tourists. They drove back to Downton and sat in the garden of their cottage, sipping tea until night fell. Shamila had never been more content.

On Friday, the thirteenth of July, Khadim took Shamila with him to Weymouth. He did not tell her how long he had already spent there or why. They parked by the Radipole lake and nature reserve and took a short walk to the town centre.

"It's jam-packed," said Shamila. "I never expected to see so many people."

Khadim told her of the arrival of the Olympic torch relay. The crowds lined the streets right along the Esplanade. The torch was on its way from Lyme Regis and heading to Bournemouth, with an evening celebration on the beach.

Khadim and Shamila stood at the railings and looked over the vast stretch of sand full of happy, smiling people. Shamila thought how lucky she was. She was having a terrific holiday with the man she loved. Khadim smiled too. Not because he was in love, but because now he didn't need to imagine how Weymouth beach might look with thousands of people on it anymore.

Meanwhile, Shamila's parents had driven up from their home in Wolverhampton. They visited her flat and, finding it unoccupied, called the police to say they hadn't heard from her for several weeks. They wanted to report her missing. Reluctantly, the officer on duty logged the request on the computer.

A photograph of Shamila was circulated to other areas, and, under normal circumstances, that would have been that. Nothing would happen. It headed for the 'twilight zone': left to gather dust alongside many other reported incidents the police abandoned as not worth pursuing. Young people move away from home. They disappear for a while without telling their parents — big deal. A boy racer pops into his local supermarket garage, fills up, and shoots off without paying; another big deal. Modern policing is about far more valuable things.

Not everyone turns a blind eye to people who break the law or fit the profile of someone who might. Only four months had passed since the Home Secretary split the old Border Agency in two. This move was followed by revelations that hundreds of thousands of people had entered the country without appropriate checks. The UK Border Force had become a separate law-enforcement body with its distinctive ethos.

A keen, young graduate had grasped the nettle. After three months in post, she retained enough zeal to check out a few of the many faces logged after returning from known terrorist training areas.

In the Central regional office, Daisy Rawlings had a grainy image of a Khadim Salah on her desk. Six months ago, he returned to Birmingham International from Faisalabad, via Karachi and Dubai. He had been in Punjab for several months. Salah was twenty-seven, held a series of jobs, and graduated from university in 2011.

Daisy added Khadim Salah to a list of 'people of interest' that she intended to persuade her superiors to let her investigate further. Daisy was not the calibre of recruit the current police service wanted. If she were to 'investigate further', she would follow the trail wherever it led.

Daisy Rawlings was like a dog with a bone when she had a cause she believed in; she did not let it go.

Back at Larcombe, Giles and his crew swept the internet for any intelligence scraps that might help narrow the field in the hunt for suspects.

"Give me a break, please," he muttered as messages and photos passed across the screen.

Something alerted him. Giles scrolled back to a photograph of a young woman.

"This girl's a beauty. I wouldn't be letting her wander off, that's for sure. Who do we have here, I wonder?"

It was Shamila Javed. One of their frequent visits to the Police National Database had thrown up the picture her parents handed the police when they reported her disappearance. Giles logged her details.

Shamila Javed was a 20-year-old student who had just completed her first year in Media Studies. The family originated from Punjab. Father is a GP. Mother is a classroom assistant. No known affiliation with any extreme groups (political or religious). Shamila has had no contact with her parents for several weeks.

Giles contacted an agent in Solihull and asked him to visit the district where Shamila studied, lived, and possibly socialised. Who were her friends? Where might she have gone? An hour later, the agent stood outside her flat and began the search for clues.

Lightning rarely strikes twice. Giles returned to the screens and picked up the latest information one of his crew had collected from a source within MI5. Last autumn, a man travelled to Pakistan from Birmingham International. The officer who talked to him had written a brief note that the visit was part of a gap year — an opportunity to meet with family members in Punjab.

When the man returned two months later, the same officer had been on duty. Again, nothing tangible except for a niggle which made him suspicious. The matter had been highlighted for his superiors to pursue. Now it was July, and they had taken no action, but a memo from a new face in Border Force stirred the sleeping giant into action at last.

Giles read the memo, noted the Punjabi and Midlands connection and waited for the man from Solihull to join up the dots. That connection could be what they sought.

Two hours later, Giles got the call. The agent had talked to Shamila Javed's near neighbours. They confirmed that she had been absent for a while, although none of them could be sure of the last time they saw her.

"Shamila was out early, you know, for the bus in term time; she studied at the Uni."

"She was always dressed smartly but didn't wear the veil. Shamila was a pretty girl, too; it's such a shame."

"I saw her in town a few times shopping and that. She always had a smile and a hello, you know. I hope nothing's happened to her."

"Reckon she's gone, mate. One of them arranged marriages. Away in Pakistan married to a seventy-five-year-old doctor her Dad found, I bet."

"I saw her with a handsome man a few times. They were up there by the café on the corner. He was older than her, but they seemed happy together."

A visit to the coffee shop confirmed that Shamila Javed had an older male companion. A customer told the agent they had been in a few times. She said they looked happy together. The girl behind the counter described the man to the agent.

Giles examined the grainy photo that Daisy Rawlings had circulated to her colleagues. Khadim Salah was their man, and he and Shamila Javed were an item. Salah had caused the border control officer to wonder why he had spent two months in Pakistan. The authorities might take a while to put two and two together. Giles alerted Henry Case. Erebus and the others needed to hear this today, not at tomorrow's meeting. Salah had to be found and fast.

Khadim Salah was ahead of the game. After he and Shamila had returned from Weymouth, he phoned the company where he rented the cottage.

"Do you have something similar out in the country? My partner and I wish to get away from things for a while."

"There's a place available in Piddlehinton, sir, at forty pounds per night."

Khadim checked where the little village lay and booked it straight away. It meant they were only twenty minutes from Weymouth and remote enough for him to get things ready for the big day without nosy neighbours prying into his business.

Shamila was surprised to learn they were moving. She enjoyed Downton and her daily adventures in Salisbury. However, she wanted to know why they were going far away from the shops. Khadim ignored her whining and reflected on what clues they left behind if any. Shamila sulked from Downton to Piddlehinton.

Khadim had been comfortable with Shamila strolling around the old city streets. He had only taken one risk that morning when they were together for only an hour. The afternoon and early evening driving around the countryside looking at old stones had been dull. But it didn't leave too many people with a lasting impression of them.

The cottage in Downton had been on a quiet street.

Khadim thought a handful of locals would have seen him, yet none saw him up close. No, there weren't too many clues there. The agent at the rental company might say the gentleman who called was an Indian because he would believe we all sound alike from the sub-continent. The employee could not describe him in detail. Any dealings he had with the company were by email and phone. As Khadim pulled up in front of the little cottage, he thought he had covered their tracks well.

Shamila was happier once she saw the new cottage. It was pretty, with roses around the door and a thatched roof.

"With luck, I will hear from one or more of my job interviews," said Khadim. "I need to check out properties in the region, like one-bedroom flats for me to stay in during the week. Looking at this brochure here that the company has provided, you can catch a bus from the War Memorial mid-morning. You can hit the shops in Weymouth inside an hour."

Shamila was content. Shopping was a passion. To learn Khadim was hunting for a bachelor pad was not good news, but she would make sure he wanted to keep visiting Wolverhampton on the weekends. The harsh truth was that Khadim wanted her out of the way for a few hours. He didn't plan to go back to the Midlands on the weekends; he wasn't planning any further ahead than Friday, 3rd August.

Khadim waved Shamila off to the bus stop at a quarter past ten in the morning. He collected a case from the boot of the hire car and took it into his bedroom; then, he laid it gently on the bed and opened it. He removed a collection of items and put into practice the skills he had learned in Pakistan. Khadim was careful to keep the vital components apart until he needed them. But there might not be many opportunities to assemble the bomb with Shamila continually standing in his shadow.

The explosive belt contained several cylinders filled with explosives. The explosive was surrounded by a fragmentation jacket that produced the shrapnel responsible for most of the bomb's deadliness. The design turned the coat into a crude, body-worn claymore mine. A wire connected the cylinders to a trigger in the middle of the chest.

Once the vest detonates, the explosion would resemble a shotgun blast. The main killing power of any bomb is not the explosion itself. The shock wave from a few explosives is small, but the fragments of the vest being launched in every direction by the explosion do the real damage.

Khadim Salah had selected the most dangerous and widely used shrapnel; steel balls that were 5mm in diameter. He had added nails, screws, and nuts to his recipe. In Pakistan, he had learned that shrapnel was responsible for ninety per cent of casualties when a device such as his exploded.

The vest now weighed twelve kilos, and despite the summer weather, he knew he needed to hide it under a suitable loose outer garment.

In Pakistan, he had watched an engineer using something he called the 'Mother of Satan'. One glance at the two fingers missing on his right hand told him everything he needed. Khadim had opted for TATP, the acetone peroxide, as the initiator, and ammonal, a more straightforward, far less dangerous material, as the primary explosive.

Khadim had smuggled a quantity of TATP home with him in a plastic bottle hidden in his wash bag. No matter how well-trained the dogs were, they could not yet detect acetone peroxide. He stored the bottle away in his sock drawer.

The sweat on his brow gathered. The clock ticked ever onward. Shamila was due to arrive on the bus at the War Memorial stop soon. He had just a few more things to do, and then he could tidy up shower, and change.

Khadim stood in the shower ten minutes later, and as the hot water battered his body, he wondered how long it would be before he stopped shivering. As he dried himself, he heard the door of the cottage squeak open.

"Hi, Khadim. I'm back. Wait until you see what I've bought."

Khadim closed his eyes in exasperation.

"Not long now. You can put up with Shamila for a while longer," Khadim told himself as he dressed.

Shamila displayed the sparkly tops and shoes she 'had to buy', and Khadim tried to appear interested. Once the fashion parade ended, Shamila showed him the other items she had bought.

Khadim looked at the pitta bread, the hummus, and the dates. He couldn't watch anymore. Khadim suddenly realised he was hungry but knew he had to wait until dark before they sat down for iftar. Khadim chose a bottle of water from the goodies in Shamila's many shopping bags and decided on a drive.

Khadim needed to do something to take his mind off his stomach rumbling.

He drove into Dorchester, topped up the hire car with fuel, and then headed back to the cottage in the tiny village. As he drove, he thought about how beautiful the countryside was. Khadim Salah shut the thought out of his mind; earthly beauty was nothing compared to paradise.

Chapter Ten

There was less than a week until the Opening Ceremony. The excitement around the country grew, even amongst those who were usually not interested in sporting occasions. The Torch Relay, the Diamond Jubilee weekend, and an occasional 'feel good' factor appeared in the news. All of this contributed to the notion that, whatever the weather, the summer of 2012 would be fun.

At Larcombe Manor, the mood brightened too. The news from the ice-house lifted spirits. So far, there had been no confirmed sightings of Khadim Salah and Shamila Javed, but at least they had something positive now. Before those two pieces of information dropped in their lap, they had been rushing around in the dark.

Erebus asked Athena and Phoenix to stay behind after the morning meeting on Monday. He had several things on his mind.

"Please do not mention what I am about to say to anyone outside this room. Do you understand?"

They nodded.

"Since I lost my beloved Elizabeth, I have been seriously considering the future. However, I need to hold the reins for the time being. As soon as you are ready, Athena, I can assure you I shall stand aside. You will lead the Olympus Project. Phoenix, you are to become her right-hand man."

Colin was startled.

"Me, sir? Surely one of the other three heads expects to be chosen?"

"If they do, then they are mistaken. You may think these old eyes miss things, but I know you two have, let's say, grown close, shall we? Even if that were not so, Phoenix, you would still be the only logical choice. Thanatos, Alastor, and Minos have been indispensable, yet they are followers, not leaders. You and Athena have youth and ambition on your side. The Olympus Project needs that in abundance as it faces an even more challenging future. I believe the two of you working together possess the necessary skills to meet those challenges."

Athena got up and hugged Erebus.

"Phoenix and I won't fail you, Erebus," she said, kissing him on top of his head.

"I wish to give you an insight into my vision for Olympus as you take it forward without me. I hope you will develop the organisation following the principles I established when we started."

"If it ain't broke, don't fix it," said Colin.

Erebus rose from his chair at the head of the table and walked over to the drinks cabinet. He gestured to Athena and Phoenix to join him. He poured himself a large glass of brandy and invited the others to fix themselves a drink. Erebus sat in his favourite chair by the fireplace, and when they were comfortable, too, he outlined his thoughts on the future of the Olympus Project.

"A collaborative, international approach to security underpins the ethos of many of today's successful independent organisations. More and more independents are tackling issues of scale that may have limited them previously with the help of global affiliations and technology. In a globalised world, an international organisation network is one way to tackle size limitations for an independent such as ourselves. Such a partnership can unlock worldwide opportunities. Olympus must seek to develop partnerships that take advantage of the benefits of global scale, shared insights, and knowledge of local criminal activity. These partnerships offer Olympus local support. The collaborative approach will allow the organisation to deliver more. Combining different but complementary skill sets through collaboration with different partners worldwide allows us to deliver integrated global campaigns. These campaigns deliver results much greater than the sum of the parts. Collaboration plays a key role. It is not always an easy choice, especially with a mix of talented, opinionated, and ambitious people. I suggest you take an objective view, use coercion, be polite, and finally, direct action to get the desired result. We live in a digital world now, and technology has influenced how we create, connect, and work together. We are more connected and accessible than ever before, and this immediacy helps us work more quickly and efficiently. Partnership and collaboration will continue to bring organisations together; in the final analysis, getting the criminals is what matters. My vision is for the Olympus Project to become a global agency for good."

Athena and Phoenix sat enthralled and listened to the elderly gentleman. Their drinks remained untouched as Erebus laid before them the projected scope for the organisation based here in the countryside just outside Bath.

"It looks as if we've got our work cut out, Athena," said Colin.

"How on earth will we finance this escalation?" asked Athena. "Indeed, how can we sustain the organisation in its current form?"

Erebus looked at her.

"When we committed ourselves to the Project in 2007, I told you that as well as my money and that of you and your three colleagues, we received support from others. People with access to funds who believed in what we did. Their financial backing depended on their secret identity. Nothing has changed in that regard. In football in recent years, the media mentioned the term oligarch for business magnates who quickly became super-rich, particularly in Eastern Europe. These people have recently been in the Middle East, India and the Far East. Our 'angels' are not oligarchs. Safe to say, their money has accumulated over centuries. The families of these men and women have travelled the highways of this nation since the Middle Ages. There is as much chance of that well running dry as Fulham winning the Premiership."

"Very reassuring," said Athena.

"Sorry, was that still a football analogy?" asked Colin, aware that he had considerable gaps in his sporting knowledge.

"Not to worry, Phoenix," said Erebus with a smile. "Oh, before I forget, you have been with us a year now, and your financial situation is becoming clearer. Our accountants convinced the Cayman Islands bank that your alter ego is no more. A year and a day have passed, and they are now happy to accept the terms of the will we sent them, bequeathing the balance of your accounts to a worthy charity. As soon as the Olympus Project has received the money, we will transfer ninety per cent of it into a personal account in your name."

"That's a sizable handling charge," cried Colin.

"Ah, but doesn't it feel good, donating to charity?"

"Who will I be then? Mr Phoenix?" asked Colin. "Will I get a card to use at an ATM? I'll need to practice my signature."

"The account will be in the name of Phoenix Holdings, which we thought apt. Our accountants will handle it on your behalf. They'll ensure it continues to make money, and you can draw any cash you need for personal use. Of course, you may continue to access Olympus funds when out in the field on direct action."

"Of course," said Colin. "Do you know when the Swiss banks might cough up?"

"As usual, they are proving a more difficult nut to crack, but be patient, Phoenix; it will turn out all right in the end."

"Well, ninety per cent OK, at least," muttered Colin.

Athena thought it was time to change the subject. It was always unseemly to discuss money. She had no idea how much money Phoenix had saved or how he had gotten it. She did not want to know. She loved him whether he was a prince or a pauper. Instead, Athena wanted to return to the matter of the future direction of the Olympus Project post-Erebus.

"You gave us an insight into the future earlier, Erebus. In modern parlance, do you have any particular ethos or mission statement to sum up what you believe the new and revitalised Olympus should aspire to?"

Erebus got up and walked back to the table. He found a sheet of paper in the back of one of his files.

"Let me quote the following:
Our mission will be to pre-empt threats and maintain national

security by collecting intelligence that matters, producing objective analysis, conducting effective covert action as directed, and safeguarding the secrets that help keep our nation safe.

"That sounds good," said Colin.

Athena giggled.

"What's so funny?" asked Colin.

"It should sound good. That is almost word for word the mission statement of the CIA."

"I thought it covered what we strive to do," said Erebus, "but generally, we do it better."

All three chorused, "Of course."

"Right, let's be serious for a moment," said Athena. "These drinks are way too strong."

"The drinks have put colour in your cheeks, my dear," said Erebus, "but you're right; we should put our long-term visions aside for now. Instead, we must concentrate our minds on the more pressing matters of the coming week."

"Phoenix won't know this, but we have a handful of agents inside the Olympic Stadium for the Opening Ceremony on the twenty-seventh," said Erebus.

"Do we know the theme of the ceremony?" asked Colin.

Erebus referred to his files again and showed Colin and Athena aerial shots of the stadium.

"The ceremony is expected to be seen by a global television audience of more than a billion. So, it had better be up to scratch. I can't imagine this Boyle fellow getting finance for another picture if he makes a cock-up of this. The show will tell the story of the making of Britain - culturally, socially, and politically. Take a look at these pictures we got from a helicopter that flew over East London at the weekend. The extravaganza will feature smokestacks, pits, and steam power as it showcases Britain's industrial history. You can expect to hear 'dark satanic mills' through the million-watt sound system."

Colin wondered what Iron Maiden and Judas Priest were doing that Friday night. If they were on stage, he would snap up a ticket, no question.

Erebus was still explaining the possible programme of events.

"The organisers have already revealed there will be light and shade. Life is about balance. I expect they'll trot out a group of bloody Morris dancers."

"As relevant to England's history as a Balti," said Colin.

"You have it in one," said Erebus.

Athena then told Colin about the people Olympus had on the inside.

"They first found out they had a part in the ceremony in January, having auditioned in November last year. We had no idea what they were getting into, but we anticipated needing eyes and ears in the stadium. They were processed and assigned various roles, from dancing to backstage work. In April, rehearsals started in Bow and then moved to Dagenham; final rehearsals switched to Stratford four weeks ago. There are two technical dress rehearsals scheduled before the final ceremony. One is today and one on Wednesday."

"We know what the official security levels are for this carnival," said Colin, "so what will this handful of agents bring to the party?"

"They are highly trained people. They won't get distracted by their roles in this show or by the hype that will surround the entire evening," said Athena. "If they see or hear anything suspicious, they will act accordingly. It's a calculated risk."

Erebus sat deep in thought. He looked towards Colin.

"Do you think we have missed a trick somewhere, Phoenix?"

"I hope not. Last autumn, I would have seen sense in having people on the inside. Back then, there would likely be an orchestrated attack by Al Qaeda on the Games. We looked at medal ceremonies being bomb targets, kidnappings, and dozens of different scenarios. We may well get something such as that. If we do, the planning has occurred far away from these shores. The terrorists won't even be in the country yet. That seems unlikely. I reckon the lack of evidence of orchestration suggests that we will need to stop a lone wolf."

"The lone wolf being this Khadim Salah, perhaps?" asked Erebus.

"If he is a suicide bomber, then the girl is probably a cover, something to make him appear to be a normal bloke with an attractive younger woman on his arm."

Athena smiled to herself. Phoenix was four years older than her.

"While I still worked with MI5," she said, "we examined the phenomenon of suicide bombing. Young males carry out most attacks, as we know. They became a weapon of choice among terrorists because of their deadliness and ability to cause mayhem and fear. What is it that motivates these attackers? The driving force is not always religious fanaticism but a whole range of things, including politics, humiliation, and revenge. A bomber's life story rarely directly connects violent militant activity and personality disorders. Most suicide bombers are psychologically normal and are light-years from being loners. Khadim Salah was a bright student who lost his way. He drifted from one dead-end job to another and then found a niche where he could be very successful. The recession saw the rug pulled out from under him. What was his response? He attended university and excelled. He got a first-class degree. The fact it was in Politics and Sociology has great relevance. Over the past three years, he has been building up his hatred for the system he sees as responsible for his redundancy. He believes it was because he was a Muslim. What other reason could there be? He was brilliant at his job, by all accounts. Someone has to pay."

"I think you've nailed it," said Colin. "He was humiliated. In his eyes, he deserved more respect."

"If this chap wants revenge, why not plant a bomb in the Olympic Stadium and claim responsibility afterwards? Why on earth would you blow yourself to smithereens?" asked Erebus.

"If he does, we'll never get the chance to ask him," said Colin. "We need to find this couple and take them out of the picture before he gets the chance to do the deed."

Popeye and Olive Oyl were returning home after an evening at the cinema. Their new mobile phones rang.

'321 my flat tomorrow.'

"What do you think it means?" asked Aaleyah.

"Nothing urgent if it can wait until tomorrow," said Farooq.

Munaf was in his flat. He turned to Abdul.

"Everything is ready. We have purchased every element. Some are in the bag on the chair by the window — the rest are at my uncle's place. I told him I needed spare storage for my books while I was away from the campus. He doesn't suspect a thing. I shall pick them up tomorrow at eleven o'clock, and when the others arrive, we can begin."

"Do you think the others are as committed to the cause as us?"

"Why do you ask? What have they said?"

"Nothing," said Abdul, "but they are too close. Their emotional connection will make them weak."

Munaf nodded. He would keep a close eye on Popeye and Olive Oyl tomorrow.

Before dawn, the two men rose and began their preparations. Their simple breakfast of a bowl of porridge with milk and one slice of toast was enough to sustain them throughout the daylight hours. Fasting during Ramadan was one of the Five Pillars of Islam, and Munaf and Abdul used it as a time of self-examination and increased religious devotion. They read the Qur'an for most of the morning.

Munaf left the flat and walked the short distance to his uncle's shop. He picked up his things and walked back to the flat. No one paid him any attention.

Abdul looked up as Munaf walked back into the flat.

"Everything we need is here now?" he asked.

Munaf nodded. He removed the bag's contents and took great care, placing them on the table. Next, he brought the other bag from the chair and added its contents to the collection.

"We have time before the others get here. Let me tell you about the pipe bombs we will carry. Pipe bombs are, by nature, improvised weapons. The steel water pipes themselves are easy to buy. You want them no more than eight inches long and two inches in diameter. Normal metal galvanised pipes are best. I bought most of these materials by buying the caps one day and then getting the pipes a few days later. They were bought from a different hardware store each time to avoid suspicion. We need to drill a small hole in the centre of one cap per pipe for the fuse."

Munaf planned to use electric fuses with wires leading to a timer and battery. Abdul viewed the components on the table with wonder. Things were getting real.

"Once we have the holes in the caps, we can attach the fuses and tape them on, so they don't move. Then we screw the cap onto the pipe tight. I've borrowed a vice from my uncle; he never uses it. So he won't miss it. We can use that to hold the pipe firmly to fill up the pipe. The manual I downloaded stated that normal firework powder works great. So I bought all sorts of bangers and stuff and emptied the powder into an old Nescafe coffee jar. That was a dirty, time-consuming job. I wore oven gloves to stop my hands from getting filthy. I put newspapers on the floor if I spilt any, and the landlord wondered what I'd been doing. Once we stabilise the pipe, cap, and fuse, we can pour in the powder. I've got a funnel thing in the kitchen drawer. We cram as much powder and shrapnel as physically possible in each one."

Munaf and Abdul were so wrapped up in what they were doing that Farooq and Aaleyah knocked at the flat door before they knew it.

"Hi there," said Aaleyah. "What are you guys doing?"

"Get inside and close that door," shouted Munaf.

"Sorry," said Aaleyah. "You did say to get here for prayers at noon."

"What did you need us here for, anyway?" asked Farooq. His eyes widened as he took in the various items on the table.

"We have everything we need," said Abdul, "and it is nearly time."

The room fell silent. Prayers followed, and then they read from the Qur'an. Later in the afternoon, Munaf showed them what they needed to do.

As night fell, everything was ready. It was time for them to eat. A simple meal of dates, followed by pasta cooked with vegetables and chicken, and a slice of plain cake with custard was washed down with cranberry juice.

Aaleyah and Farooq made their way back to their respective digs.

"I'll see you in the morning," said Farooq. Aaleyah nodded and stood silently by the doorway into her apartment block.

"We only have two messages to go," she said.

"Until tomorrow then," said Farooq, not wanting to think about it.

Back at the flat, Munaf and Abdul studied the results of their handiwork. Munaf was satisfied.

"We have done well, Abdul."

"Roadrunner," he said.

"Do you have your uniform ready for tomorrow, Roadrunner?"

"I do, Spider-Man," said Abdul with no hint of a smile. "We must be the best Games Makers we can be at Greenwich Park. Many people are relying on us."

He glanced at his watch as Abdul retired to his room to sleep. He had forgotten the Opening Ceremony had been on the television tonight. He wondered if it had gone well.

The newspapers and the media were ecstatic about the extravaganza that had taken place at the Olympic Park last evening. Twitter was in meltdown with ten million tweets. The first day's events were due to begin.

The four students were on duty, ready for a ten to twelve-hour shift. Aaleyah had a ten-minute bus ride to the swimming events; the journey for the boys was just over forty minutes. Bright-eyed and bushy-tailed in their purple and red uniforms, they welcomed, directed, assisted, and comforted visitors of all ages and from every corner of the world. It was a long day, and they were exhausted by the end.

Deep in the Dorset countryside, Khadim and Shamila were lying low. Of course, she didn't realise it as she thought they were just chilling and getting to know one another better. It seemed to her that Khadim wanted to spend his day as a devout Muslim should during Ramadan, fasting in quiet contemplation. Shamila was cool with that.

Khadim allowed Shamila to take the bus into Dorchester on Monday to shop, and they drove to Lyme Regis together on Wednesday to stroll on the Cobb. The weather was delightful. Khadim thought they were far enough along the coast from Weymouth to pose little risk. It would be Friday soon enough.

At Larcombe Manor on Thursday morning, Colin lay on his bed. He tried to think of a way to tell Athena that he would be away for the day tomorrow. She was bound to want to know where Colin was going. If he were evasive, she would smell a rat. Therese had texted him to remind him about Greenwich Park. Colin was catching an early train and would be in the park by eleven o'clock.

A few hours in her company wouldn't be too much of a hardship; far better to keep her sweet than to provoke her. Therese could expose him. Now that Erebus had told him he would soon have one and a half million in his bank account, keeping Therese sweet was paramount.

Colin had at least done his research, and he now knew that it was horses he was watching, not blokes kicking a ball. It was a slight improvement, but he was desperate for something to break in the hunt for Khadim Salah, and he could go elsewhere instead.

Since the prison break mission, he had been starved of

action. Most of all, he missed the buildup and the planning he found so fascinating, pitting his wits against the complexities of the job at hand. He loved working out in minute detail how he would complete a successful mission. On the other hand, to react at a moment's notice to an impending crisis was alien to him. Colin did not like it.

There was nothing for it; he had to bite the bullet. He must tell Athena the truth about the London trip. He leapt from the bed and made his way towards the main house.

No sooner had he poked his head around the door to his room and entered the corridor when Rusty shouted out to him.

"Come and look at this, mate."

The bell saved him. Colin turned and followed Rusty's voice. His ex-SAS buddy was looking at images.

"Don't tell me," sighed Colin, "you want to know if I've ever seen any this big?"

"No, mate," said Rusty, "it's not a porn site. It's a CCTV feed from Lyme Regis."

"Lyme Regis," asked Colin. "Where's that when it's at home?"

"On the Dorset coast, you ignoramus. Twenty-five miles from Weymouth."

"Where they're holding the sailing events. So what?"

"Check this couple out."

"Khadim Salah and Shamila Javed; pleased to make your acquaintance. When was this?"

"Yesterday afternoon."

"Let's get over there then. Why are we waiting?"

"Hold your horses, Phoenix, Erebus, and the others haven't seen this yet. We've only just intercepted it. Henry said Giles had people up through the night scrambling through CCTV footage within a thirty-mile radius of an

Olympic venue. Have you any idea how much that was? We are talking needle and haystack territory, mate."

Colin was itching to be doing something, not hanging around and waiting for a green light to go to Lyme Regis. They must stop this couple from doing whatever they planned to do.

Rusty viewed the footage again.

"I know the spooks reckon this Salah fellow spent time in the old country last year and had him recorded as a potential terrorist but look at them. Are we sure? Look at the way she's gazing lovingly at his face. She's in love. They're strolling arm in arm on The Cobb; they don't look bombers to me."

Colin stared at the screen.

"She's gazing at *him*, Rusty. The guy's not looking at *her*. He's checking out everything around him, keeping his eyes on the floor, when those two older women walk by them. There, do you see? No, this one's clever; he's using the girl as a decoy. He wants people to think they're the perfect couple. As a loner, he'd stand out from the crowd. This way, he'll blend into the happy crowd spending the day at the seaside."

"Well, you're probably right. You usually are, mate. I'll pass this to the bosses, and they can decide who goes to locate these two and sort the problem."

Colin left Rusty and headed off to see Athena. As Colin walked across the lawn, it dawned on him that he had his Get Out Of Jail Free card, if he volunteered for the Weymouth mission. Colin could send a message to Therese telling her a rush job had come up on the South coast. He could say he couldn't get out of it, and there would be nothing to tell Athena.

Colin tried to get in to see Erebus. He thought if the

boss viewed the evidence of the Lyme Regis CCTV, it wouldn't do any harm if he sat in too. He'd be in the prime position to be picked for the mission. Unfortunately, Erebus was off-site for the rest of the day, visiting his solicitors. Athena saw Phoenix loitering in the corridor.

"The little boy lost look doesn't suit you, Phoenix," she said, running her nails up the middle of his back.

"Rusty tells me we got a break in the Salah case. He's in Lyme Regis. I reckon I should get over there pronto."

"I've assigned Hayden Vincent and Kelly Dexter to that job. They are picking up a former sniper in Yeovil on the way. I reckon they should be positioned sometime before noon. If these two terrorists target the sailing programme, they still have over a week to strike. We've got people checking the live feeds from the tourist webcams in Weymouth and Portland. Once we get a positive sighting, we can let the agents know. If Jack Mould gets a clear shot, he's to take them both out, no messing. We have a clean-up crew from Bournemouth on their way. It would be great if they could remove any evidence from the beach. If not, I have a backup plan."

Colin was impressed. Athena was on top of her game, all right. Erebus was away, and she had assumed control and sorted out the actions necessary. There was nothing left for him to add.

"OK, it looks as if you've got it covered. I might pop up to London tomorrow to get a flavour of the Olympics, you know if that's okay? It won't take long. I'll be back by nightfall."

"Not so fast," Athena said. "You didn't say anything about getting tickets. You hate sports. What's going on?"

"Nothing, honestly, but after Erebus told me my money

was available, I thought it was time to look for something on which to spend it."

"You don't need me along, too?" said Athena.

"Not just now," said Colin, "but thanks for the offer."

Athena had to get on with Olympus's matters, so she kissed him quickly on the cheek and told him to have a good day. As Colin made his way outside, he gave a massive sigh of relief.

"Hurry back tomorrow, Phoenix," Athena called. "You might find you have a guest waiting for you."

Colin congratulated himself on dodging the bullet. He now had the chance to keep Therese sweet and something to look forward to when he got back to Larcombe.

The rest of Colin's day was quiet and uneventful.

In London, it was yet another busy day in mobile phone activity.

"543."

Chapter Eleven

The morning of Friday, the third of August 2012, had arrived.

Popeye and Olive Oyl received their call to go to Munaf's flat. Both had been up before dawn, praying and eating a light breakfast. Finally, they dressed in uniforms and were ready to resume their Games Maker duties. Today was to be their final day.

While the two young students collected their bombs, Colin listened to the weather forecast. Then, he sat on the train pulling out of Bath Spa station to Paddington.

'The UK is in an unstable south-westerly flow with scattered showers, but most showers will fall in the west and south-west. On Friday, central and eastern Britain will begin fine with hazy sunshine, but clouds will build with a scattering of showers by the afternoon. A few showers might reach the southeast of the UK through the morning. These will then die away in the afternoon with fine and sunny weather to end the day. Moderate southerly breezes will develop, becoming fresh and gusty over the southwest of England later in the day. Afternoon temperatures in London should be around twenty-one degrees Celsius.'

Typical thought, Colin. I should have brought a coat. English summers weren't what they were when he was a boy. Sitting in an open stand watching bloody horses as they trotted around while it rained was not what he would be doing given a choice.

Colin checked his watch. The train got him into Paddington before ten, and it took just over thirty minutes to reach the Park. Colin looked out of the window at the wide-open spaces. He wondered if the descendants of the deer that Henry VIII hunted in the Park all those years ago were still in residence. Would the organisers have rounded them up and moved them elsewhere during the Olympics?

He sent a text to Therese, telling her he'd meet her at half-past ten by the Royal Observatory. As the train pulled into Swindon, he got her reply: -

"I can't wait. I missed you."

Colin did not take much notice; he was still scanning the platform for Andy Partridge.

At Greenwich Park, the second day of the Men's and Women's Team Dressage was underway at eleven o'clock. The crowds were building, and as the spectators emerged on the other side of the security cordon, the temporary open seating began to fill.

Spider-Man and Roadrunner left the flat a few minutes after Popeye and Olive Oyl. Munaf told them he would call again. When they received the message, they knew what to do.

In Piddlehinton, Khadim Salah and Shamila Javed made an early start too. They also rose early, prayed, and Khadim packed the car.

"Are we going somewhere nice today?" Shamila asked Khadim.

"I thought we could go into Weymouth," he replied.

"What, to the beach? What shall I wear?"

"I think you should wear the shalwar kameez, the one you wore the first day we met; that would be perfect. I shall wear traditional clothing too. I have an embroidered kurta that I wear on special occasions, and with a dhoti and a pagri, we will show these English people what fine Punjabis we are.

Shamila was beside herself. Surely today, Khadim would tell her he would ask her father if they could be married. She ran to her room to change into her most elegant outfit.

Khadim was in his bedroom changing too. He carefully donned the jacket and then the outer clothing. He checked himself in the small mirror on the dressing table. He looked bulkier than usual, but he could carry it off.

He turned on the radio as he reversed the hire car into the street and headed towards Weymouth.

'If you are heading off to the sailing today, then there is a thirty per cent chance of a shower in the morning. With luck, it will then be a dry afternoon. Expect around twenty knot southerly winds off the Weymouth coast and temperatures of around eighteen degrees.'

"I hope it doesn't rain, Khadim; it will be a shame."

"We won't let it spoil our day, Shamila."

Meanwhile, his phone rang as Colin stepped off the train onto the platform at Paddington station. Commuters and staff turned their heads as Judas Priest welcomed their arrival in the capital.

It was Rusty.

"Where are you, Phoenix?"

"Paddington. I've just arrived."

"You need to get to Stratford, mate; it's urgent."

"What's happened?"

"Giles picked up a video posted on YouTube thirty minutes ago. It's already going viral. A student called Farooq Habibi uploaded it. He wore a Games Maker uniform. He's been at the swimming this week, but I guess they won't be coming into work today."

"Did you say they won't be coming?"

"His girlfriend has been volunteering there, too; she's not in the video. Giles is trying to find out who else hasn't turned up for work today so that we can get names. They were due in half an hour ago."

"What's on the video?"

"There are many quotes from the Qur'an on violence and attacking non-believers. So that's us, mate. Oh, and he rambled on about Arabic posters."

"Did he say what they planned to do? Are these two in it together, the boy *and* the girl? Is Salah connected to this in any way? What have we missed?"

"That's it, Phoenix. In the video, he says *they* are carrying out suicide attacks today. The lad's scared stiff, and he wants to live. By the sound of it, he has something to live for - this girl student - by the sound of it. Salah is heading for Weymouth if our sighting of him is a clue, but whether they met somewhere, who knows? Giles hasn't found a link yet. Unless he turns up something else and fast, our best bet is that these two kids will be together near Stratford and the Olympic Park."

"Oh, cheers. That narrows it down."

"We've got people on the ground already, mate, don't worry. They'll meet you as soon as you get over there. If you're up there on a jolly today, I'm guessing you aren't carrying a gun?"

"I'm naked as the day I was born. Sorry love."

"What was that?"

"Frightened an old lady at the ticket machine. She snapped her head so quickly; it nearly fell off her shoulders. Right, I'm on my way to Stratford. I'll be there around half-past ten. Who am I meeting?"

"Do you remember Brad? We worked with him at Oxford Circus. He transferred from Birmingham in April. Brad's squad lives in the Chiswick area. We're scanning CCTV for sightings of Habibi. The deadly duo from Devizes is heading for the beach with their plus one."

"Jack Mould, the sniper. Is he any good?"

"Jelly was one of the best we had."

"Jelly? What do you mean was?"

"Jelly Mould, you plonker; it's just a nickname. Dark humour from those who lie around picking off targets further away than I can see. It was because he never had even a quiver. We're in safe hands, Phoenix, don't fret."

Colin stood on the platform; it was just after ten o'clock. He waited impatiently for the train to arrive.

Farooq and Aaleyah were outside Jamie's Italian inside the Westfield Stratford City shopping centre. The enormous retail space had been open for a year. The pair still wore their Games Maker uniforms and carried their official bags. The pipe bombs they had collected from Munaf's flat were inside. When they left Munaf and Abdul, they had turned to one another at once and said, "I can't do this."

"I know, Aaleyah," Farooq had said. "Can we stop using these stupid nicknames he gave us too? I am ditching my burner phone as soon as Munaf rings us. We should hang on to them until he calls. He'll never know we aren't going through with it. Whatever he and Abdul do is up to them. I want to stay alive and be with you."

Farooq took Aaleyah back to his flat. He told her he was recording a video and planned to upload it to the internet.

"What are you going to say? Can I be in it, too?" asked Aaleyah.

"Not if you don't want to."

Farooq turned on his computer and started work. The finished product was not a slick presentation, just an outpouring of emotion from a naïve young man. He was a student experiencing love for the first time, caught in the enthusiasm and ideological miasma surrounding life at his university. He did not want to die.

Farooq quoted verses from the Qur'an. He said why he wanted the West to suffer at his hands. He cited several examples that only warranted a brief mention in the media but seemed significant to him. Farooq talked of the posters at the shopping centre near the Olympic Park that welcomed shoppers in Arabic but incorrectly translated. That was unforgivable, he said. Farooq mentioned respect a lot.

"Our words carry no weight, so we shall talk to you in words you understand. We give our words life with the blood of your people. Our religion is Islam - obedience to the one true God, Allah, and following the footsteps of the messenger Muhammad (peace be upon him). My mission was to protect and avenge my Muslim brothers and sisters with my death. I do not want to die; I want to live. Until we believe you respect and treat us as equals, you will always be our target. We will still make sure our bombs get used today. If Allah's will is that we survive, so be it."

Minutes later, the video went live.

A sudden flurry of activity on the internet followed. #gamesbomber trended on Twitter in minutes. The social media storm soon alerted the ice-house, and Giles viewed the video. He acted at once.

Back in London, Farooq and Aaleyah had left the flat. They set off to Stratford with no real idea of what they would do. Then they wandered around the massive shopping centre into the Olympic Park.

Aaleyah was still the firebrand she had always been. Getting to know Farooq and liking him made her question whether she needed to blow herself to bits to get across her message. But, as she listened to her friend speaking to the camera and pouring out his feelings, she realised they could still contribute to the cause. She was not prepared to go as far as Munaf and Abdul, but it would be helpful in its way.

It was a minute before half-past ten. Therese stood by the Royal Observatory. Where was he? She rang Colin, but it went to voicemail. Therese waited.

It was half-past ten. Farooq and Aaleyah were still wandering, riding the escalators, waiting for the call from Munaf.

One hundred miles west of Stratford, someone from the surveillance team at Larcombe shouted, "Yes."

Everyone in the room jumped.

"What have we got?" asked Giles.

"I've got them. The students are heading for the escalators at Westfield Stratford shopping mall on the first floor. I'm looking for them now on the second floor; please hold."

"Right, we know where to send Phoenix, Brad, and the others. We need to get moving to stop them from setting off those bombs. It's been a few hours since he uploaded that video. Why the hell are they waiting?"

At ten thirty-four, Colin had reached Stratford station. He walked across towards the entrance to the Westfield. Brad spotted him and trotted over to him.

"Good to see you again, Phoenix. Nasty business, this one, isn't it? We've heard from Larcombe that they are inside the building. We've identified the girl, too; her name is Aaleyah Fayad. Let's get over there, and you and I can find a quiet spot. I've got a choice of toys you can choose from to play with later."

Colin followed Brad into the complex. Two minutes later, he had the comforting feel of a Glock in his jacket pocket. The search for the two Games Makers could begin.

Farooq and Aaleyah waited for Munaf to ring. They had run out of floors to explore. Farooq had taken the Nando's escalator to the third floor and spotted the entrance to the Casino. That was as good a place as any. He removed his bag from his shoulder and opened it. He set the timer for noon. Farooq ensured nobody was watching and stuffed the bag into a litter bin. He made his way back to the second floor.

Aaleyah waited for him over by the InSpiration multi-faith space. The volunteer staff didn't arrive until eleven, but it was okay to sit there and pray. He joined her, and they sat together.

"What have you done with your bag?" she asked Farooq.

He told her. Aaleyah grabbed his arm and pulled him to his feet. She headed off towards the escalators.

"We had better find somewhere to leave mine now. Let's go back downstairs."

"Two people in uniform, running," cried a voice at Larcombe.

"Got you," said Giles and called Brad.

Brad received the information they wanted. The two would-be bombers were on the move. They had descended from the second floor and were now on the ground floor.

He contacted the rest of his team. They sat in the van one hundred yards from the scene. Brad was confident he and Phoenix could take care of these two kids; he didn't want the place swarming with agents; it would attract too much attention. Instead, he wanted them close on standby to summon them to deactivate the bombs and remove the bombers. Brad rang their squad leader and told him to move inside the building at once and head up to the second floor.

Brad hoped the capture and removal of the bombers and the discovery of the bomb's position would happen without bloodshed.

Because Phoenix had joined them at the last minute, they weren't 'miked' up, so he had to call him. Colin had his phone in his hand and scrolled through his missed calls and text messages from Therese. He was about to send her his apologies when Brad's call interrupted him.

"Both targets are in the Gallery. Where are you?"

Colin looked around for a clue. A clock above him ticked over to 11:13.

"Chestnut Plaza, heading for The Street, by the looks of it. Do I keep heading in this direction?"

"Roger that. I'm near Cherry Park Lane by Marks and Sparks. I'll keep an eye out, and if the CCTV picks them up again, they'll let me know where they are heading. I will call you, but if they keep moving the way they are now, I'll be behind them, and we'll have them trapped."

"Keep your gun out of sight until we need to use it, mate. There are too many people around in here."

"OK, Phoenix, I'll keep my cool, don't worry."

Brad rang off. His earpiece crackled at once.

It was from Giles. "Habibi no longer has his bag; repeat, Habibi no longer has his bag."

"Shit," swore Brad. He rang Phoenix.

"One bomb has been deployed in the building, either on the second or third floor. I'm calling my crew to track it. I sent my lads that way already; maybe this is our lucky day."

"OK, Brad, I got that. I am outside Hugo Boss. No sign of anyone as yet."

"I've seen them. The bombers are running towards you. Something spooked them. I'm in pursuit."

Brad and Colin ran. Farooq and Aaleyah had vanished. As the two agents met, breathing hard, they looked around them wildly, searching for the movement of two purple and red shapes.

"How did we miss them?" said Brad.

Colin turned back and looked up The Street. The place was heaving. At eleven fifteen in the morning, with the Olympics in full swing, it was only natural that the area would teem with people.

Brad received a message in his earpiece. He breathed a sigh.

"They found the pipe bomb and disarmed it. Timer set for noon."

"Thank God," said Phoenix. "One down, one to go."

Suddenly, Brad pushed past him and sprinted.

"There they are, in the middle of the walkway. I've no idea where the pair hid. It could have been any of the shops along here."

Shoppers, sightseers, spectators, and the odd, mildly interested security guard watched as the two agents barreled towards the two Games Makers.

"Take the lad," called Phoenix. "I've got the girl."

Farooq and Aaleyah realised they couldn't escape. The two agents caught them and grabbed their arms.

"Neither of them has a bag, Brad," shouted Colin.

"Where have you put it?" demanded Brad.

"Where have we put what," said Aaleyah with a defiant look. "What's it to you anyway? You aren't coppers?"

Brad scanned the gathering crowd of onlookers. They needed to remove these two out of here pronto. He called the driver on standby in the van and told him to expect company. Then he contacted the agents upstairs.

"We have another device on the ground floor. We know roughly which part of The Street it's in, but no idea when it's due to blow. Get here right away."

Colin watched the two students leave the shopping centre. With luck, the youngsters would crack first and tell them where they placed the second bomb. Aaleyah looked like a tough cookie. He took his phone out of his pocket and sent Therese a text.

'I'm running late; something cropped up. I hope to meet up with you soon.'

Seconds later, he got a reply.

'OK, see you xxx.'

Colin consulted his watch again - 11:20 - it had been ages since breakfast. He looked around. He was sure he had passed a café earlier.

"I'm going back to get some grub and a drink," he said to Brad.

Brad nodded as his agents approached. The bomb disposal expert collared Brad at once.

"There's not enough time. It's not possible to search every one of these units. We have to evacuate the building. I rang the police and told them there was a bomb in the litter bin by the casino. I told them it was detonating at noon.

The alarms will sound any minute now, and the tannoy system will get people out of the building. They can't risk it; they must evacuate, even if they think it might be a hoax. There are far too many people in here. Hopefully, the other one is on the same timing device as the one I disarmed. If the bombers talk, we can ring again and tell the police where to look for the second device. They can get the army bomb disposal people in to deal with it. They have thirty minutes if we're lucky. The police are on call for the Olympic Park, anyway."

"A good call, pal," said Brad. "We had better head back to the van. I'll ring Phoenix to update him."

Brad sent Phoenix a text message and followed his crew outside to the van.

As Brad reached the outside door, he got a reply.

"I got a chicken tikka masala, mate. Sorry if it stinks the van out, but I'm starving."

The clock ticked on to 11:30. All hell broke loose.

Colin shook his head. His ears were ringing.

The blast had come from twenty, thirty yards behind him and to his left. He had just left that café. The same restaurant was full of customers enjoying a bite to eat and a cold drink on a warm summer's morning. Happy, smiling customers blissfully unaware that someone would leave a bomb on a chair or under a table set to go off at half-past eleven. They were unaware that someone would leave with their companion and abandon them to their fate.

As Colin moved on unsteady legs towards the café, he recognised the familiar charcoal-like smell of gunpowder mixed with blood and burned flesh. It was thick and bitter, overpowering everything. He tasted it in his mouth.

The young girl on the till smiled when he paid for his sandwich and can of coke. As she placed his change in his outstretched hand, her fingers felt so small, soft, and warm. She trailed her fingers lightly across his palm and giggled as he turned to walk away.

Colin recalled the small group standing outside the café, deciding what to get and who went in to buy it. He pictured the elderly couple in the corner nursing their cups of tea, just people-watching. The tables were full of parents with young children in the middle of the room. He remembered the noisy teenagers he stared at who sprawled over a table by the back wall. Why hadn't he seen a Games Maker bag?

He stood now where the gaily curtained windows and the doorway had been. His head was clearing. Colin forced himself to remember, but he knew he had not seen a flash. Instead, he heard a noise similar to a firecracker; it was that which struck him most. He had felt no heat, and there was no rush of wind. Instead, the blast threw him forwards onto his hands and knees.

Outside the devastated café, there were people like himself: confused, shaken, and walking around in circles, wondering what had happened. Colin saw a few people with bloody faces picking themselves up from the walkway.

Inside, bodies lay scattered on the floor of the café. Although it seemed like the bomb had exploded ages ago, only a minute had passed. The coppery, bitter smell of blood invaded Colin's nose. The old chap in the corner tried to put out the flames on his wife's back. As Colin looked at what remained of her face, he realised her husband's efforts were a waste of time.

The tables where the families sat had gone too. What remained were tables and chairs shattered and body parts everywhere. There did not appear to be any survivors in this part of the café. Colin swallowed hard and switched his attention to the back wall. The teenagers were unnaturally quiet. The tableau was surreal; one had lost both her legs. She might still be alive, her mouth open, but so far, she could not seem to decide whether she wanted to scream or not. Her three companions sat in the same positions as he left them. The shards of wood and slivers of glass sliced through arteries, penetrated brains and vital organs and forever wiped away any thoughts of a gap year.

Staff members appeared from the rear of the building. They were kitchen staff. They picked their way through the rubble in shock at the horror in front of them. Finally, one of the chefs called out a name and dropped to his knees behind the remains of the counter.

"Ally," he screamed.

Colin was there in seconds. The young man was hysterical. The pretty girl who had flirted with him minutes ago sat on the floor. She had lost her right forearm; the fingers she trailed across the palm of his hand had been blown away. Colin could still feel her light affectionate touch; he fought to keep control of his emotions. Black blood covered the stump.

Colin knelt by the young chef and beckoned to one of his colleagues.

"Look after this lad, mate, will you? Try to calm him. Help will arrive soon."

Ally breathed heavily; she looked up at him.

"Am I going to die?"

Colin reassured her as best he could. He grabbed a shredded tablecloth, ripped it further for makeshift tourniquets, and tied them around the remains of her arm to stem the bleeding. The blood and ash now blackened her outfit with a blue and white t-shirt and white skirt.

The Games' euphoria and the crowds' cheers for the medal winners seemed so far away. Colin heard no national anthems nor cries of encouragement for runners or swimmers; no flags were waving or bunting, fluttering in the breeze. He could hear sirens. He heard alarms. Colin could hear the screams of people in pain. He listened to a tannoy announcement, telling people to stay calm and to evacuate the building.

Colin stayed with Ally until the police and paramedics arrived. They started work on her at once. Ally was still breathing when they loaded her on a trolley and whisked her away in an ambulance.

Colin sat on the floor where the counter had been and spotted the cash till for the first time. But, unfortunately, the force of the blast had embedded it in the wall.

Brad found Colin still sitting on the floor in the café.

"Time to go, my friend; the centre is being evacuated. This place will be crawling with police, paramedics, the military, and the media in no time flat. We need to make ourselves scarce. There's nothing more we can do here."

Two minutes later, they sat in the van, trying to drive away from the shopping centre. Traffic was gridlocked: police and emergency services were everywhere. Thousands of people had been let into the Olympic Park to clear them away from the buildings. Brad and Colin knew they had accounted for both bombs. But, sadly, they had been unsuccessful in avoiding any bloodshed.

"Any joy with those two kids in the back?" asked Colin.

"We have had tears from the boy. The girl isn't saying a word. We found two phones on each of them. One looks as if it was for personal use. The other only had a few messages on it. Brief coded messages in their inbox—no outgoing calls. So we have a problem, Phoenix. They either had a handler who sent them in to bomb the Westfield that we still need to find, or they are not the only bombers on the ground today."

"We're certain there's no connection between these two and Salah in Dorset?"

"Larcombe is convinced he's a lone gun. However, we can't be sure they aren't part of a cell."

Colin looked at his watch. It showed 11:50.

"If there are others, they might not be Games Makers. They may have also wandered around the building in ordinary clothes. If they planted their bombs, then in ten minutes, the Westfield could be a mess, but at least it will be empty."

"If there *are* others in the Park, tens of thousands of people are in the firing line. The fact of the matter is that we can't help them."

Colin's phone vibrated.

Another text message from Therese.

'Hurry, the horses are lovely.'

At Greenwich Park, the morning's dressage session of the Grand Prix was well underway. The weather remained warm and dry. Stands of temporary seating were packed with thousands of spectators in good spirits. The atmosphere was electric. British competitors had done well in front of their flag-waving, cheering fans.

Spider-Man and Roadrunner stood at their posts, directing people to first aid centres and toilets; they helped late arrivals to find their seats.

Munaf Mansoor kept looking at his watch. It read 11:52.

Abdul Bashir helped an older woman back to her seat.

"Thank you, dear," she gushed. "You Games Makers are doing such a wonderful job. We are so grateful."

Abdul was embarrassed and scuttled away as soon as possible. It was 11:53.

In Weymouth at 11:53, Khadim Salah and Shamila Javed shuffled through the security gates onto the beach. Traffic had been heavy, and it took several minutes to get to the seaside resort and find a parking space. The streets teemed with holidaymakers, locals, and Olympics visitors.

It was eighteen degrees, with a twenty-knot breeze. It was sunny and dry.

"This way, sir, madam," said an attendant at the gate.

"I'm afraid you won't be able to take that through, sir," he said to Khadim.

Khadim removed a sheath from his belt.

"This is a ceremonial dagger; here, keep it for me. I shall reclaim it from you when we return."

The queue behind them grew longer and more frustrated. The crowd wanted to run onto the beach, to join in the fun.

"Come on, granddad, get a move on. Let them through," someone shouted from behind Khadim.

"Do you mind if my female colleague searched the lady, sir?"

Khadim had prepared for this. He pushed forward.

"Is it not disrespectful enough that you hold these Games during Ramadan? You also want to shove my female companion and me; this is discrimination."

Seconds later, Khadim, Shamila, and the people in the queue behind rushed through the gate and onto the sands. The crowds still milled around. There was a real buzz on the Live Site, and Khadim was now where he wanted to be.

Shamila lost sight of him in the scramble to find a spare piece of sand; she stood fifteen yards to his right, surrounded by happy, smiling people waving flags. Everyone nudged her, and she got a few stern looks and an elbow in the ribs when she tried to push her way towards her man.

It was 11:57

Colin and Brad still edged their way through the traffic in Stratford, inching their way further away from the Westfield. Giles contacted Brad.

"I've got an update on the students. Farooq Habibi, the video star, and Aaleyah Fayad attend London Metropolitan and Queen Mary University. They have known associates. Habibi is a member of the Islamic Society at the university and was recruited by Munaf Mansoor. Fayad was friendly with Abdul Bashir at QMU. Mansoor and Bashir are Games Makers volunteering at Greenwich Park. Both signed in as normal this morning."

"Greenwich Park?" asked Brad.

"What about Greenwich Park? Colin asked.

It was 11:58.

"It could be trouble," said Brad.

On the beach, Khadim Salah anxiously waited for the clock to reach noon.

Jack Mould breathed slowly and steadily.

Kelly Dexter sat in the van; alongside her was Hayden Vincent.

The Samaritan's logo on the van's sides persuaded a warden to let them park on The Esplanade for fifteen minutes.

"Don't let me find you here when I walk back," she said.

"Don't worry; you won't. Thank you for being a star," Kelly had replied.

The view from the van was perfect. Jack waited.

"Do you have a clear shot, Jelly?" asked Hayden.

"Affirmative," replied Jelly.

"Whenever you're ready," said Hayden.

Gold, Silver and Bombs

At Greenwich Park, Spider-Man typed a text to Roadrunner, Popeye, and Olive Oyl.

He pressed send.

"632."

Khadim Salah knew nothing of Munaf Mansoor and his coded signals.

He had his timetable and edged his hand towards the buttons of his tunic. It was time to trigger the bomb. Khadim's hand trembled, but he held his nerve.

Roadrunner was the only one to receive the call from Spider-Man. The phones belonging to Popeye and Olive Oyl rang, but no one answered.

One of Brad's crew alerted him from the van's rear and relayed the message.

"I wonder what '632' stood for?" said Brad.

Colin looked at his watch. It was almost twelve.

"Boom?" he said.

The big screens at Weymouth broke away from showing events at sea; there was a lull in the racing. Then, they switched to Greenwich Park for an update on the Grand Prix dressage.

Jelly Mould saw Khadim Salah tense. His rifle pointed through a modified air vent on the side of the van. At this distance, he could not miss. He fired.

Shamila had moved to her left, still trying to push her way through the crowds to get back to Khadim. She spotted him as his head exploded. Shamila collapsed to her knees, screaming. Blind panic replaced the happy atmosphere as people desperately tried to escape and get anywhere away from the nearly headless body, which stained the golden sands. Dozens of people got hurt in the stampede.

Two pairs of hands scooped Shamila Javed from the sand and got her up the steps onto The Esplanade. Then, they bundled her into the back of the van. Hayden Vincent joined her and Jack Mould on the inside.

Kelly Dexter pulled away from the kerb and threaded her way through the traffic as it slowed to a crawl. Ahead of her were desperate drivers trying to discover what had caused the commotion on the beach.

The stretch of beach home to the Live Site lay deserted, apart from Khadim's body and his jacket bomb.

In minutes, the police, the emergency services, and men in suits from the secret service descended on The Esplanade like flies.

The big screen still showed images from Greenwich Park.

Spider-Man and Roadrunner had moved into their agreed positions at either end of one of the open stands. They had set their timers to noon.

Therese Slater sat near the end of the row with an empty seat beside her as she watched the latest competitor in the ring.

She had almost given up on Colin.

Therese felt her phone vibrate in her pocket.

Both bombs detonated.

It was carnage.

The police, emergency services, men in suits, holidaymakers, former Olympics spectators, and security staff at the gates at Weymouth stared at the big screens.

The only person not watching the scenes from Greenwich Park was Khadim Salah.

Chapter Twelve

Colin looked at his phone. It showed 12:02.

"Message still not delivered," he said to no one in particular.

"With the mayhem going on around Stratford, it's no big surprise if the mobile system goes into meltdown. Just think of New Year's Eve," said Brad.

"I sent a text to Greenwich Park," said Colin.

"Hang on," said Brad. "Giles has got something... fuck. Say again?"

Colin sat staring straight ahead as Brad listened to Giles.

"Two suicide bombers have hit Greenwich Park: several dead, dozens of seriously injured, a hundred walking-wounded. The only good news is that they got the bomber in Weymouth. Unfortunately, they had to shoot him on the beach amongst ten thousand people, but at least he didn't have the opportunity to detonate his bomb.

"Each event at noon and the ice-house still say they're unconnected?"

Colin seethed. He wanted to reach Greenwich Park; he tried Therese again.

"Can we get over to Greenwich?" he asked Brad.

"We can try," he replied, "but it will be chaos, like this place. I can't see us getting near, mate, sorry. So I reckon I should head home, drop my urchins in the back in a safe house in Chiswick with my lads. Larcombe can decide what to do with them after this mess. I can drop you at the nearest tube station."

"We've only moved a half-mile in this traffic jam, Brad. I'll run back to Stratford and take my chances that the trains are running. From what I remember, the DLR will take me via West Ham over to Cutty Sark. So I'll be heading in the right direction. Drop me here. Cheers. It was almost good working with you again."

"Cheers, Phoenix. I hope you find who or what you're looking for safe at Greenwich, mate."

Colin was already running along the pavement. Why did he feel so concerned about Therese? Was it guilt? She had been desperate to see him. He could not have left to meet up with her with the situation as it had been at the Westfield.

He thought of the young girl in the café too. Had she made it to the hospital in time? The trains were running. As the train journey began, he had more time to be alone with his thoughts.

It was 12:20.

Shamila Javed had stopped screaming.

Kelly Dexter negotiated the traffic jam around the docks and floored it on the relief road. They arrived in Yeovil in thirty-five minutes. The Bournemouth clean-up crew had left for home; they could do nothing now. Athena's backup plan would have to come into play.

Kelly dropped Jack Mould off at his house. Jack cleaned his rifle as Kelly headed for the Frome turning. Soon he could put his kit away in the loft until the next occasion Olympus needed someone taken out. Jelly cracked open a can of lager and sat in his conservatory. He wasn't thrilled with his work today. Far too easy, like shooting fish in a barrel.

Hayden Vincent glanced at his watch. It was 13:00.

He gazed at Shamila Javed, who sat opposite him. The young girl was in shock.

Hayden spoke to her quietly. He explained to her about Khadim's training in Pakistan. He said he had used her as a cover because the authorities would not suspect a young couple. Shamila listened and sobbed. She felt so ashamed. What would her family think of her? Those nights when she ached for Khadim to come to her bedroom, they slept alone. She had believed he stayed away because he loved and respected her. What a foolish young girl she had been.

Hayden knew after Frome that Kelly would drop Shamila off with Henry Case at Larcombe. After that, it would be a while before the young woman saw her family again.

Colin soon discovered that the train service had suffered from the mayhem of Stratford and Greenwich. It was after one o'clock when Colin arrived at Cutty Sark. The scene as he walked across towards Romney Road was a mirror image of the Westfield. Emergency services and police darted in all directions. An army bomb disposal unit had arrived, and helicopters circled overhead. A HEMS helicopter had landed in the Olympic dressage arena to pick up another casualty.

No way he could get near the stands. They were now a mangled heap of wood and metal.

He rang Therese again.

There was no reply.

A St John Ambulance man walked towards him, pale and drawn.

"How many died?" Colin asked.

"Seven confirmed deaths. A few looked bad when they went in the ambulances. They have been working on one woman over there for a while now. It doesn't look good. She's a fighter, though."

Colin ran in the direction that the man had pointed. Half a dozen people surrounded a body on the ground. A doctor or a paramedic tended to her. Colin pushed through the protesting voices. He barely recognised Therese.

Another man in blood-stained scrubs caught Colin's arm. Colin looked at him. The man shook his head solemnly.

Colin sank to his knees. Therese opened her eyes, and her eyelids fluttered. She struggled to speak.

"Took your time," she said hoarsely. Her eyelids fluttered once more, and she was gone.

"I'm sorry," said the doctor. "I have no idea how your wife hung on this long with her injuries. It was obvious she didn't want to leave without seeing you."

"Not my wife," said Colin. "A friend."

He stood up, and as he turned away, the doctor said to his colleagues,

"Time of death confirmed at 13:08."

Colin somehow left the Park. Thousands of people still milled around, too shocked to move. Strangers comforted one another. Officials did their best to help the authorities, but a major incident such as this was beyond anything their training programme had imagined.

Colin walked for what seemed ages until he spotted

Deptford Bridge station ahead. He had to return to Larcombe. Colin needed the security blanket that Olympus, Erebus, and Athena provided him. He was devastated he hadn't been able to help to save those people. Therese had died too.

Colin considered killing her himself so she could never reveal his true identity. He had never loved her, yet she had fought for an hour, against impossible odds, to stay alive until he reached Greenwich.

She deserved better. Colin resolved to avenge her death. This episode of bomb attacks might have ended. Others would surely follow. The Phoenix would be ready.

The hour-long trip via Canary Wharf and Waterloo delivered Colin onto the platform at Paddington at last. There was a train due to leave in a few minutes. Bath Spa and home were only just over an hour away.

Although the concourse was busy, and the tannoy announcements echoed around the old terminus, the mood was sombre. London was in mourning for the lives lost.

Colin slept fitfully on the train, dreamt nightmarish dreams, and passed Chippenham before he awoke, still lost and alone. He rang Larcombe for the transport section to rustle up a taxi. He stood outside the station at Bath Spa and waited for five minutes for his lift to arrive.

As people passed him, their conversation concerned the bombings. He caught snatches of what they said,

"Wasn't it terrible? All those people dead."

"Over thirty, they said just now on the news."

"Where were the police? That's what I want to know."

"All that money they spent on security for the Olympics."

"Who shot the Indian bloke on the beach then? Was that the SAS do you think?"

"He was a Pakistani."

"Who, the bloke who shot him?"

"No, the man on the beach; his family came here from Pakistan."

Colin saw the taxi with the Olympus logo arrive. He jumped in the back, and they headed for Larcombe.

If what he had just heard was anything to go by, the next few weeks would be challenging for many people: the families of those killed and injured, the Olympics organisers, who had to decide whether the Games could continue or not, the authorities, and, last but not least, Olympus.

There would be questions for the authorities on how the London bombers got through the screening process to become Games Makers. Questions, too, over how they got their pipe bombs into their targets. They would have to explain how Khadim Salah, a person of interest, smuggled a jacket bomb onto Weymouth Beach.

As for Olympus, taking Salah out in such a public manner had been Athena's call. Colin was not overly critical of her decision without knowing the full facts of how things developed on the beach, but it did pose the question. Once the authorities had checked every potential section of their forces to discover who had fired the shot, the spotlight would switch elsewhere. Would Olympus be caught full beam?

Back at Larcombe, everywhere was a hive of activity. Erebus and the others sat in a top-level meeting. Henry Case had a young girl from the Midlands in Hotel California for a quiet chat. Giles and his crew in the surveillance section monitored the aftermath of the three incidents.

Colin logged the Glock into the armoury so that Brad had it returned in due course, and then he went to his quarters to check for any messages. There was nothing for him. So Colin checked to see if Rusty was in his room.

"You're home safe and sound then, Phoenix," he said. "Someone will be pleased."

"Has someone been looking for me then?"

"Her Ladyship, of course."

"I looked into the manor house on my way in, but they're in a meeting."

"I think they are discussing damage limitations, mate. Athena took every precaution. We didn't have eyes on those two before they reached Weymouth. There was a possible window in the car park where they might have taken him out, but Kelly couldn't get Jack in close enough because of the traffic. The beach was cutting it fine. If this Salah fellow had been trigger-happy, there would have been many more dead people reported in the papers tomorrow. Fortunately, he stuck to his noon deadline, and Jelly took him out."

"We are bound to see attention concentrating on whichever organisation carried out the kill. The authorities will know it wasn't one of theirs, and, although the British public may never learn that, the authorities will still want to find the shooter."

"That's where her Ladyship was clever, mate. Jack's rifle is L115A3, and he is a wizard when it comes to fiddling around with the kit he uses. He got a few rollickings in the SAS from his superiors, but now that he's freelance, he does what he pleases. So when they dig around and locate the bullet in the sand or wherever it ended up, everything on the type Athena suggested he used will scream CIA."

"Bloody hell, that was clever."

"Exactly. It should deflect the attention away from Olympus and silence the spooks because they used the CIA as advisers on London 2012 security. Why wouldn't they have had agents on the ground at Weymouth? With luck, they will not query it with Langley because they will look stupid. So that the public doesn't think our security services are complete tossers, they will claim it as their kill."

"It sounds like a masterstroke."

"Your day out was buggered up, mate, wasn't it?"

Colin could not tell Rusty everything, but he filled him in on what happened at Westfield Stratford. He told him he had gone to Greenwich Park to see if he could help. He didn't mention Therese.

"Do you think the Games can continue?" asked Rusty.

"They carried on in 1972 at Munich and again in 1996 at Atlanta. I guess that the IOC and the government will put on a united front. They'll state that the Games should carry on as planned to show that acts of terrorism will not cow the world."

The two friends chatted for a while, and then Colin said he needed to shower and change.

"You whiff, mate, but sometimes it's good to talk," Rusty said as Colin got up to leave.

"Thanks, Rusty. You're a pal."

An hour later, Colin sat at his computer, watching the news updates. The St. John Ambulance guy had it right. Eight people died at Greenwich, and well over a hundred were taken to the hospital. Several of those suffered life-changing injuries.

The café had yielded the highest number of fatalities, with twenty-two dead. An older man and a student were the only survivors. The student was critically injured.

"Ally didn't make it," Colin said, thumping the desk.

A knock came at the door. It was Athena.

"Thank goodness you're okay," she said, running to

Colin and wrapping her arms around him. "I was so scared that something had happened to you."

Colin rested his head on her shoulder, and Athena felt moisture on her skin. Colin cried softly.

"Phoenix," she said, "what is it?"

"The girl in the café, Ally. She didn't make it. She served me a sandwich and a can of coke. I walked out of the door and up The Street. The next thing I know, I'm on my knees. She had lost half an arm. She was in a bad way. Do you know what she asked me? She said, 'Am I going to die?' I told her not to worry; everything would be OK. Now she's dead. She was so young."

"Many people died, Phoenix; we saved a lot more. Unfortunately, we cannot be everywhere. You did everything you could."

"You made a good call at Weymouth Athena; the ammo idea was pure genius."

"Not just a pretty face, Phoenix. Do you want me to stay with you tonight?

Colin nodded. He knew that the night they had planned was on hold. But he couldn't face the night alone. They lay on his bed and held one another until dawn. Sleep was a luxury for Colin. Most of the time, he lay there, listening to Athena's steady breathing and seeing the faces of Therese, Ally and the other people from the café.

The morning papers and the TV news bulletins were full of the horrific details of the attacks. They could attach names and faces to the people who had perished. The media photographed and filmed families visiting relatives in the hospital. Concerned, haggard faces filled newspaper pages and TV screens.

Erebus called Colin and asked him to come over to the main house.

"Bring Athena with you, old chap, if you please," he said as he ended the call.

"He knew you were here," Colin said.

Athena smiled. "I told him I would see you when I left the meeting yesterday."

When the room had its full complement, Erebus began,

"The Prime Minister will address the nation at ten o'clock. He will say that the Games resumed as per the original schedule this morning. Terrorism must not be allowed to win—everything you would expect him to say. There will be a memorial service in St Paul's next Sunday morning. The IOC will reschedule events to allow the competitors to have the service relayed to them in the Olympic Stadium. No events will take place on that day.

The government has asked the UK population to be on the alert. Television adverts, full-page spreads in the news and posters the length and breadth of the country will carry the following message,

If you are walking or sitting and a suicide bomber strikes nearby:

At the first flash or blast, hit the ground and get as low as possible to avoid debris and smoke. Shelter behind something and expect another bomb. Get yourself and anyone you can to an exit and get outside. Once you have made it out of the area, keep away from buildings or structures that might collapse because of the first blast or any other bombings that could follow.

Take precautions to prevent radiation sickness. Be aware that an explosion may have been 'dirty' or a radiological dispersion device. If you are within one mile downwind, you are in the radiation danger zone. You should always presume that you have been exposed to radiation. Ensure officials are aware of the fact and follow their instructions. Do not eat anything. Drink water only from a sealed bottle.

Thanatos looked across at Colin. He said, "I suppose you can find something funny to say about that, Phoenix?"

"I believe that to be a very apt message, Thanatos. Far better that people know what to expect. If our intelligence is correct, then this spate of bombings is over, for now."

Rusty chipped in, "Far better these adverts than just printing a load of t-shirts with 'Keep Calm and Radiate' printed on the front."

Erebus examined the file in front of him. How did Rusty know the Home Office was considering that?

Everyone needed time to heal. Olympus would lie low for a while and gather strength for future battles. Erebus decided to close the file for now.

Next in The Phoenix series

vinci-books.com/nothing-ever-forever

Illusions shatter, destinies collide. Nothing is ever forever.

Phoenix races against time as detectives Hounsell and Wheeler navigate a deadly path from flood-ravaged Somerset to the Diamond Jubilee. With the Royal family targeted by suicide bombers, Tayler's gripping thriller keeps readers on edge, where nothing is ever forever.

Turn the page for a free preview…

Nothing Is Ever Forever: Chapter One

Monday, September 3rd, 2012

The Olympics were fading from the headlines. Every day, something else crept into the headlights of the media's all-seeing eye. Memories for those involved faded a good deal slower. The athletes would keep their successes and failures for years to come. Spectators at the packed stadiums could always say, "I was there."

Those caught up in the bombings in the capital and those who saw the would-be bomber executed at Weymouth bore the scars and the memories forever. But, at Larcombe Manor, time and tide waited for no man as its agents continued to carry out direct action against those who sought to bring the nation into disrepute.

Phoenix had been in the thick of the action in London. Kelly Dexter and Hayden Vincent were in Weymouth. Others had been positioned around the country, ready to strike where required. But, throughout August, Rusty had been stuck at Larcombe, waiting to join in the fun.

On the first Monday of the new month, that time arrived. Erebus invited Rusty to join him in the orangery alone. Rusty was slightly surprised; Phoenix generally attended these special meetings with Erebus. Now and then, the old gentleman condescended to letting the tough ex-SAS sergeant join them. A face-to-face meeting was a privilege not to miss.

Rusty arrived at the orangery at the appointed time. He wore a clean t-shirt for the occasion. Erebus nodded at Rusty and noted the slogan across his chest; SAS–Super Army Soldier. He passed no comment.

"Thousands of foreign domestic workers live as enslaved people in Britain, suffering sexual, physical, and psychological abuse by their employers; over fifteen thousand migrant workers come to Britain every year to earn money to send back to their families. Many endure conditions that amount to slavery. They can suffer physical and psychological abuse. Thousands are not allowed out alone. They never have a day off, work all the hours God sends, and receive a pittance. Foreign diplomats are among the worst offenders. Unlike those brought in on a domestic worker visa, their workers cannot change their employer and face being homeless or deported if they run away. To prosecute diplomats for treating their workers as enslaved people is extremely difficult. One young girl was trafficked from Nigeria to London when she was twelve. The girl's employer worked as a cultural attaché at the Embassy. The young girl was a domestic servant. Behind closed doors, she was raped and beaten. Aged fourteen, her employer threw her into the street. What had been her crime? She asked for a day's holiday. The attaché left her with nothing; terrified and alone, she could do nothing but sit on the street, waiting for her abuser to change his mind. He relented in the morning, and she returned to household duties and be at his beck and call whenever he wanted her. In June this year, she took her own life by drinking bleach. Her employer was adamant that there had been no signs that the girl was unhappy. She had been a good worker, always willing, and they missed her smiling face around the house. Extreme mistreatment such as that is commonplace. Migrant domestic workers are in a uniquely vulnerable position. Thousands of miles from home, they rely on that single employer for their accommodation, work, and immigration status. Mostly, they are isolated and don't mix with anyone. When this young girl died in June, a woman who cooked for the attaché contacted her family in Bandung to tell them what she knew. She was frightened of going to the police because her employer told her she faced deportation if she didn't have her visa and documents. The cultural attaché retained those, and he intimidated her too much to ask him to return them. We intercepted her story in text messages she sent to Indonesia. The cook said this child worked from dawn to midnight. The young girl feared what might happen to her at any time. The cook told them what had happened to the young girl and suspected her employer had raped her. That had been the reason for her taking her own life. The older woman feared she faced assault too if she kept working there."

"Beggar's belief, doesn't it?" said Rusty. "I find it difficult to get my head around the massive numbers involved."

"There are more servants in the UK now than in Victorian times, Rusty. This is contributed to by the growth of childcare and the lower cost of domestic staff," said Erebus.

"I'm hoping that folder in front of you holds the identity of the bastard involved. Excuse my language, Sir."

"Everything's there, Rusty," said Erebus. "I want this job

carried out without delay. I believe the bastard concerned has outlived his usefulness as a cultural attaché to these shores. Please arrange for his repatriation at once."

"Consider it done, boss," said Rusty, and he picked up the file from the table and left the orangery to return to his quarters to prepare.

Rusty often sat in with Phoenix to watch the master planner at work. He had picked up a few tricks of the trade in the past two years. But, with the hours of training that Rusty gave Phoenix when he first arrived at Larcombe, it seemed only fair it became a 'two-way street.'

Solomon Okonkwo was forty-six. He had been with the High Commission for three and a half years. The high-rise apartment he occupied was impressive and situated in Marylebone. Rusty always imagined that these blokes gravitated towards Mayfair or Knightsbridge. Their government picked up the tab. Rusty flicked through the information that Giles and his team had put together.

He was interested in learning that five million bought you more space in Marylebone than in the more upmarket areas of central London.

"Who knew," asked Rusty, to nobody in particular, "how the other half lives, eh?"

Rusty read further. Marylebone had transformed itself into a great destination with a lovely village feel and, some would argue, the best high street in London. Marylebone's international diversity with Russian, American, and African inhabitants was part of its charm.

Rusty checked the easiest route to Northumberland Avenue to get to the Embassy. He had photographs of his target and could pick him up from there and follow him home. While Solomon was at work, he wanted to look at the apartment block itself. Gaining access would not be an issue. Phoenix knew at least half a dozen methods, tried and tested, and half a dozen that never failed. One of those was sure to serve his purpose.

Rusty believed Solomon Okonkwo deserved to pay the price for his actions, but he went through the data on the young girl just the same. Olabisi Promise Chukwu had been only twelve years old when she arrived in the UK on a flight from Lagos. An elderly relative, said to be an uncle from her village, accompanied her.

Olabisi arrived at Solomon's new apartment only days after he had collected the keys from the letting agents. The diplomat stayed at a five-star hotel for the first two months after taking up his new position at the High Commission. Solomon was a single man with specific needs. Olabisi carried out the domestic duties and soon discovered the other more personal services required of her.

As well as Olàbisi, Solomon employed an Indonesian woman, Nurul Ruby Pohan, a thirty-nine-year-old mother of four, who had worked in London for seven years. Mrs Pohan came to the flat seven days a week to cook.

Rusty looked at the photographs of the two desperate women. Then, he studied the long list of crimes that diplomats were responsible for in the past year. They included robberies, sex attacks, fraud, grievous bodily harm, drink-driving, and shoplifting. One suspect had made a bomb threat.

"You couldn't make it up," muttered Rusty.

International treaty rules give immunity from prosecution to diplomats and relatives living with them. Rusty was appalled that serious offenders escaped justice. The privilege granted exemption from arrest or detention.

"Well, in my book, Solomon's immunity doesn't exempt him from having a nasty accident."

Everyone at the Olympus Project agreed. Serious offenders escaping justice was not an option.

Rusty went through his outline plans once more. He felt happy. Transport could be arranged for the morning to have a day in the big city. He looked at his watch. Yes, he had time to drop in to see the lads in the armoury — time to choose the proper kit and then walk to the pool. A hundred lengths should give him time to go through every step of his plan just once more. One can never be too careful. 'Fail to prepare; prepare to fail' was Phoenix's mantra. If it was good enough for him, it was good enough for Rusty.

The following morning, Rusty was up bright and early. The transport would arrive at the stable block at seven-fifteen. The seven forty-three train from the old Spa station would arrive at Platform Five at Paddington just before a quarter past ten.

Rusty collected his kit bag and started the journey. As the train sped through the Wiltshire countryside, he thought through the timetable for the first part of his mission. Straight ahead to the Tube, then the Bakerloo Line to Northumberland Avenue. That should get him outside the Nigerian High Commission before eleven.

The concourse wasn't that crowded on this Tuesday morning. Rusty strode through the slow-moving crowd of commuters, tourists, and students. Why were there always students around, no matter what time you travelled? Late for wherever they ought to be, he imagined. Either that or they selected a course where lectures were scattered throughout the week, ensuring lots of free time.

Twenty minutes later, Rusty studied the front doors of the building. There was no disputing the place had character. His mobile phone vibrated in his pocket. He had received a message from Giles. Giles had hacked into the CCTV in the vicinity and checked that Solomon Okonkwo had arrived for work. Giles confirmed that Solomon was definitely inside the building. The coast was clear for Rusty to pay a visit to Marylebone.

Rusty had another short ride underground via Green Park, and he craned his neck to see the floor on which his target lived. Rusty knew that his choice had been perfect as the crick in his neck increased. What he needed to do now was gain access. It was time to use one of Phoenix's ruses. He removed a clipboard and Hi-Viz waistcoat from his kit bag.

He strolled up to the nearest pedestrian crossing, donning his disguise as he went. As he waited for the lights to change, he kept an eye out for any movement at the front entrance to the apartment block.

There! A postwoman with a trolley. It was early September, and she was wearing shorts, but then they wore shorts, whatever the weather these days. In her case, it was a mistake. The postwoman was old enough to be his mother, with legs that should stay hidden by law. The lights changed; as the mighty noise of traffic paused, Rusty crossed the road.

He hoped that a bit of charm would win the day. He held back for a second as she searched through her bunch of keys. Finally, the woman found the one that allowed her entry into the foyer and the post boxes on the wall.

Rusty sprinted forward.

"Here you go, sweetheart, let me get that for you," he said, holding the door back to get her trolley through.

"Oh, thank you, my love," the old postie cooed. "I'm getting too old for this game."

"Too old?" said Rusty. "Don't be daft. The council has

sent me around to check flats on the top floor; they keep hearing pigeons in the roof spaces. I might have to get rid of vermin later."

"Bloody nuisance, pigeons," the postie agreed, dishing out the post. The pile disappeared fast.

"Nearly done?" asked Rusty. "They can wait for me a few seconds longer; I'll help you get out without scratching those pins."

She was putty in his hands. She slotted the last gas bill into No 84 and wheeled her trolley back to the door. Rusty let her out.

"Have a nice day!" he called after her.

"And you too, love, you too," cried the postwoman.

Rusty had already reached the lifts. Floor after floor slipped by in silence, and then he was there. Finally, when the doors opened, the only thing Rusty heard was his breathing. It was quiet as the grave, which was perfect.

Getting inside Solomon's flat presented no problems. The ability to pick a lock was one of the many skills that Rusty had acquired over the years. Once inside, he moved around quickly and quietly, just in case people were at home in the adjoining apartments. More than likely, the occupants would be at work. These weren't flats a single mum with a nipper could afford on benefits. So Jeremy Kyle seeping through the walls was out of the question, which was always a blessing.

Rusty crept towards the windows. He peered out behind the curtains to ensure that nobody watched him from the flat across the street or idly glanced up from street level. There was no one. He tried to open the sash window, but it was stuck or secured by something.

"Back to the kit bag," he muttered. "Just as well that I collected a few bits and pieces from stores."

Fifteen minutes later, the window opened. It slid up and down smoothly, perhaps better than it had done for fifty years.

"Job's a good one," said Rusty. "Time for lunch, I reckon."

Taking as much care returning to the foyer as he had on the way up, Rusty exited the apartment block. He shared the lift with a Jewish couple and met a lady with sunglasses and a large handbag sashaying into the foyer. Nobody challenged the man with the hi-viz waistcoat and clipboard. Why would they? People who could afford these apartments didn't talk to 'the help', did they?

Rusty removed his waistcoat and stored it along with the clipboard in his bag.

He planned to find a decent pub for a pint and a bite of proper nosh. Two hours later, fed and watered, he strolled through Regent's Park. Rusty made a mental note to thank Phoenix for telling him to take twice the cash you thought you'd need on a mission. Rusty thought that was overkill, but a pint and proper nosh set you back a pretty penny around here.

Nurul Ruby Pohan was due to get to her employer's flat at six o'clock. She was going to prepare a meal, cook it, and serve it at seven-thirty as usual. Everything would be in the dishwasher before eight. Nurul would be out the door as fast as her little legs allowed before Solomon got any ideas.

Rusty made his way back to Northumberland Avenue. He wanted to arrive in plenty of time. These cultural attaches didn't work late. So Solomon might leave early.

Rusty wandered the street opposite at just half-past three. There was a crowd of people going in and out of the building. Rusty concentrated hard on making sure he didn't miss him.

At around half-past four, the door opened. Solomon Okonkwo strode through it majestically. He was a big man, suited and booted every inch the gentleman. A black limousine glided to a halt. Solomon bent forward to open the door, sliding elegantly into the back seat. Rusty desperately searched for a taxi. Two minutes later, he was in pursuit. Afternoon traffic in London can be slow, so his target hadn't got that far ahead. Ten-pound notes in the top pocket of his driver got Rusty a shortcut, and the gap soon closed to a manageable distance.

Rusty paid the rest of the fare as he got the driver to park near the apartment block. He crossed the road between stationary vehicles as the traffic started to build in preparation for the evening rush hour. Where was a postie when you needed one? He didn't have long to wait. A couple let themselves into the building; they were young and looked single. Maybe the guy had brought the girl from the office back for a 'quickie'? They were so engrossed in one another as they moved entwined to the lifts that they didn't notice the door didn't close behind them because of Rusty's right foot.

As the lift ascended, Rusty slipped into the foyer and called the lift. His luck held. No one else was coming home just yet. The lift doors opened, and he pressed the button for the top floor. Rusty checked the gun in his inside jacket pocket. He didn't plan on using it except as a frightener. He pressed the buzzer on the door to Solomon's flat. The door swung open.

"Come in, Mrs Pohan. I've been waiting for you," said Solomon Okonkwo, wearing only a towel. "Who are you?"

Rusty stepped forward and grabbed the cultural attaché. Despite being a big man, he was weak and no match for the trained SAS operative. Rusty kicked the door closed and bundled Solomon into the lounge, expertly zip-tying his wrists and ankles in seconds.

Solomon was shouting now. He demanded to know who the hell was in his flat. Rusty slapped a strip of duct tape across his mouth to shut him up and carried on with his preparations.

"Who am I? Why am I here? I'm your worst nightmare. It's time for you to pay for causing the death of Olabisi Promise Chukwu."

Solomon's eyes widened as Rusty opened the sash window to the fullest extent. He looked out onto the early evening traffic. As he turned back, he saw that Solomon's eyes widened even more. Rusty shoved him unceremoniously to the ledge. Then he cut off the ties with a knife, ripped the tape away and held on to the towel. Just a gentle shove was all that was necessary after that. Solomon screamed. The traffic still moved along at a steady pace. Nobody looked skywards, not at once, at least.

Rusty had already moved away from the window. He folded the towel neatly and put it away in the airing cupboard, and then he tidied up the flat and made his way towards the door. He paused and wondered whether to leave a note for Nurul Ruby Pohan. She wouldn't need to cook tonight; she shouldn't worry about the randy attaché anymore. He thought just a few words would suffice; something along the lines of 'Solomon has left the building.'

Sunday, September 23rd, 2012

After the Olympics, there were troubled times in the capital. Indeed, there were concerns across the country. Lights

Gold, Silver and Bombs

burned late into the night at Larcombe Manor. Nevertheless, the members of the Olympus Project and its agents vowed to continue the fight against terrorism, battle with organised crime, and fight for justice in whatever arena they deemed ripe for direct action.

When Rusty returned from disposing of Solomon Okonkwo, Erebus asked him at the Wednesday morning meeting whether everything had gone to plan.

"No problems whatever, Sir," replied Rusty. "Everything fell into place, you might say."

Erebus smiled. "You played your part well, Rusty. A few pedestrians were shocked when the naked former cultural attaché dropped in. But a vote of thanks must go to Giles and his team in the ice-house. They have created a series of transactions that show that Solomon Okonkwo withdrew significant amounts of his nation's funds to finance a serious betting spree. It's a toss-up who will uncover it first: the police or the High Commission. Either way, his death will be ruled a suicide. The poor devil couldn't face the truth about his attraction to the fillies."

"Oh, excellent, Sir," said Rusty. "I approve of that."

Among death, there's life; hasn't it ever been the same? In dark days at Larcombe, they decided that a criminal should pay the price for his crimes. Even so, there were still brief but enjoyable occasions when Annabelle Fox and Colin Bailey, now known to his colleagues as Phoenix, spent time together.

Their relationship had matured in the last few months. So late on this particular September afternoon, as they lay together in his bed, they planned a few days from the pressurised conditions they had suffered for so long.

After this year's absence, there was a Festival at Glastonbury in 2013 in late June. Soon, the tickets were going on sale. Athena traced a circle around Phoenix's left nipple with a long slender finger. Colin knew that this was a set-up for something he wouldn't enjoy. Colin listened. He said his piece.

"The prospect of a muddy field full of teenagers pissed up, drugged up and effing and blinding throughout the weekend isn't that appealing. Athena," he protested.

"But darling, Glastonbury is a highlight of the 'alternative season'. It's the place to see and be seen."

Colin stared at the ceiling. For the past couple of years, he had spent almost every waking hour avoiding people seeing him; he did most of his best work when invisible.

"Look," purred Athena, "there are plenty of luxury camping providers online. I've checked out a yurt package at around six thousand that will give us luxury showers and toilets. In addition, there's a private access road, gourmet restaurant, round-the-clock security, and extra goodies."

"Suppose you get custom-made wellies for that price?" grunted Colin. "SIX grand!"

The circling motion stopped. A sharp pinch left Colin grabbing for Athena's arm, and seconds later, he flipped her over onto her back.

"Are you sure I can't persuade you to come?" asked Annabelle Grace Fox as her long slender fingers moved further down his body.

Colin decided it was pointless to resist.

In due course, Athena would secure the tickets. Then, she would book the yurt. So, all things being equal, Annabelle Fox and Colin Bailey were going to be at Worthy Farm throughout the Festival weekend at the end of June 2013.

It was becoming imperative that Athena and Phoenix remained close. In the months since Erebus had lost his beloved wife, Elizabeth, he looked to have aged ten years. The old gentleman had been dropping heavy hints of his imminent retirement. Erebus travelled up to London on Olympus business on several occasions. Their leader returned to Larcombe early in the morning and was reticent on the matters discussed.

Several years before, he had indicated to Athena that he wanted her to be his successor. As the Phoenix became a prized asset of the Olympus Project, it was plain his position at the top table was inevitable. When Erebus realised that Athena and Phoenix had become involved, it sowed a seed in his mind. They would make a formidable pair, heading up affairs at Larcombe Manor after his departure.

When Olympus snatched Colin Bailey from the waters below Pulteney Weir in the summer of 2010, he heard of the Project's aims and objectives. Erebus had a vision. He had his family's wealth behind him. The half a dozen senior Olympus members who lived at Larcombe, whose true identities were hidden by their given mythical personas, contributed as much as they could afford. The amounts available for the Project were plentiful, but the scope of those initial aims and objectives was more far-reaching. Erebus told Phoenix that other silent partners shared the same beliefs, and their financial backing was essential.

Erebus had been the sole contact with these financiers over the years. It was time for him to convince them that Athena and Phoenix could assume responsibility after he had gone, and together they would bring their vision to fruition. Late-night returns from London suggested that this had not proved easy.

The day after Athena and Phoenix finally agreed on sharing a yurt next summer, Erebus chaired the usual morning meeting in the Manor house. Senior members and other attendees entered in dribs and drabs. The conversation centred on the gun and grenade attack last week in Manchester in which two female police officers died. Police caught their killer, but the agents were concerned about the ease of getting hold of weapons in the UK.

"At one time, this was unthinkable," Rusty said to Phoenix. "If it happened in the States, we'd shrug and accept it. But we would swear blind it could never happen here. Now it's as easy to get a gun as a morning newspaper."

As the last straggler took his seat, Erebus tapped the table to bring the meeting to order.

The first matter on the agenda concerned an incident near Banbury at the beginning of the month. Thanatos had prepared another lengthy report. Their eyes glazed over as he delivered it; Mondays were always a trial.

"Cropredy village is five miles north of Banbury in Oxfordshire. Every August, its inhabitants welcome an invasion of up to twenty thousand music lovers for Fairport's Cropredy Convention. Organised by the folk band, this outdoor extravaganza has been held annually since the 1970s. Cropredy Bridge on the River Cherwell was a major battle in 1644 during the English civil war. King Charles engaged the Parliamentarian army led by Sir William Waller. As the battle loomed, the villagers took care to protect the most valuable item in their church. If the Parliamentary forces won the battle, there seemed every chance the lectern would become part of a cannon. So the villagers hid it in the river to enable its recovery with ease. But when they went to retrieve the lectern, it wasn't there. So instead, the damaged lectern reappeared further up the river many years later."

"Who won?" asked Phoenix, trying to sound interested.

"It was a stalemate, but both sides sustained heavy losses. The local historical society was on their monthly expedition in the first week of September, looking for relics from the past relating to the Civil War period..."

"Am I going to enjoy where this story is going?" muttered Athena.

"Exactly," continued Thanatos, "they dug up human remains instead of the odd shoe buckle or fragment of a musket. It didn't take long for someone to realise that the body unearthed from the ground wasn't a Roundhead or a Cavalier."

"Heavens," exclaimed Rusty. "Are you saying they emasculated the poor bastard?"

Phoenix stifled his laughter with difficulty. Erebus looked down the table, peering over the top of his half-glasses.

"Children, please. Continue Thanatos, but can we dispense with the frills?"

Colin glanced at Thanatos; he had somewhat cruelly dubbed him, Alastor and Minos as the Three Stooges. Although on his arrival at Larcombe, they appeared to be 'yes' men, they seemed to be in awe of Erebus and jealous of Athena's relationship with the old man. They were overly wary of him too. After being closeted together since the Olympus Project began, the originals made it plain the newcomer needed time before being accepted into the fold.

Chris Rathbone, known as Thanatos, was in his mid-fifties now. Thirty years ago, he was a SAS sergeant working with the FRU in Northern Ireland. Thanatos had spent five years in deep cover as a mole in the UDA. What he experienced there left physical and mental scars. After a stint in Bosnia, his country abandoned him despite thirty years of serving his country with honour. His identity was now known to the IRA. They knew he had been supplied with the names of suspected members by his army paymasters and leaked them to the UDA. Despite informing them of his death threats, no protection had ever been offered to Thanatos by the MoD. The Olympus Project had been his saviour; Larcombe Manor was his safe house.

Colin knew, deep down, that Thanatos fought his demons daily. The lengthy reports, with the bells and whistles, were a way of occupying his mind, reducing the time for those horrors that he had witnessed and taken part in for his country to creep inside his head and send him over the edge into insanity. Colin resolved to show his colleague due respect in the future.

He and Athena would become the senior duo at Olympus HQ after Erebus retired. The others needed to consider them a valued part of the team. Thanatos continued.

"I'm afraid this body could stir up a hornet's nest, Sir. As you will recall, there was a lot of activity straight after the effective prison break we orchestrated. The chase continued across the country for weeks. The police found nothing. The media assumed that Muslim extremists released these prisoners, maybe even Al Qaeda itself. Our borders leak like a sieve, as we know, so the public was pleased to accept that a dozen men could disappear to a place of safety. More wander in and either find a job or sign on for benefits every day. So a handful going the other way was an easy pill to swallow. There was no possibility of anything relating to the prison break linking to Olympus. Any trace of possible CCTV evidence, the vehicle movements involved, and the vehicles themselves were gone. Other events in the weeks after the Olympics deflected attention from the problem until this happened."

"Have they identified the body?" asked Erebus.

"It was one of the clerics and a member of the terrorist cell the authorities caught after 2005. When our clean-up crews dispersed the bodies around the Midlands, they got over-enthusiastic, it would seem. So rather than follow the 'one body, one grave' principle we adopt, one crew hacked a couple up and buried them in a shroud like a jigsaw."

"What do you mean, a jigsaw?" asked Erebus.

"The head and legs of the cleric were in with the torso of the bomb-maker, Sir."

"Unbelievable," said Erebus. "Get Henry Case to sort out the buggers involved, and please make sure that our systems are updated and rigorously followed in the future. Don't we have Standard Operating Procedures for this method of disposal?"

"Of course," replied Athena. "I will see to that myself, Erebus. We must assume that the authorities now realise that the prisoners are dead. Why are they keeping this knowledge from the public? How did they handle things with the historical society at Cropredy?"

"If the police and the secret services know that nobody rescued them, then who do they think killed them?" asked Phoenix.

Erebus stood up from the table and walked over to the window. He gazed across the lawns towards the old stable block and the ice-house. As the others sat and waited for him to consider what steps to take, he thought of everything they had achieved over the past five years. The vision was still crystal clear in his mind. The organisation was sound. Any minor setbacks, such as this ill-advised desecration of their victims' bodies, would be dealt with swiftly, but it wouldn't damage the integrity of the whole operation. Thanatos was almost correct in his statement that nothing could be traced back to Olympus. Erebus resolved with a sad heart that the two loose ends that might potentially give the authorities a scintilla of a clue must die.

"Perhaps I can suggest an answer to your question, Phoenix," he said, returning to his chair at the head of the table. "I expect them to concentrate on organisations that have been vocal in attacking Muslims in this country. Several groups will come under scrutiny. As for Athena's question about news coverage, no doubt the authorities have closed things down tight, as they are wont to do, in the interests of national security. They don't want to spook these white extremist groups fighting against the Islamisation of Europe. They want them to carry on spreading their vitriol and remain unaware of their close surveillance. Do you have anything to add about the Sealed Knot weekend warriors, Thanatos?"

"Well, Sir, as I said earlier, they found the remains and contacted the police. The local free paper recorded the discovery in a single paragraph together with court appearances of a drunk driver and council tax defaulters. It didn't attract any great interest, hidden away in that manner. However, a few keywords proved enough for that first publication to be picked up by Giles and his team in the icehouse. They then put search routines in progress to track the forensic results when they became available. They identified the bodies and forwarded an email to the police. The message was intercepted and amended in due course. The police emailed the secretary of the historical association. They informed him that although the bones were human, as suspected, they had been buried for well over a century."

"The bodies have only been in there a few months. They didn't swallow that, did they?" said Phoenix.

"One imagines a few ramblers on a Sunday afternoon scavenger hunt find the sight of a decomposed body more than their stomach can handle," said Erebus. "Eyes would be diverted rapidly. I doubt they could account for what they saw to the police or a reporter if one got a whiff of a story. For the time being, Giles can keep the surveillance in place to see what comes of it. With the police forensics staff swamped with work, I doubt they'll follow up the lead. We might have dodged the bullet."

Thanatos had finished. Erebus looked at his watch.

He nodded towards Phoenix and Rusty.

"Perhaps you'll join me in the orangery in an hour, gentlemen. I have a matter to talk about with you."

Phoenix and Rusty left the room together in silence. They walked across the lawns to the stable block and their accommodation.

"See you in an hour then. Phoenix," said Rusty.

Phoenix went into his quarters, closed the door, and set to work on cleaning his gun.

Nothing Is Ever Forever: Chapter Two

As Phoenix and Rusty entered the orangery, they found Erebus tending the ornamental plants scattered around the room.

"I hope you will look after these when I'm gone, chaps," he said. "I should hate to learn they just withered away."

"My Granddad had a greenhouse," chimed Rusty. "I used to help him in the summer holidays."

"This is an orangery, dear boy, not a mere greenhouse," snapped Erebus.

"Athena and I will ensure the plants come to no harm, Sir," said Phoenix. "I love this place. You have always invited me here for our meetings, and it's a place of solitude. It's good to escape from the Manor house or the other buildings and spend time here. Athena and I will use it as our base for quiet contemplation."

That seemed to appease the old gentleman. He smiled briefly; then, it was back to the grave matter in hand.

"In the folder on the table are the names of the two

clean-up crew operatives responsible for the faux pas at Cropredy. I have instructed Henry Case to interview the other crews. They will visit Larcombe over the next few days for a 'refresher' training course. It may involve visiting the place you refer to as 'Hotel California' to learn what procedures they followed when they disposed of their prisoners. But, again, I pray that we are only dealing with an isolated case."

"Dealing with, Sir?" asked Rusty, with a puzzled expression.

"Did I not make myself plain in the meeting?" asked Erebus.

Phoenix picked up the file and opened it. There were photographs and background reports on the two men. His mate looked over his shoulder, and Colin heard the sharp intake of breath.

When Colin arrived at Larcombe, he had spent many hours under Rusty's tutelage. Rusty had been a SAS veteran when selected for the first intake of the Special Reconnaissance Regiment in 2005. He had shown that his temper was as fiery as the colour of the hair on his head. Four years later, he fought with a superior officer, and they asked him to leave. In the past three years, Rusty had trained dozens of agents for Olympus here at Larcombe. That sharp intake of breath suggested that Rusty had trained these men or served with them in the SAS or SRR.

"Are there any questions?" asked Erebus.

"None," replied Phoenix.

"If it has to be, then I'm prepared to carry out your orders, Sir," said Rusty.

"No choice, I'm afraid," said Phoenix. "They screwed up. Bodies can't be left for anyone in power to find. Once identified, it would pose several uncomfortable questions. There will be a record of their being helped at Larcombe by the charity to cope with their PTSD.

"We must keep an acceptable level of detail," said Erebus. "The Charity Commission insist on it. Just recall what nightmares their last visit caused. We can't invite them here, as with the others that Henry Case will interrogate and retrain if they smell a rat and go to ground. It would be the devil of a job to find them if that happened."

"With training they received in the service, plus the upgrade they got here, then it will be a tricky job anyway, Sir," said Rusty.

"I trust the two of you can cope?"

The two friends looked at one another and nodded.

"With the right planning and attention to detail, we can work miracles, Sir," said Phoenix.

"Happy hunting; you have forty-eight hours. Any longer, and news of the other crews arriving here may filter back. The job needs completing before they get wind of what's happening."

With that, Erebus left. Colin and Rusty stayed in the orangery for a further thirty minutes devising a plan of action. Then they returned to the stable block to pack their things. Fifteen minutes later, they visited the ice-house and collected the required tools to finish their task.

Colin ordered transport, and just over an hour after Erebus started the walk back to the Manor house, the two agents were on their way towards the Oxfordshire countryside.

They arrived a mile from their target at two-thirty in the afternoon. On the trip up, Colin and Rusty went over the plan repeatedly. The pair developed strategies for each eventuality they foresaw. Colin knew that for Rusty, part of keeping his mind so active was to push any thought he was being sent to kill former colleagues to the furthest corners of his mind. Colin was calm. He didn't know the clean-up crew members. Erebus said they had to go. That was enough.

"I'll go ahead and put the first phase of our plan in place, Phoenix," said Rusty.

"Right," replied Phoenix. "I'll give you an hour. Let's synchronise our watches. On my mark, the time is 14.35. Mark."

"Check," said Rusty and got out of the van. He collected his kit from the rear and set off across the fields.

Colin sat in the van and waited. Finally, when the clock ticked forward to 15.20, he, too, left the van with his kit and set off at a brisk walk towards the target.

Al Stratton and Terry Wright-Jones lived in an isolated cottage on the outskirts of Great Bourton, just a few minutes up the road from Cropredy. So they had been ideally situated for the cleaning task when handed it. The bodies of the cleric and the bomb maker were retrieved intact from another Olympus safe house in Banbury. They had transported them through the village at night and planned to bury the bodies in the countryside.

Both men had been Sergeants in the SAS and served in Bosnia and Iraq. They had years of experience between them. When the black marks against their names for insubordination and unnecessary violence towards prisoners during interrogations mounted up, they found themselves surplus to requirements and back on 'civvy' street. After working for various security firms and debt collection agencies, always just staying one step ahead of the law, Olympus approached them.

While they trained at Larcombe, they received warnings

that they were drinking in the Last Chance Saloon. Rusty and the other instructors had tried to break them, but they kept their noses clean throughout their training period. For the past three years, they had been used on various operations and, although surly and distant with their colleagues, they followed orders well enough. No black marks existed against their names in the reports that Rusty and Phoenix had seen.

The drink was their downfall. Stratton and Wright-Jones returned to the cottage on the night in question and went indoors. Their task had been to bury the two bodies, a half-mile apart, in areas with the minimum pedestrian footfall.

"Sounds like hard work, Terry, for two ragheads," said Stratton.

"Sod it," grunted Wright-Jones. "Let's have a drink first."

One thing led to another, as it often did with these two. Dawn was a distant memory before the drinking ended, with both men passed out in the lounge. But, the devil will make work for idle hands. When they awoke, hung over and irritable, they chopped the bodies up in the outhouse behind the cottage. They then planned to bury them on either side of the same field, three minutes from where they sat in the house.

"They can wave to one another," chuckled Wright-Jones.

"Fat chance," muttered Stratton. "We'll separate them. Then they'll know what it felt like for our lads to stand on an IED and get blown to kingdom come."

They filled the shrouds with parts from each of the mutilated bodies, and Stratton and Wright-Jones buried the remains on opposite sides of a field near Cropredy Bridge that night.

Gold, Silver and Bombs

Colin looked across the open ground towards the cottage. Everything was quiet; it was undoubtedly isolated. There was no traffic sound anywhere. Just a few birds were singing in the trees to break the silence. Through his glasses, he picked out the outhouse. He could barely see the grill of an old Ford van parked to the side. Stratton and Wright-Jones were home.

A hedge ran the field's length to the lane in front of the cottage to his right. He needed to backtrack twenty metres and use the cover to reach the target by 15.35 when Rusty expected him to make his move.

He crawled backwards until he could safely hunker down and run towards the cottage under the cover of the hedge. Colin rechecked his watch. Fifteen thirty-two.

He stashed his kit under the hedge and put his SIG Sauer P226 into the waistband of his trousers. It felt cold but reassuring against his spine. He strolled up to the front door, knocked and waited.

Stratton opened the door. "What can I do for you, mate? Hang on, don't I know you?

Colin nodded. "I was nearby and wondered if you guys wanted to join me for a beer. I'm parked up the road and staying in the pub in the village tonight."

"That sounds great," said Stratton, standing back and inviting him to come inside. "Why don't we have a few beers? You can tell us what you've been doing. Phoenix was your name if I remember right? One of the blue-eyed boys at Larcombe. Met up with you on that prison break caper."

Colin stood his ground. He didn't want to go inside the cottage alone. However, there was no movement from inside the building. So plan A had been for Rusty to gain access from the rear of the house and take out whichever operative didn't answer the door. Colin would then dispose of the other man at the front when he was distracted by events behind him.

Colin heard a faint crunch of the gravel behind him and the unmistakable touch of cold steel on his neck.

"You'll have to do better than that, Phoenix," sneered Wright-Jones. "We spotted you ages ago. It doesn't take a genius to work out why you're here. Someone must have uncovered our handiwork. The old boy sent you to clean up, didn't he?"

Wright-Jones continued talking as Stratton patted Colin down and found the gun. He looked at it and turned it over in his hand. Then suddenly, he whipped his arm across Colin's face knocking him to the ground.

"We're going to take a short drive," said Stratton. "One way for you, I'm afraid."

"Move," growled Wright-Jones and shoved Colin forwards. Colin stumbled and fell again. Stratton pointed his gun at him, and the three men headed towards the outhouse and the old Ford van.

Colin experienced a sinking feeling. Plan A had long gone down the drain, and these two old hands had skipped several other scenarios in the playbook. What could he do? He was unarmed and with Rusty nowhere around. Had they spotted him as well? Was his best friend in the van? Had they killed him, or were they destined to die side by side?

Colin thought over the past thirty months working for Olympus. Athena's face drifted in and out of focus. His head was still spinning from the pistol-whipping Stratton dished out. With so much to live for, was this how it would end?

"Ah well," he sighed as he stumbled to the van's rear,

and Wright-Jones opened the doors. "Nothing is ever forever, is it?"

Stratton shoved him towards the empty van, but Colin resisted. He wasn't getting in without a fight. Stratton tucked the Sig Sauer in his belt and grabbed hold of Colin, bundling him into the back and slamming the doors. Colin cracked his head on the bulkhead and lay there stunned.

He heard four muffled reports.

His head hurt; nothing made much sense. He curled up in a ball and waited for the van to pull away. He tried to think about making one last-ditch effort to save himself when they reached wherever these two planned to kill him and bury his body. What had happened to Rusty?

The van doors were suddenly thrown open.

Colin gathered up his strength and sprang from the van. Stratton and Wright-Jones lay in the yard, dead. Both had been shot in the back of the head. Exit wounds at the front destroyed any chance of their relatives viewing the body. The familiar smell of death that should have attacked his nostrils was not in evidence. All he could smell was the authentic smell of the country.

"Thank God for Plan Q!" said Rusty, who appeared by his side. Colin saw his teeth as his mate grinned at him but little else. Rusty was in full camouflage gear, his face blackened.

"Thought my number was up," shuddered Colin. "What happened?"

"I could tell as soon as I got in the neighbourhood that the cottage was an ideal spot. It's almost impossible to get close without someone spotting you, especially when well-trained like this couple. I had to use everything I'd ever learned to make my way undetected into the garden at the rear. I had to improvise. I burrowed into the compost heap near the back wall. It meant I was six feet from the van doors. Then I waited for your conversation at the front door. Terry came out and crept around the side of the cottage. I would break cover then and ride to the rescue, but I thought that might end up with a firefight. I didn't want to risk it. Sorry you got roughed up, mate. Once I knew they planned to take you off in the van to get rid of you, I stayed hidden until they put you inside the van. They were a few feet in front of me, walking towards the front of the van, when I stood up and took them out. They never suspected a thing."

"Thanks," said Colin. Although it was alien to him to show emotion, he wanted to throw his arms around his friend and hug him, but the stench was awful.

"First things first," said Rusty. "Let's get these two into the van. Then I'm going indoors to have a shower or two. A change of clothes and a beer will help. Maybe this pair has a stock of food in the house we can grab too. Then I reckon we watch telly and wait until nightfall."

Colin couldn't believe how Rusty could remain so cool.

"You knew these two guys; I got the impression you weren't happy doing this job when Erebus laid it out for us."

"They crossed the line, Phoenix. When they joined Olympus, they agreed to follow the rules. I might have been unhappy about the mess they made of disposing of the prisoners. I might have questioned that Erebus thought it serious enough to dispose of them. But they were prepared to kill you without a second's thought. I couldn't allow that, mate."

The two friends bundled the bodies of Stratton and Wright-Jones into the van. Later that night, they would be driven back to Larcombe to their final resting place in the crowded pet cemetery.

The two agents took showers and spent the evening in total silence. The food was prepared and eaten. They each drank a can of beer. The TV was watched and then switched off at the mains as midnight approached — no point leaving it on standby.

Rusty drove the old Ford through the lanes in darkness until they reached their transport. Colin followed Rusty back to the outskirts of Bath in the Olympus van. They swung between the pillars at the entrance to the estate at just after two in the morning.

At three o'clock, an electrical fire was instigated at the isolated cottage near Great Bourton in Oxfordshire. The fire burned swiftly. It's great living in the country, miles from anywhere, unless you need a fire engine. Unfortunately, before anyone noticed the flames and summoned the fire brigade, the blaze reduced the cottage to little more than a shell.

Tuesday, September 25th, 2012

"Back so soon, gentlemen?" asked Erebus as Phoenix and Rusty strolled into the morning meeting.

"Mission accomplished," said Rusty.

"Everything went according to plan, Sir," added Phoenix with a grin at his pal.

Henry 'Head' Case looked up from the reports he read.

"I think we may need to apply for planning permission for an extension to the pet cemetery if we have to bury many more bodies. As we speak, a work detail is in progress, ferreting away the two you delivered early this morning."

"Sad business," said Erebus, "when we have to bury two

of our own. I'm afraid they were 'off-message', as they say in modern parlance, so we had no alternative. I believe we can draw a line under the Cropredy affair now and move forward."

Athena had not seen Colin since he left the meeting yesterday, so she was unaware of the near-death experience he had endured. He and Rusty's blasé comments when Erebus had spoken to them were to protect her as much as keep the full facts from Erebus. There was time enough to tell him what had gone on when he debriefed the operation later, almost certainly in the orangery.

"I don't suppose we missed much while we were away yesterday?" asked Colin.

Athena smiled.

"You couldn't have picked a better day to be off-site. The Avon & Somerset Police visited us."

"What on earth for?" asked Colin.

"They were looking for you, Phoenix," said Erebus. "Or more precisely, they asked after a troubled serviceman who raised a few doubts in the mind of one of the Charity Commissioners earlier this year."

Sir Julian Langford QC, known to his colleagues as Minos, the judge of the dead in the Underworld, took up the story. Another of the Three Stooges, Minos, was nearly sixty years of age. After a long career in the law courts watching criminals evade justice or receive softer and softer sentences for serious crimes, he had retired a disillusioned man. A family tragedy followed. His young son Harry committed suicide. He bought the drugs online as simple as downloading a CD onto his iPod. Minos joined Olympus after reading the advert placed by Erebus in The Times; he was a valuable and contented member of an organisation able to make a difference.

"You will recall the Data Protection Act raised a few issues concerning the personal information we hold on our people here at Larcombe. The Commissioners required us to complete a questionnaire, and then the ICO inspectors descended on us without warning for a review of our answers. The visit was said to be in an advisory capacity. They offered practical advice on how we might improve things should the need arise. Of course, we took our normal precautions when strangers visited us. The ice-house was locked down, and only a skeleton crew remained in the stable block. I did my utmost to show them that our records were in an exemplary state. If they looked out of the windows of this room, they would have seen a few service members tending to the flower beds or cutting vegetables from the kitchen garden. The whole picture we try to portray at times is what you would expect to see when lads return from the theatre of war suffering mental problems. They engage in a modest level of activity and exercise to complement the counselling they receive while the mind repairs itself. The interviews went well. We schooled the candidates we chose, and everyone kept to the script. They were poised to sign us off with distinction."

"Then I walked in and stuffed everything up," said Phoenix.

"I'm afraid it complicated matters, Phoenix. There's no denying that," Minos replied. "Rather than debriefing the Swindon mission as you expected, you realised the situation and collapsed in a heap. That allowed us to get you out and concoct a cover story. We avoided answering awkward questions about who you were and where you had served. We thought we had pulled the wool over their eyes. But, unfortunately, the senior Inspector chewed over events on the train journey north and, in due course, sent a report to the

Charity Commission to cover his backside. They decided his concerns about what went on behind the walls of the Olympus Project were significant enough to call for further investigation. With the Leveson and Savile inquiries prominent in the news, it was inevitable in the current climate. So they invited the police to at least confirm this serviceman's identity and current status. Was this the right place for him? Had we mistreated him here even?"

Henry Case joined in at this point. "Minos and I met to talk about your case. Phoenix in the aftermath of the visit. We thought it politic to create a plausible persona for you that would satisfy the ICO if they came calling again. We have to keep sweet with the Charity Commissioners no matter what. We have kept the authorities and the public at arm's length for five years."

"So what happened yesterday then?" asked Colin, who had felt a slight chill running down his spine since he heard the police had been asking after him.

"Two officers arrived mid-afternoon without warning," said Athena, "a female Detective Inspector and a uniformed sergeant. They travelled across from the county force HQ at Portishead. These days it's where their Criminal Investigations people are based. They wanted to speak with you. During their advisory visit, they asked to interview the serviceman who fainted before ICO staff members. I called Henry Case, and he brought over the paperwork we had prepared."

"We informed them that Warrant Officer Second Class Garry Burns was the soldier they had seen collapsing. We said Burns was a veteran of several trips to Iraq. After he returned, medics diagnosed him with severe PTSD. Burns could still function and work from time to time, but there were several days a month when Burns got emotionally unstable. After leaving the military, he had spent several years having random erratic episodes, and his GP just chalked it up to his excessive drinking and temper issues. When Burns came here as a volunteer, we got him to cut back on his drinking and stopped him from fighting everyone in sight. He did things he was not proud of over there, as did many of his colleagues. We offered to counsel him on his mental issues and arranged weekly visits with a social worker. That social worker got him into sessions with a psychologist and quarterly sessions with a psychiatrist. Those sessions helped him find his way back. It was slow at first; several months passed before we built the trust that enabled him to share his experiences in a vulnerable and truthful way. It can be a real battle to enter willingly into therapy, open up to a stranger, and hope they don't tear you apart and judge you. Finally, after talking to others and taking drugs for depression, sleep disorder, and mood swings, we judged him to be 'relatively' healthy. The police learned that a virus caused the incident during the ICO visit. I showed the detective the MO's report on the matter. As he had entered the Olympus Project as a voluntary patient, we couldn't prevent him from walking away. We told them we preferred that he had stayed here, among friends and fellow service members who understood the hell he had suffered. But he was adamant he felt well enough to make it on the outside on his own. We said that he left Larcombe Manor to travel the world in July. We haven't received a card from him so far."

"How did this DI react to that?" asked Rusty.

"Difficult to tell. The woman was young, too young, I thought to be a DI," said Henry Case. "She read through every scrap of paper we had prepared for his so-called personnel file. The DI asked for copies, which we provided.

She asked for a specific date when Burns volunteered himself for treatment. She studied his ID extremely closely."

Athena tried to reassure Colin.

"Don't worry, Phoenix. We chose Garry Burns for a reason. He did serve in Iraq. Burns arrived with the first intake the week the Project opened for business. His records before he joined the Army at sixteen and throughout his time served will stack up when they check. He was with us until September 2010, when he went missing on a mission in West Africa. Burns was trying to track members of Boko Haram, and his handlers lost radio contact with his party. Nothing was ever heard from them again. Henry merely picked up the threads of his life here at Larcombe as if he had never left. You joined us in July and underwent training and facial reconstruction in your first three months with us. As far as that Detective Inspector was concerned, you were Garry Burns when the ICO inspectors visited."

"Wouldn't they spot the difference in our appearance?" asked Phoenix.

Henry Case stood up and walked over to a whiteboard. He placed photographs onto the board and secured them, one by one.

"This is Garry Burns with his mother and father at Barry Island, aged seven. This picture shows Private Garry Burns at seventeen in Rheindalen. Here we have Garry Burns again, with half a dozen other squaddies on a beach in Tenerife. He's about thirty in that one. When he joined us, we took this photograph for his ID card. He was thirty-eight years old in November of that year, which was 2007."

As 'Head' Case stuck that final photo on the board, even the antique clock on the mantelpiece seemed to pause; the likeness to Phoenix was incredible. Then, without saying a word, the intelligence head placed Colin's latest photograph alongside that of Garry Burns.

"Meet your twin, Phoenix," said Henry. "The surgeons made minor alterations to your features in September and October, perhaps unwittingly, maybe with a nod to a fallen comrade, but as you can see, the resemblance is uncanny."

"The police know how you looked on July 1st, 2010, when you went missing in the River Avon in Bath. You moved a few miles from the city to be with us, and we altered your features. Nobody you knew before that time thinks you are alive, let alone know how you look now," said Athena. She hoped her lover could see there was little cause for concern.

While this conversation was taking place at Larcombe, the young female DI reviewed her findings with her boss in the Criminal Investigations offices at Portishead,

"His paperwork shows that Burns had PTSD after his experiences in Iraq. Unfortunately, I couldn't talk to him as he had waited until his early forties to take a gap year. I expect he's trekking towards Machu Picchu as we speak with a bunch of people half his age."

"What did you do with the ID photograph?"

"I contacted the ICO inspector who raised the query and sent him a copy. He forwarded it to the colleagues he had with him on the visit to Larcombe Manor. Every single one of them gave him the same reply. 'That's the man I saw; I'm almost sure that's him.'

When I pushed the senior inspector to say whether he was one hundred per cent certain himself, he said, 'No, I couldn't swear to it. My colleagues agree. We think it's the same man, but we wouldn't want to swear to it in a court of law. Please remember; it was a long day. We had trawled through reams of paperwork and carried out interviews with officers of the charity and service members receiving help. Their stories were harrowing; we have no concept of the conditions we ask them to endure when we allow our politicians to send them off to such places. Then just as we were bringing matters to a close, the door opened, and this man entered the room. He stood there for less than five seconds, then collapsed in a heap. He received attention from two charity officers at once, and stewards came in to carry off the poor devil. I challenge anyone to say they were certain in those circumstances. If he wasn't the man in the photo you sent me, then he's his twin.'"

"That's as far as we've got, I'm afraid."

"Forget the ICO people; they can't help us any further," said her Chief Inspector. "Forget the charity, too, for now. Everything points to them doing a great job. Let's see if we can find this, Garry Burns. We can't afford to commit many resources to this; there's no evidence of a crime. Perhaps we can post a notice on the relevant backpacker sites, asking if anyone has seen him. Leave his photo on a few forums and ask him to contact us. I'm not sure what else we can do."

At Larcombe Manor, the morning meeting had finished. Rusty and Phoenix had then brought the elderly gentleman up to speed on the clean-up crew mission in the orangery. He was concerned about the tap-dancing they had resorted to finishing the job.

"My fault, chaps, I suppose," he said. "I should have given you more time to formulate your plans. How are you holding up, Phoenix? Is everything clear in your head over the police business yesterday afternoon?"

Colin looked at Rusty.

"Do you mind, mate?" he said. Rusty took the hint and left them alone.

"That detective paid particular attention to the ID

photograph, Sir. She pored over it for several minutes. What did she see in the face of Garry Burns? Could she have thought that maybe Garry Burns reminded her of someone she knew?" said Colin. "I was in Oxfordshire yesterday afternoon, miles away from Larcombe Manor. How can I know that female Detective Inspector? Yet I'm positive I do."

"She identified herself as DI Zara Wheeler, and her colleague was Sergeant Toby Drysdale," said Erebus.

"There you go," sighed Colin. "She worked with my nemesis, Phil Hounsell. Hounsell and Wheeler were on my tail from Durham to Manchester and then to Bath. I kidnapped Hounsell's wife to get him to back off and allow me to travel freely to London. I had unfinished business. Everything went south when I got back. Instead of releasing her and disappearing as planned, I was running for my life with coppers on my tail. No doubt Drysdale was one of them. I remember Ms Wheeler well; no wonder she made DI at such a young age. She's as sharp as a tack. If she thinks there's any doubt about the truth of the story we gave her yesterday, she'll keep gnawing at it like a dog with a bone. That picture holds the key to the slight possibility of a cover-up job. Deliberate or not, my facial reconstruction leaving me with features so similar to Burns may well have given us a problem, not a solution."

Erebus had listened to Phoenix intently.

"You may be worrying unnecessarily, dear boy," he said. "When they left yesterday, they believed that Burns had gone to see the world. Where would they look for you if they peel away enough layers of the onion to expose you as being alive? Not here, just minutes away from the city where everyone thinks you died. They might try to trace Burns's movements and will come to a dead end. So I suggest you keep a low profile for a while. As for Burns, Giles may have to magic up a cover story in a few months; a tragic accident while swimming off the Great Barrier Reef could suffice."

Colin reluctantly had to agree; he was no doubt worrying about nothing.

Grab your copy...
vinci-books.com/nothing-ever-forever

About the Author

Ted Tayler is the international best-selling indie author of the Freeman Files and Phoenix series. Ted lives in the English West country, where his stories are based. He was born in 1945 and has been married to Lynne since 1971. They have three children and four grandchildren.

His thought-provoking mysteries appeal to readers of Sally Rigby, Joy Ellis, Pauline Rowson, and Faith Martin. His action-packed thrillers are a must for fans of Mark Dawson and J C Ryan.

Gus Freeman's cold case investigations are carried out with reasoned deduction rather than bursts of frantic action. In each of the 24 books, unsolved murders are accompanied by romance, humour, and country life. The core message in the 12 Phoenix novels is that criminals should pay for their crimes. Unfortunately, the current system fails to deliver the correct punishment, so Phoenix helps redress the balance.

Acknowledgments

The love and support of my family; without them, this would have been impossible.

www.ingramcontent.com/pod-product-compliance
Ingram Content Group UK Ltd.
Pitfield, Milton Keynes, MK11 3LW, UK
UKHW040119190326
469155UK00004B/1231

9 781036 700508